1 8 6 6 - 1 9 9 1

125th

ANNIVERSARY

BOOMFELL

Douglas
Hobbie

A John Macrae Book

HENRY HOLT AND
COMPANY
NEW YORK

Copyright © 1991 by Douglas Hobbie
Published by Henry Holt and Company, Inc.,
115 West 18th Street, New York, New York 10011.
Published in Canada by Fitzhenry & Whiteside Limited,
195 Allstate Parkway, Markham, Ontario L3R 4T8.

Library of Congress Cataloging-in-Publication Data
Hobbie, Douglas.
    Boomfell / Douglas Hobbie.—1st ed.
        p.   cm.
    "A John Macrae book."
    I. Title.
PS3558.03364B66   1991
813′.54–dc20   90–24021
                                                           CIP

ISBN 0-8050-1534-5

Henry Holt books are available at special discounts
for bulk purchases for sales promotions, premiums,
fund-raising, or educational use. Special editions
or book excerpts can also be created to specification.
    For details contact:
    Special Sales Director, Henry Holt and Company, Inc.
    115 West 18th Street, New York, New York 10011

FIRST EDITION

Book designed by Claire Naylon Vaccaro
Printed in the United States of America
Recognizing the importance of preserving
the written word, Henry Holt and Company, Inc.,
by policy, prints all of its first editions
on acid-free paper. ∞

10   9   8   7   6   5   4   3   2   1

BOOMFELL

In September, which to him had always meant the fresh start of a new year, Boomfell sold his first house for Odyssey, and on a Saturday night, in the grip of a prodigal mood, he took his wife to Cyrano's. The bar was a narrow room of facing mirrors: old wood, brass, cut-glass chandeliers—*crawling*, Val whispered, with undaunted graying couples expensively turned out as befit Cyrano's on a Saturday night. Boomfell was slightly wrinkled and out of season in his weathered corduroy jacket, while through a throng of men sporting blazers, pinstripe, the odd seersucker, he possessively—one hand on the small of Val's back—steered his pretty companion. In black pants and the new lavender blouse she shared with their daughter, Val stood out. Men, Boomfell noticed, noticed her. They wedged themselves between women on stools and Boomfell raised his hand for drinks.

"Let's relax, all right."

Shy of surprises, Val wished she'd been told where they were going. Cyrano's made her feel out of it. "And you." She gave him the once-over, shaking her head at the sight of Boomfell. "Pitch this thing, Charlie." She tugged the sleeve of his jacket—more than ten years old, the dingy color of a good mustard. "You'd think you were out to shoot grouse."

"To put it solemnly, this is a special occasion. One guess."

Val correctly guessed the farmhouse in Northfield. She was pleased, of course. Then, as she looked at him, her clear eyes narrowed thoughtfully. "Charles Boomfell," she said, as if recalling that name from the past. "Who would have thought?"

For years now they'd been managing on Val's income and Boomfell's haphazard jobs, waiting for something to give. He'd painted houses, he'd worked in Archangel's Bookshop and had served as soup-and-salad chef at the Uncommon Kitchen; he'd cut cordwood for a season and had tutored high school students preparing for their SATs—anything to avoid the likes of what he was doing now. Nothing happened. No one was interested in *Revisions*, his free verse epic of daily life. Everybody says boring, Phoebe Orlando reported long-distance. She was a tax attorney who had set herself up as a literary agent after failing to find lawyer's work in New York City. Boomfell had been given her name by Archangel's writer-friend at the New School. Personally I can get into it in a certain mood, she said, but, Charles, you can't expect people to sit still for this kind of stuff anymore. And his first book, *Disillusions*, brought out by Painted Desert Press, the short-lived Southwestern outfit that had offered him vital encouragement at a difficult time, hadn't it disappeared like smoke? Like smoke signals, cracked the tax expert. He thanked her for her efforts on his behalf. Phoebe Orlando! From the beginning he had found her name hard to believe.

For two years he'd been trying, haltingly, to write his way into something new. Val was loyal—she wouldn't be the one to say quit—yet this, he saw, was more plausible to her: the sale of a farmhouse to a potter for ninety-six five.

The stress of futile labors, borne just so long, had suddenly become insupportable. The worried crease between Val's eyes had deepened so that now she often seemed to be anxiously—or angrily—frowning. Their daughter, Ruth, at present lost in the thralldom of erratic teenage life, began making judgments out loud about her parents' life. The cost of everything went up every time you turned around. One night in February, alone with a bottle of wine, Boomfell read *The Summing Up*,

2

Maugham's bitter turn at truth telling. There was a sentence in that thin volume that oppressed his conscience and pierced his confidence. Under cover of darkness, stealthily as it were, he did what was necessary—read the book, took the test—to get a license to sell real estate. Briefly he had attended classes, seated at a little red plastic desk in the fluorescent glare of the ten-year-old community college classroom, numbered amongst the very sort of hapless halfhearted drudges—bored, all but burned out on the allure of betterment—who had haunted the night classes in Freshman English it had once been his duty to teach. That experience had proved so disturbing he couldn't even share it with his wife and at least let off the steam of his humiliation, so discomposing that during this period and for months afterward he had been unable to read— even lightweight contemporary novels, even Samuel Pepys, his hero of the moment, even *The Yearling*, which he had been reading aloud to Ben all winter. Boomfell unable to read had begun to feel like Boomfell unable to be.

Several months later he called Louis Weisman at the Odyssey Realty Company looking for a game of tennis. Weisman got him the job. Boomfell's friend seemed to feel, What else is new? In one way or another, for whatever reasons, everyone seemed to be kissing illusions good-bye. I've never had any illusions, said Boomfell. Weisman winked: You do now, Charlie.

"I'm glad Muler got it," he said. At first the bank had been reluctant to give the potter a mortgage. "He loves the place and he knows what he's doing. He won't ruin it."

"It's a dream," said Val. "Northfield is beautiful."

If things had gone differently, the sequestered farmhouse in the remote hill town was the kind of place they would have liked for themselves. That was one theory of happiness.

I didn't know you could get a life out of pots, he'd said to Muler. They were on the front porch, checking out the view that went with the property. From here, facing north, you were on top of the world: hazy mountains piled up in successive shades of gray, blue, violet. The meadow sloping before them, bounded by woods, was deep green and featured an oak as old as the stone walls. Muler was a man in his forties with a ponytail, and four children under ten. It's what I do, he said, that's all there is to it. His tone was defiant, and unfriendly. I admire your perseverance, Boomfell told him. Muler said, Don't bother. Let the potter be happy hidden away in the hills with his pauper's pride, his garden, his wood-burning stove—in the house Boomfell had sold him. Tonight Boomfell was determined to enjoy a taste of ordinary indulgent pleasure at Cyrano's.

"Forget the men," said Val. "Look at the wives. Can women want to stand around looking like this in these hairdos, howdoing each other to death? Is that what I get to be in twenty years if you make big money in real estate, Charlie? One of these fluffy, puffed-up ladies no one listens to." Boy, she added, the drink was going straight to her head.

Boomfell watched her in the mirror behind the bar—a receding series of Vals—as, with eyes closed and chin up, she drew her hair back from her face with both hands. The gesture had a startling effect on him, as if he had been tapped on the shoulder just then in Cyrano's and had turned to face an old girlfriend from fifteen years and thousands of miles ago, whose existence, until that moment, he had forgotten. Unexpected desire, an old friend always welcome, began to swell in Boomfell from a neglected source of deep strong feeling for his wife.

If he made big money in real estate, he told her, he would buy her a hot fudge sundae with extra whipped cream and two cherries. How did that sound? And Boomfell, impetuously seizing the memory that had come to mind, recalled their long walks through the city and along the river to his tiny, tawdry apartment on Marlborough Street, where they would slide the twin beds together and pull the shades. How did his shy studious roommate, Freddie Ray, silently endure their

4

irrepressible laughter, the invariable wall-banging wrestling match that was their clumsy athletic push-and-shove version of—innocent word!—foreplay. Then, life was foreplay. "Sunday afternoons in the Gardner Museum, Val. My balls used to ache." Boomfell rarely went in for such nostalgic rhapsodizing with his wife or anyone else. Generally, he didn't regard the Boomfell of those years, his young know-nothing self, with much generosity or affection. Just now, he did. "Isn't it incredible, Freddie Ray turned out to be gay."

Yet Val, if she was listening at all, hardly seemed susceptible to Boomfell's rendition of student romance. She was far more interested in the Saturday nightlife of Cyrano's as reflected in the mirror behind the bar. She was looking hard at something there, and then she turned toward the busy room, boosted herself on tiptoe, craning her neck to see over the crowd.

"Charlie," she said, and tugged his sleeve. "I could have sworn . . ." She pointed. "Doesn't that man by the framed mirror look the spit and image of Eliot Singer?"

Poor Singer had been the only friend to remain at the university where Boomfell, along with a dozen other casualties in humanities, had left off seven years before. (Had it been that long? Seven years?) Friday nights they would get together and deplore their state of affairs—the ignorance and incompetence of students and certain colleagues, the tedium of teachers' chores such as grading exams and attending faculty meetings—and these typical beery sessions of faultfinding formed the basis of their friendship. But while Boomfell did little to ingratiate himself in that small world—what could he do?—clever Singer guarded his ass, coyly courted the right people, volunteered for committees, flattered wives at parties to which out-of-it Boomfell was seldom invited, and generally demonstrated a sparky interest in his job. He distributed numerous memoranda on pink paper pertaining to matters in and out of the department. He made a point of dropping in on older faculty members for advice, saw to it that people of so-called consequence received copies of his papers on Swift, Dryden, and Pope, submitted course syllabi to his chairman for approval, and was an occasional contributor to the school newspaper. Singer, Boomfell noticed, skillfully adopted a balanced position concerning controversial matters, which permitted him to side with most sides. He sent UNICEF greeting cards to a long list of people it behooved him to remember during the holiday season, and received numerous holiday greetings in return. Singer devoted days and weeks to maintaining useful correspondences, composing lengthy applications, dreaming up long-range projects, and in this way wangled helpful contacts and managed to weasel his way into research grants and expense-paid conferences to San Francisco, New York City, New Orleans, England. Apart from Boomfell, Boomfell soon realized, Singer only formed personal relationships with people he might meet along the steep uphill path of anticipated promotion. All in all, Boomfell often reminded himself, he only did what any able ambitious young man would do in order to become a full-fledged and respected member of his profession.

Yet, while he shrewdly and steadfastly careered ahead according to his own daily schedule of set goals, Singer never spoke of any of this to Boomfell, but continued to come around Friday nights and deride the colleagues who coddled him, mock the meetings he never missed, dismiss his duties as trivial, and agree wholeheartedly with Boomfell that it was all a waste of precious time and that the only way to make the best of a bad situation was to sit tight and do your work. I admire that, said sad Singer, propped on an elbow, his enormous hand concealing half of his long sallow face. If there was any justice, the poet's single-minded devotion to his task was bound to pay off.

6

His successes filtered down to Boomfell indirectly, as faits accomplis, and if Boomfell brought up such matters (I hear you've become a tenured one of the boys, Eliot. Nice going), Singer would respond with a casual contempt for his own good fortune (yes, it seems I may be able to remain in this hole forever. Maybe mediocrity is my niche), as if he and Boomfell agreed that Boomfell's precarious and untenable position was an enviable one. During his second year Singer's much re-vised dissertation on Swift was accepted for publication by the University of Chicago Press (but what is the point, he replied to Boomfell's enthusiastic congratulations, of a book that will be hastily read by a handful of dullards for the sole purpose of pointing out its shortcomings amongst themselves and putting their hollow competitive fears to rest), one of its chapters was delivered at the winter meeting of the MLA, and the author was promoted to associate professor.

At school Boomfell only saw Singer in passing, particularly after the second year, and it gradually became clear—at lunch in the faculty club one of the few times Boomfell set foot there, in the lobby of the library following a lecture on black holes, in the corridor between classes—that in the company of his staid colleagues, Singer really did not like his Friday-night friend lurking familiarly over his shoulder with knowing winks and wry wisecracks. At such awkward moments, Singer addressed Boomfell in the distant polite tone reserved for strangers or persons whose cheerful advances were not to be encouraged. So, all passion spent, hey, Eliot? leered Boom-fell at the reception that followed a faculty reading of *Samson Agonistes*, in which Lantini was Samson and Singer was Sam-son's father. Maybe fifty people had shown up. Just insane, was what Boomfell thought of the whole charade. Insane and hilarious. Singer was unapproachable. Why, good evening, Charles, how have you been?

That bizarre performance was also insane and hilarious and memorable, especially memorable to Boomfell, because of the presence onstage—in a black skirt and white blouse—of Wanda Gwertz, the cellist, who accompanied the actors at rather random intervals with fragments from a Bach suite. Presumably it was hoped that a touch of music would give the deadening affair the illusion of life. Wanda Gwertz was the reason Boomfell endured such nonsense at all. She was his maiden voyage, as he thought of it in retrospect, through the straits of adultery, which led from the safe becalmed bay of marriage to the treacherously open seas of obsession, humiliation, and after Wanda, other women. Rhymes with Kurtz, he once joked to her, never imagining the darkness he would discover within Boomfell as a result of their yearlong entanglement. *Samson Agonistes* was the occasion that introduced Wanda Gwertz to Boomfell's sometime friend, Singer.

Val forthrightly scorned the man and considered each and every Singer accomplishment a matter of wheedling, worming, or weaseling his way, rather than the result of intelligence and diligence. Why does he come over here, Charlie? Why do you sit up with him until one o'clock in the morning? If he thought you were competition, he'd knife you in the back at the drop of a hat. I enjoy him, Boomfell stated simply. Singer was smart, for one thing—one of the few people whose thoughts on poets and the presidency, movies or school gossip, gave Boomfell pleasure. Furthermore, their first year at the school together, Singer was the closest thing Boomfell had to a friend. Saturday mornings they would meet in Lovejoy, the only two people working in their offices on the weekends. Saturday afternoons they would get together for tennis, soccer if it was fall, or in the springtime of the first two years, the rejuvenating thrill of intramural softball (the one redeeming joy, Singer said, of being born American). He's only doing what he believes is expected of him, Boomfell said to his wife in Singer's defense, and the truth is he's good at it.

But Singer's friendship was puzzling and Boomfell had been unable to decide whether Singer had chosen him to be

8

his privileged confidant as he maneuvered ahead, or whether Eliot Singer somehow imagined that Charles Boomfell might someday be useful to know. His motive in maintaining the relationship might have been something else altogether, or there may have been no motive at all. Maybe Singer likes me, he once suggested to his wife. Eventually the Friday-night visits fell off, which was all right with Boomfell, and by Boomfell's fifth and final year at the school he only saw Singer by chance, at a distance.

Even after they had moved, however, and put that life behind them, the Boomfells still received a UNICEF card each year, one week after Christmas, in which the scholar still wittily belittled his drone's life of joyless toil and concluded with self-deprecating allusions to some work in progress, each card bearing the postmark of a different distant city—thus keeping Boomfell abreast of his successful career. One year he alluded to a wife, almost parenthetically, as if this remarkable news could be of no interest to them. And in fact a married Singer had no reality for Boomfell whatsoever. In memory, the man remained a bachelor.

For his part, Boomfell didn't answer these glad tidings, and with each passing year he was slightly more surprised to find, amongst his Christmas bills, the envelope bearing Singer's unmistakable calligraphy. Such persistence was annoying as well as mysterious.

Yes, at a glance this might have been Singer. Black ringlets on his neck, the cavalier mustache Eliot had grown in the third year, a svelte jacket the color of a plum. Boomfell could imagine Singer in this jacket without any trouble at all. Grinning too pleasantly, he surmised, at whatever the people with him could be saying. But what brought his former colleague most to mind was the man's stooped posture. Towering Singer slouched like a humpbacked lady who had grown up trying to keep big breasts a secret—as if he had never been comfortable with his imposing height.

"You know it's not altogether unlikely," said Boomfell. "Wouldn't he love to be teaching at one of the schools around here?"

But no—good Lord!—this in fact was not Eliot Singer sauntering into Cyrano's right out of nowhere. Only Boomfell knew his unpleasant excitement at the prospect. Singer he wouldn't want to see.

"When I think of Singer," said Val, "I think of long white feet with blue veins. Isn't that strange?" She shuddered.

These, in fact, were the unforgettable feet that had made their appearance the August evening fastidious Singer surprisingly showed up at Boomfell's back door in a blue oxford shirt, clean khaki shorts, and new, rather Roman-looking sandals—to say good-bye.

"Poor Singer."

"There was nothing poor about him," she said. "I wonder who he married. That would be interesting."

Singer's life as a man had always been an obscure matter. With two or three brief lapses—unforgettably, for Boomfell, Wanda Gwertz—Singer seemed, almost seemed, above the fervent fiddle-faddle of everyone's main joy and desire. No one was above it, Boomfell believed, a monadnock monumentally upthrust amongst the various ranges of the inside self, the cloud-covered peak never to be reached. For a while he imagined Singer lived in the grip of a profound never-to-bloom latency—like Freddie Ray. Or maybe here was a living example of textbook sublimation, Singer's overpowering ambition drying up healthy appetites. Maybe the poor son of a bitch, damaged in childhood, tossed and turned in an ongoing nightmare of sexual repression, his bachelor's apartment an onanist's fantastic lair. But frankly none of that fit Singer. Certainly, religion had nothing to do with his monkish disposition. No, Boomfell said to Val, you never knew what arrangements

Singer had made to satisfy or silence the overbearing boy between his legs.

His wife was not amused. She was frowning. She glanced behind her as if to see who might hear what she was about to say, then, pouting thoughtfully, she looked at Boomfell. "He wanted to go to bed with me. Did you know that?"

Boomfell laughed. That shy phrase—"go to bed"—was funny. The solemn heavy-duty expression on Val's face was funny.

"I'm serious."

"Lantini and Dean Reilley wouldn't have approved," he told her.

"Skip it."

Pressed against his wife in the warm crush of the crowded bar, Boomfell went on evoking the old days: Bagels from Ken's, shared first love of *Ulysses*, their single monthlong breakup, love letters by Boomfell, long Sunday afternoons playing with their genitals as if these private parts were amusing and fascinating pets.

"He was really far more interested in flirting with me than he was in discussing all that academic abracadabra with you. Eliot could be damned charming, Charlie. He charmed the pants off everyone there, including you."

"Forget Eliot Singer. God, we were innocents," Boomfell persisted. "Fellatio might as well have been the name of Romeo's friend."

"Ssh. I'm telling you something. Do you want to hear it or not? I was washing the dishes and he was standing against the stove watching me and he started telling me what an attractive woman I was. My hands were this and my hair was that and my eyes were something or other and how comely I was in this ratty old corduroy jumper I had on. You weren't home. It was Friday night and you took Ruth sliding or something. He was very sure of himself. He said he hadn't met an interesting woman since he'd gotten there. I was interesting, right? I could feel him watching me as I did the dishes. He made that huge fire, remember?"

This was a night—now that you mention it—that Boomfell remembered well. There had been a fire on the ice. The waterfall was frozen. He and Ruth held hands and drifted along the perimeter of the pond while young boys recklessly displayed their flash and flair. His daughter, new to skating, was a penguin in her snowsuit, cautiously jerking along with short abrupt strokes. One time Boomfell stayed behind by the fire while she determinedly scuttled off on her own. The band of boys flew by. He lost sight of her in the dark, the shadows of trees, amongst other skaters, and he was momentarily alarmed to an extent the circumstances hardly warranted—as if his little Ruth had skated out of his life.

At home the lights were out in the front rooms of the house, and from the car Boomfell could see a writhing forest of flames reflected on the white living room wall. The freezing air outside was redolent with wood smoke. Entering through the front door, arms full with Ruth, skates, a bag of beer, Boomfell found himself intruding upon a silent scene. Singer, settled back in the Boston rocker with a pipe in his mouth, and Val, snug in a corner of the couch with her stockinged feet cozily tucked up under her, were both staring into the hazardously large fire as if, Boomfell recalled clearly, they'd just received some sobering news. Warm enough, everyone? Val took Ruth off to bed and didn't return. Boomfell opened a window to let heat escape. Singer said in effect, Charles, I have something to tell you. Boomfell said, Let me get a drink first. That's real winter out there tonight, Eliot. When he returned to the room, Singer began talking about energy, the practicality of the wood-burning stove compared to the far less efficient yet elemental open fire. Ideally, one would want both. So, what's up? Boomfell asked. Oh, I've just been sitting here quietly tending the fire and tying one on against your return. However, Singer was not the least bit drunk. The following morning Val complained that he had wasted her evening. She wanted to read, but he wouldn't go home. Boomfell remembered the book she'd been reading at the time: *Emma*, a blue-green paperback. He remembered her grungy green corduroy jumper.

"Ruth and I didn't go sliding. We went ice-skating. At Slade's Pond."

"It had been a long time—forever—since someone had talked to me like that. He was getting all turned on while I'm standing there with my hands in the sink. My head was spinning."

"Remember Ruth's blue snowsuit with the weird frosty reindeer? God, she was gorgeous. You don't think you're ever going to forget, but you do forget. That little person is no longer with us, Val; she's gone. Yesterday she went out of the house looking like a bona fide woman. She's mad at me because we aren't taking a sabbatical to England or France or New Guinea like half her friends." He tipped up his whiskey. "Singer could have burned the house down that night."

"I didn't see it coming at all. I didn't see Eliot Singer that way. He was very frank and relaxed about it. He thought we'd have a nice time. We should try it out." She paused, then asked, as if putting the question to herself, "Why haven't I told you this before?" She sipped her drink. "When do we get to eat around here, Charlie? I won't be able to taste the food."

"That lonely bastard," said Boomfell. "Not even one consoling kiss on the couch, Val?"

"It wasn't a joke. I thought about it a lot afterward. Eliot was intriguing. I thought he looked like a tall Thoreau, odd but appealing." Val encircled her tan wrist with clean slender fingers. "He had huge hands."

"Then, why not? You wanted to. Later you wished you had."

"Because of what you've done to me in this marriage probably. I couldn't go out and meet someone if my life depended on it."

13

This, however, was not a welcome turn in the conversation. He didn't want their big night at Cyrano's to become an occasion to air grievances. "Come on," said Boomfell. "I'm kidding. Why are we getting into this at all, an insignificant flirtation ten years old? I was on another track altogether. Marlborough Street in the sixties."

"It wasn't insignificant."

In the mirror the tall man who had put them in mind of his former friend raised his arms with animation—the climax of his story, thought Boomfell. His friends of the evening, an attractive older couple, laughed. Grand time at Cyrano's, examples of wit, tidbits of gossip, genial argument, intimations of desire, hints of larger issues in the backs of our minds. Our thin human fun, he thought. The man was handsomely balding. When Boomfell looked away from them, he met his wife's eyes observing him in the mirror. Her serious eyes.

"All right, then you might as well know, Charlie." She permitted this new note to resonate, as it were, in the suspended air of the barroom. "I did have a thing with him." Pouting, Val looked into the icy suds of her piña colada and began to stir with her straw. "When I saw that man come in, I had an impulse to tell you about it because it just doesn't mean anything to me anymore. The whole thing is so far away. Then I decided there wasn't any point. Now I've told you. So."

Boomfell pleasantly grinning.

"Don't ask me any questions because I'm not going to talk about it. Period."

"He used to ask Hyde for advice just to humor him—old folded-up senile Hyde, who happened to head the tenure and promotions committee. Lantini, with his high blood pressure and his bad back, rode a bike every day, so Eliot went out and bought a bike, and they could be seen, Singer and Lantini, riding their bikes to school together in their tweed jackets and striped ties and funny little phony berets. He actually bought a beret, Valerie, except Lantini's was blue and Singer's was black. Oh my God. He used to avoid me in the halls—at concerts and lectures he didn't know me. *Samson Agonistes*, Val. *Samson Agonistes*. And here's a detail I'll never forget, all right. I'm in the outer room waiting to see Lantini, who has summoned me to discuss my future, and who should I hear in his office with him but Singer, Val, right. They're flirting away in there like they're on a date. Singer has him purring with gentle laughter in the palm of his hand. And then I hear Lantini saying, Now, our Charles Boomfell is a mysterious fellow, Eliot. I'm sure you know him as well as any of us. What's this I hear about a book? And Eliot Singer, who had seen my manuscript in the flesh and was one of the few people I'd ever made the mistake of talking about it with—Val, do you know what he said? I wouldn't be the one to ask, Walter, I rarely see Boomfell. There are those who wonder if such a book exists. I left the room in shock. I never kept the appointment with Lantini. For shame. There are those who wonder if such a book exists, Val, which is simply another way of saying there are those who wonder if Charles Boomfell exists. Right? And on top of everything, he had those feet with the toenails. Right?"

During Boomfell's speech Val watched the bartender mix drinks. Nor did she look at him now. "Does Charles Boomfell exist now, Charlie? You just sold your first house." Glancing up into the mirror, she added, "Believe it or not, I believed in you."

"Once? Twice? What?"

"I don't know. Friday mornings for a while." Her initial anxiety, if that's what it was, had given way to an air of bored indifference. "I thought he liked you. I wouldn't have done it if he didn't like you." She turned to him and gave the lapel of his corduroy jacket an impatient yank. "The lumberjack. Boomfell the bumpkin. I don't know why he said that to Lantini. You should have asked him."

"For a while?" he asked. "How long?"

But she wasn't giving any clues to the chronology or the duration, or to the reality, of the affair—the thing—between Eliot Singer and herself. "See, I shouldn't have told you. I'm not going to say another word about it." She was going to the women's room.

"Well, was it okay?" Boomfell took her arm to detain her, and bore down upon his wife with a look of some urgency. "Was it fun?"

"Don't bully me. I know what you were up to with God knows who."

"But fun, Val. Our friend Singer wouldn't be my idea of fun."

"Right, I made it up, Charlie. Don't believe me." She freed her arm. "I'll tell you one thing, which I know interests you a great deal."

"Shoot."

"It," said Val, and she held up her index fingers as if this were a fish story, "was unreal."

Boomfell watched her cut her way through the packed room to the arched doorway. Singer's double touched her back as he let her by, then Val's bright blouse was lost in the dim light and the crowd and the dazzling mirrors of Cyrano's. Good-bye.

You can't imagine how remote and out of reach this seems to me, Singer once said to Boomfell following a scene of domestic peace and order in which adorable Ruth and Ben had kissed their father good night, kissed their father's strange giant visitor good night, and been led off to bed by their pleased, pretty mother. If I envied you anything, Boomfell, sad Singer had said, it would be this. With his large hand he gestured to the walls and ceiling of the room where they sat, to this house, Boomfell's home, to this whole heart of the family man's life.

Forgetting himself in Cyrano's, Boomfell groaned.

He remembered looking up from the puzzling and unpleasant realization of another checkmate, from the evening's second

16

game of chess and his second defeat, to find Singer watching him with nothing of the victor's predictable air of irrepressible triumph, but rather gloomily, shruggingly, as if to say, Sorry, I wish you could have won. The sting of Singer's weary superior refusal when Boomfell pleaded in vain for a third game stung more now, some ten or eleven years later. How about one more game, Eliot, just one more? Not tonight, Charlie.

The hollow courtesy with which Val and Singer had always greeted each other, Boomfell had always interpreted that as an untested yet tacit antipathy. Val would excuse herself for the night ten minutes after their guest had shown up and Boomfell would be left to explain: She's been on the go since early this morning, Eliot, don't take it personally. God love us!

He remembered a discussion of *Madame Bovary—mon dieu!*—in which he had long-windedly argued against Singer's too sympathetic view of Charles, that pathetic fool, until at last a bored Singer came to his feet—it was late; he had to get to bed—and told him that he considered the whole matter academic and really didn't give a damn about any of the characters in that perfect book. It was the sentences that interested him. He had placed his hand on Boomfell's shoulder. Why had this stuck with him?

A great deal of Singer had stuck with him—his morose good looks, his astute silences and shrewd asides. Boomfell could recall a discussion of divorce in which he had boasted the mettle of his own tempered marriage—still kids back then, for crying out loud!—while this expert on eighteenth-century English literature sat with legs crossed, and nodded, grunted, grinned. In his unbearable black beret.

But if Singer had known his wife, so to speak, why then should Boomfell feel known? If he had in fact fucked and fondled Val Friday mornings for a while, why should Boomfell feel defenseless and found out? He did, he did. Eliot Singer—Boomfell's secret sharer! This seemed far worse at the moment than the mere licks and moans of adultery. Once Boomfell had read to Singer from his manuscript, nothing he did easily. Singer smiled, unforgettably, and said, Not bad.

There are those who wonder if such a book exists. His visits had stopped at that point, but when Singer unexpectedly dropped in on them the following August, Boomfell welcomed him as cheerfully as ever, and listened as sympathetically as ever to the new professor's most recent complaints and the continuing chronicle, both comical and cruel, of Lantini's fatuous ways. Just as if revelation of that remark had not occurred. No, he wouldn't give Singer a cold shoulder at this stage of the game and, along with it, the satisfaction of attributing such last-minute hostility to a Boomfell case of sour grapes now that Boomfell was on the way out. No, he'd be a good sport and leave Singer answerable, where Boomfell was concerned, to his own conscience. Laugh, everyone. Laugh and spit.

Wasn't it mammoth gall to have come by at all? They'd already begun packing; labeled boxes were stacked in the living room. There, towering above them in his new sandals, and tanned as a cheerleader, Singer took down their new address in his little notebook and slipped it into the back pocket of his khaki shorts. He capped his fountain pen and clipped it to his shirtfront, Boomfell recalled, seizing upon every detail with pale fire. In no time, Singer told them, you'll have put these years behind you—unlike me. (Just as if, in those jobless days of rising inflation, it had been Boomfell's good fortune to be fired.) The man added, Maybe I'll get down that way to see you one day. Extending his hand to Val—his hand!—he said, Well, I guess this is it. Val stepped up on tiptoe and placed her hands on his broad shoulders to bestow one quick kiss. Without further ado, she left the room. At the time Boomfell only imagined it had been a distasteful duty for her, performed with such dispatch. He had imagined she was as impatient and fed up with Eliot Singer's pomposity and presumption as he was.

Boomfell, Boomfell, Boomfell.

The author of "Swift and Stella: Speculations on a Secret"—Boomfell still had his signed copy of the article somewhere—then turned to his former colleague and they shook hands. Oh, one last thing if it isn't too much trouble, he said. I believe I lent you my *Hero with a Thousand Faces* at one point. Voilà: the point of Singer's eleventh-hour call. Yes, yes, yes, chirped Boomfell. Of course; no trouble. He scrambled to the basement and found the oversize paperback amongst a stack of unpacked *National Geographic*s and *Ranger Rick*s. Boomfell had borrowed it at Singer's insistence—a must, Charlie—at least two years before. Ah, you do have it, said Singer. So I thought.

Outside on the front steps he placed his hand on Boomfell's shoulder for the last time. His height endowed Singer with a patronizing and sometimes patriarchal manner. Now look, Charlie, don't vanish on us forever. Let's keep in touch. If you ever have any longing for this place, just remember the winters—and think of your unfortunate friend.

Take care, Eliot.

Boomfell watched him walk across the lawn to his white Raleigh ten-speed, which stood against the ten-foot birch tree he and Val had planted two years before. Tall, stoop-shouldered, glum. He was an incongruous giant, all arms and legs, on the elevated racing seat, slenderly hunched over the curled handlebars: a sublime praying mantis. Without looking back, the cyclist raised his arm as he glided down the slight grade. Boomfell waved back, although Singer wasn't looking, and he was touched, despite himself, as his Friday-night friend rounded the bend in the road and disappeared from view.

Maybe he likes me, Val, in his own way. Wince!

God yes, a great deal of Singer had stuck with him. Not to mention, for instance, the lonely nightlong vigil the lowly Boomfell kept outside a tiny rented house, huddled in bushes, waiting for Singer's faded Plymouth Fury to leave—not to mention, that is, the blond cellist from California, Wanda

Gwertz. No, thought Boomfell, shutting his eyes to the slide show of trite repellent scenes featuring Singer, Gwertz, and Boomfell, which had switched on at the back of his brain. Not tonight.

Quite by accident, via these egoist's worries, he stumbled upon the question of his wife's needs. What loneliness, longing, and neglect . . . ? But when he took two minutes to sift through highlights of those years—their first house, its view, Val's vigils and marches, the blizzard, Ben's mysterious flu, the death of Grandma Welsh, their first canoe—it seemed to Boomfell that if ever there had been a mellow plateau in the course of their married life, that was it, despite, for instance, the Gwertz episode. Nestled, no less, in a rural countryside changing with the seasons like scenes out of a Grandma Moses calendar, that had been the period of their life—believe it or not, I believed in you—when he and Val had come closer than ever before (or since) to what he would have dared to call—oh word!—happiness.

Thanks in part to Eliot Singer, everyone? Your weaseling, wheedling, worming Singer? He even complained about our beloved pastoral countryside, Val. Nature annoyed him. He was indifferent to fields and streams, irritated by cows and farmers, afraid of dogs and the dark. He hated weather, for the love of God—wind, rain, cold, heat. When Val, holding back a tear, told him the story of their terrier's tragic death by snowplow, Singer was holding back a smile. Each detail of country life only contributed to his constant lament for his lost New York City—a sob story poured out to no one but Boomfell. Lantini, a city boy himself, turned country gentleman, would have been surprised to know that Eliot intended to abandon them and unspoiled beauty at the first decent opportunity.

No, she couldn't have done it, not with someone who didn't care whether birds and ladybugs lived or died. Or if she could have done it after all, she never could have concealed it so well, with such a seasoned deceiver's ease and skill and scorn of spouse. Of course not. Not to have picked up one filthy hint of anything the whole time, how could that have been possible? Oh, good joke, sweetheart. The very night of our little celebration. You carried it off with real class. But why wasn't Boomfell laughing? Because the mood and manner of her off-the-cuff confession had been altogether convincing, was why. Because he knew her—she was his wife—and he knew when she was not joking.

Walking home one evening through new snow, briefcase in hand, he entered their warm welcoming kitchen to be greeted by the garlicky aroma of roasting lamb, his favorite meal, and then, more rare, the happy hug of a radiant rosy-cheeked wife. Charlie, you're home! Livelier, prettier, yes, cheerier than ever. The day had been a Friday. For Boomfell also remembered—trudging down memory lane in spite of himself—that the next morning, Saturday, the whole smiling family had gone sledding down a favorite hill not at all far from their house. Four Boomfells bundled up together on the Boomfell sled, caroling hoots and hurrahs as they flew down an ideal hill on a picture-perfect morning. Happier than ever, Val.

See, I shouldn't have told you.

In the room-length mirror behind the bar, reflecting everything, he was the glaring example of a person out of place, out of season, out of sorts. Does Charles Boomfell exist now?

A dozen stools from where he stood Boomfell spotted anyone's idea, he thought, of an attractive young woman alone on a Saturday night, bravely waiting for something to happen. He held his drink above his head and made his way to her side.

"Hi."

"You know I've never even been picked up, Charlie. I don't even know what that's like."

For the first time in years, Boomfell found himself observing his wife as he would any woman. She hadn't worn a bra, he supposed, in years, and yet in a sense—in the sense of desire—he hadn't noticed. Val had applied gloss to her lips. Just on the line of her jaw, an inch below her left earlobe, all but concealed by makeup: a small mole. It had always been there. In the gentle light of Cyrano's, the lines in Val's face didn't amount to anything worth worrying about. Boomfell considered her capable beaten-up hands: a ten-dollar wedding ring.

Dormant lust for his wife, swelling in Boomfell earlier, now made him bold and, huddled over her, he began to recount joys of sex drawn from their real life. Dirty talk Boomfell wouldn't have expressed to anyone but Val and, even then, in only the most uncommon and unaccountable mood of shared lewdness. He praised the feast of her femaleness, lavishing laughable alliterative language on the various edibles of her anatomy. He recalled their delayed discovery, after years of marriage, of hitherto forbidden orifices, which had temporarily turned them into two venturous virgins again. Once, at the licentious urging of Boomfell's blue language, not unlike his present prompting, Val succumbed to unnatural acts with a vegetable from the garden while a breathless Boomfell watched from across the room like a drugged ape.

"That turns me off," said Val, "not on." He was being abusive. "Describe me savoring a piece of salmon, Charlie, if you want to be titillating."

Boomfell persisted, pestering his wife's ear with nonsense, and a little premarital scene in the woods, in which Boomfell happened to recall schoolgirlish knee socks, a pleated wool skirt, a handmade cabled sweater, as well as the joy and difficulty of making it against a tree, something in this moment seemed to take hold and Val didn't tell him to stop as he stammered to recapture the slippery thrill and urgency of that awkward upright maneuver. Like trying to hold broken eggs in your bare hands without spilling. . . . But his hold on

22

the erotic began to slip and the focus on the merely physical became blurred as the context of their walk in the woods came back.

It had been Thanksgiving at Grandma Welsh's, Val's little old sharp-as-a-tack grandmother, and the first holiday Boomfell had spent amongst Val's large holiday-spirited family. By three-thirty the eating was over. Now I can die, Grandma Welsh declared. Everyone was "stuffed," and "adjourned" to the stuffy living room. In their warm sated state, half the holiday company dozed off in old slipcovered furniture while afternoon shadows lengthened along Grandma Welsh's Oriental rug and the band of roving cousins raised cries of play outside. Boomfell, the family guest, as stuffed and warm as the rest, endeavored to present an interested face to garrulous Uncle Guy, who held forth on unions, Jews, new cars. Bursting, that's all, with stopped-up longing that had been building for days, coming to a head all morning during his three-hour drive to the country. Just aching for this schoolgirl on the couch in the wool skirt and furry sweater whom he hadn't seen for a week, hadn't been alone with yet all day, and who had now abandoned him altogether for her older and plainer sister, her manipulative mother, her boring elderly aunt.

"Remember?"

"Yes."

Drowsy numbness overtook stuffed warm Boomfell at last, and when he least expected it, his hand was plucked from his lap and this smiling wide-awake anthropology major he'd known for two months or so was asking him if he'd like to take a walk. Oh, I guess so. Just suffocating, everyone, with want. I'll show you my favorite tree. Endearing Grandma Welsh, "tipsy" by now, her stockings rolled down around her ankles, said, My tree my arse; you haven't been back in those woods for years. General laughter. Can I come? asked a little cousin. Why don't you stay here, chimed the older sister, the mother, the aunt.

Was it his obvious lust that commanded such respect? He was a thief stealing out of the room with her.

"We were kids. Babies."

"You wrote me that letter," said Val. "I thought it was great."

Then the beautiful air, crisp as an apple, bare trees, dead fragrant leaves, and the edgy oozy excitement of being stuffed with Thanksgiving dinner plus puffed up with desire for this warm near person. The cheers of children hounded them across the lawn. They strolled into the woods behind the house—oh, casually—as though they themselves could not have dreamed that the tender picture they made kicking up leaves would become, at first touch, a torrid X-rated scene of clinging and clawing containing everything: torn underwear, helpless animal sounds. The sky behind the bare trees was the color of bittersweet. There, Val said, is that a tree or not?

Then—and now—Boomfell placed his hand on Val's shoulder. We can't, darling . . . really, the kids. That adult word—darling—which she never used as an adult. But they were already up against the mightiest elm tree Boomfell had ever seen and everything was already under way. And as the young ardent Boomfell begins to spill the eggs and as the present Boomfell began to run out of words again (and then . . . remember), Val, his wife, turned her face into his shoulder and placed her hand on his chest just as she had done then (so it seemed), which affecting gesture brought Boomfell all the way back to that memorable late afternoon in the woods behind Grandma Welsh's house.

This was that person!

"My poor little grandmother."

Boomfell felt they had entered a realm, call it, of unlooked-for possibility. When she raised her head—this, he thought, is that person—an old response prompted him to proffer a kiss, which touched an old responsiveness in Val. As of old, Boomfell and wife kissed.

24

Big deal! But it was a big deal—if not quite the sort of white lightning Henry James employed to strike innocence with knowledge. Expert sex between Boomfell and Val, long since a single-minded, self-serving matter, mastered along tried-and-true lines of mutual give-and-take, didn't involve kissing, even at its abandoned best. They hadn't kissed each other, really, in years. Memory of the feeling flowed back as from another life altogether, and Boomfell recognized that here was the kiss he had always half expected on the occasion of each first kiss with anyone new—the measure of all that desperate hugger-muggery—and the authentic kiss to which no one else's kiss quite measured up.

Valerie Welsh!

His wife drew back to glance at him inquiringly, unsure of herself or Boomfell or the place, then she closed her eyes and this kiss of yesteryear, more novel and exciting in its way than any of the eroticism Boomfell had been drumming up for them—reminiscent, almost, of making love to Valerie Welsh against her favorite tree—momentarily resumed in the bar-room intimacy and anonymity of Cyrano's.

Yet even as they partook of this first kiss in years, Boomfell knew—surely Val knew—that this would probably prove to be their last kiss in years as well. If it had once been the real thing, it no longer was. Holding his wife close, he looked into the mirror. Anyone might have taken them for a pair of devil-may-care adulterers set free in a foreign city, rather than, as they appeared to Boomfell at that moment, two lonely, vaguely disappointed people.

Does Charles Boomfell exist now?

The man who at a distance had seemed the spit and image of Eliot Singer reached over them for drinks. No, there was nothing of Singer's intelligence, audacity, or melancholy in this man's face.

"You don't love me anymore," Val said coolly. "You never say so."

25

Boomfell tipped his ear toward her and asked, as if he hadn't heard, "What?" Her boldness, this daring, stunned him.

With her index finger she traced the outline of his old jacket's crinkled lapel. "I don't think I love you anymore either."

Cyrano's burly host, his voice raised above the general hubbub of the place, announced "Boomfell." Their table was ready.

Before they reached the arched doorway that led from the glitter and noise of the bar to the reserved velvet formality of the dining room, Boomfell caught his wife by the arm and said, just loud enough for her to hear him, "Of course I love you, goddamnit."

"Sure you do."

Guilt and shame and lust were his constant companions. Lust lorded it over the other two, sulking hangers-on who went along kicking the dirt, never having any fun, always whining to get back home. Wandalust. An old Volvo wagon, a certain green, still had the power to make him turn away or, in a more fanciful mood, follow with hungry eyes until the streetlight changed, and the car turned left or right and was lost to view. It was her misfortune to be Boomfell's maiden voyage through the straits of adultery, which led, in this case, to the up-and-down sea of obsession with its squalls of hurt feelings and rejections, its little deserted islands offering fake respite, remorse, more lies, which led ultimately to the halting journey back to the mainland rather than, as they sometimes pretended was possible, a new sunlit shore, white beach beneath emerald hill, where you could live in your skin, there was plenty to eat, and the people were friendly, a place that justified and forgave all the waste and risk of getting there. It was the misfortune of her name—Wanda—to become, for him, something like the pained sound an old man might make stubbing his toe in the dark.

At first sight she was sitting on the carpeted floor of a frugal academic's dowdy family room, holding the slender leg of a harpsichord. She had taken off her red leather shoes. Her stockings were black. The wall-to-wall carpeting was oatmeal. Before the night was over he was sitting on the floor holding hands with her stockinged foot. Under interrogation—intense

27

Boomfell's mode of conversation in those days—she turned out to be a cellist, new to the music department. She swam, for exercise, and wove rag rugs for relaxation. When he spoke of the happiness of musicians, fluent in their universal language, buoyed above the prevailing muck by ageless works of genius, and the task itself an enviable matter of mastering the possible, she said, Music is dog-eat-dog; I've been killing myself since I was six.

Lost in his libido, he squandered time and energy like an infant. They spent most of the year tugging at one another's crotches at every opportunity, then breaking up and making up, months went up like smoke in banal anguishing almost as stimulating as secret screwing had been. The fun of torment, he wrote in his notebook. She moved three times in six months. Twice, catching up with her on moving day, he helped her cart her single-girl's stuff, an old oak table, an iron bed, her bricks and boards that made a bookcase. A driven man, he sped into the sunset on the arrowlike interstate at blind speeds, not to return until the small hours of the morning, either enraged or elated depending on whether he'd found her in her tiny apartment. One afternoon, following a thunderstorm, he cracked her bedroom door with his fist.

Although she was vain, and pretty in an odd way, it soon became apparent to Boomfell that she contrived to look as plain as possible when he was around. Unwashed hair looped behind large ears, face scrubbed clean of makeup, which in Wanda's case often concealed the rashes and blotches that flared up uncontrollably during periods of stress to mar her fair complexion. Her ugly-duckling strategem amused him. Obsession hungered for imperfections. No one would want this woman—save Boomfell.

One weekend she went to stay with a friend because, she told him with what seemed real alarm, she'd discovered large footprints in the moist tulip bed under her bedroom window. By means of merciless interrogation, poking and prodding until she bawled the man's name into Boomfell's wide-eyed face, he learned that she had spent the weekend at the White Horse Inn with Eliot Singer.

Obsession entered a new shameless phase. He spent most of a night returning to her little rented house on Grand Avenue at hour-long intervals, waiting for Singer's faded Plymouth Fury to be gone so he could come tapping at her door to find out what the devil she thought she was doing to him—to Boomfell. Unbelievably, the car didn't leave. Undeniably, it was Singer's car: three missing letters left the rude word MOUTH in chrome on the left-hand corner of the trunk for Boomfell, hour after hour, to read. MOUTH MOUTH MOUTH. Unbearably, by quarter to three, the lights in the house had gone out.

He pounced on pale wan Wanda as she wheeled her three-speed bike into her overgrown backyard the next day. Questioning, reviling, but also kidding around, jokes from Boomfell about Singer's nose, his ass-licking ambition, his humped back, although the night before he'd been beside himself at the thought of this back humped above his smothered Gwertz. In the thick of crisis and hate he could still make her laugh, winning her over again, while he caught a whiff of the sex between them and the thrust of their pillow talk. Once he got his foot in the door it was only a few steps back to the bedroom. Endings followed endings.

She practiced a minimum of four hours a day even on her worst days, even on the worst days of the depressing Boomfell debacle when he could do little more than run—five, ten, fifteen miles—and fret. Wanda, after all, had a career under way. Regularly, she was off to Boston, New York, New Haven, to play in some string ensemble or chamber group, at some festival, some church or university affair. It took years of Ruth's violin lessons, years of subsequent concertgoing, for Boomfell the ignoramus to realize how good she was—very good—and how hard she worked to stay that way.

During the first months of knowing her he would let himself into her house, silent as an assailant if he heard her at work, and sit for half an hour before leaving as unobtrusively as he had come, not wishing to break her concentration. He admired the manly way she straddled her beloved cello with her legs, her square-assed upright posture, her dead-seriousness. The expression on her face—her puckered brow—was something like the expression on her face when he made leisurely love to her. Listening hard to bring something inside out, something outside in. Her fingering was remarkable. Her vibrato could cause vibrations in the pit of his stomach. More than one humid afternoon he had come upon her wearing nothing but a dish towel over her left shoulder as she played. She didn't intend to be enticing. When she practiced, Wanda hardly seemed to know he was there. That was hard to believe—discipline and determination that blocked him out—but it was true. Later on, when to intrude at all would have disturbed her, he stayed away during her customary practice times. Long afterward, even now, he thanked his stars that he had maintained that shred of sanity. There had been days, to be sure, when he could have put his foot through the gleaming back of her priceless instrument, her enviable and unassailable refuge.

At the end of April he and Val went to a faculty recital. The second half of the program was Wanda Gwertz. She wore a simple black dress. Nothing, not even a music stand, stood between her with her cello and the cruel world, it seemed to Boomfell just then. Silence! he wanted to shout as the restless audience settled down. Marilyn Reilley clicked down the aisle, late from her intermission smoke; he could have wrung her simpleton's neck.

The first note caused his gut to jump. He was as nervous as he had been the first time little Ruth performed her dizzying Suzuki solo, "Perpetual Motion," for a dozen child violinists and their tense, grinning moms and dads. In no time, however, he saw that Wanda didn't need him holding his breath for her. She was in command. He sat back more comfortably, loosened his grip on his knees.

Her face, as she played, was as changeable as the ups and downs of her relationship with Boomfell. She was severe and authoritarian, almost angry, during passages of rapid virtuosity or mounting force. Her torso tipped and swayed, her full lower lip protruded arrogantly, her nostrils flared with her studied breathing. Then, the music sweeter, she turned away, presenting her profile to the audience, turned away from this big member of the violin family as if resisting its cloying, too seductive sound. Here, he considered, was her lifelong friend, her loyal comfort and opposition. Several times Wanda Gwertz swooned, seemed to swoon, seated alone onstage in the university's paneled nineteenth-century auditorium.

She concluded with Bach's Suite no. 5 in C Minor—the only piece Boomfell, having heard it before, recalled by name. He recognized the movements he'd listened to her working on in the bare white-walled living room on Grand Avenue. During the sarabande, the cellist's head fell back, pale neck exposed, eyes closed. Her lips moved as if mouthing the sounds she was making. He too, he considered, weirdly identifying with old wood and gut that stood on one leg, had stood like that before her seated figure, similarly embraced by her whole body. But mere lovemaking had never done this to her face, elicited such surrender. Giving them her all, the entranced stranger, as she suddenly struck him, was unusually attractive, beautiful to everyone present, he imagined—a soul who had thrust herself above the rest of them. He looked at his lap in alarm. Val had placed her hand over his. When he glanced toward her, she was facing the stage, evidently moved. What did this mean? What was she saying?

The brisk gavotte came as a relief. At last, when the Bach suite ended, he was relieved.

Huddled over her cello then, Wanda looked momentarily lost. The applause—Boomfell's hands roaring—might have had nothing to do with the woman onstage. Her smile, as it gradually appeared, was more radiant, that was the word, plain happier than any smile she had beamed in his direction. She must have had him in mind during the Bach suite, he assumed, somewhere in the back of her mind. But when he sought and met her eyes as they panned the audience—there, wasn't she looking directly at him?—Wanda didn't seem to know Boomfell was Boomfell.

Her performance was a revelation to him, yet revelation of the real Wanda didn't provoke him to leave her to her first love, the antique overlord, four feet four, that sang between her knees, aglow in its honeyed patina.

For two weeks she visited Nova Scotia, then drove down the Maine coast, dropping in on old friends at the Pierre Monteux School. When she returned she agreed to meet him for dinner. Boomfell couldn't think straight all day. Just as he was leaving his office to pick her up, at the last possible moment, she called and told him she couldn't make it after all. Her father had suddenly shown up from somewhere, she explained, and wanted to spend the evening with her. She was whispering over the phone because she was in this amazing personal library—you'd love this, Charlie; it's your dream of a library—and didn't want to be overheard. She called her father Dad. Indirectly, as it were, he quizzed her about Dad's friend, the house, the room she was then standing in. He was able to picture the whole scene without any trouble: Wanda in a cotton dress whispering over the phone in the paneled room of a huge fake Tudor in a nice neighborhood. She was impatient, yet she was able to answer his questions without hesitation. There was a ship's portrait over the mantel, a large oak table, two walls of books, an Oriental rug—like the one in your living room, she said. Heriz. Hey, I remembered!—a view of the backyard with a clump of birches in it. Dad's friend was an endodontist. I've got to go, really, she said. Wily, clever, quick-witted. You can't do much about the prerogatives of father-hood, said Boomfell the father. He believed her.

He believed her.

Nevertheless, the moment he hung up he instinctively, if this was instinct, phoned her tiny downtown apartment.

She answered immediately, she hadn't even moved away from the phone. Following his evil hello, a smug grunt, there was silence on Wanda's end. For Boomfell it was a moment of terrible satisfaction. You bastard, she swore, that's not fair. You shouldn't have called back.

He didn't call again. Heriz. Hey, I remembered! What did it mean, to come up with that off the top of your head? Was it a gift? Part of his obsession, he thought, had been trying to get to the bottom of her. There was no bottom. The idea of her standing in her cramped and steamy efficiency kitchen, in underwear probably, whispering over the phone as if she were in the tall library of a stranger's gracious home—inventing the room for him, his dream of such a room—while Dad drank cocktails outside by the pool, the crazy desperation of it seized his imagination. He had to stop doing this to her.

It was like the big sleep was over, here comes spring (it was actually another fall), time to wake up, and bearish Boomfell emerged from his cave with a half-assed grin on his face, blinking at the bright life all around him. There was Val and Ruth and Ben again. There was his own backyard, his neighbor with a beer, a stack of unread books, his running shoes. Wanda Gwertz was over. He no longer wanted to phone, or write letters on yellow paper, or prowl her street at midnight, or run into her by chance at an evening of Ravel or anywhere.

Then, from one of her music friends—oh, by the way, said Sue List—he learned that she was gone in more ways than one, self-exiled without a word to a gray island in the Atlantic, a place he had never laid eyes on. Wanda had joined the Atlantic Symphony Orchestra. For Boomfell's intents and purposes Nova Scotia didn't exist. When it turned up in an issue of *National Geographic* on his coffee table, "Nova Scotia: The Magnificent Anchorage," he didn't look at the pictures.

A year later, while Val and the children were away, he ran into Singer at the grocery store. The bachelor, who seemed overly happy to see him—they hadn't met socially for months—invited Boomfell to dinner.

Singer's apartment, located at the rear of a sprawling Victorian place surrounded by porches, was one long room plus a standing-room-only kitchen. Boomfell had been here before, but not, come to think of it, since Wanda Gwertz had been here. It was easy to imagine her sitting on the edge of Singer's enormous bed, which dominated his meager dwelling. There was a Victorian love seat, worn rose velvet. That would have gone well with the white dress she had liked the look of herself in that summer. Between bed and couch stood a card table covered with a white tablecloth and fastidiously set for two. Two white plates; goblets for water and wine; extravagantly ornate silver handed down to Eliot, Boomfell learned that night, from an elderly aunt; off-white candles in brass candlesticks; a rose, for the love of God, in a crystal vase. Was this how the room had looked to Wanda Gwertz the evening Singer stuffed her with Cornish game hen, anesthetized her with wine, and persuaded her to spend the night? From the outset, Boomfell felt he was on a date, or revisiting a date, a scene of undoing.

Aside from the table setting, this might have been the temporary room of a poor student rather than the home of a professional man in his thirties. Plants would have helped, he thought. Books would have helped, but Singer kept most of his books at school. Picasso's *Swimmer*, tacked above the bed, its corners curling, was the only thing on the walls. Three neat stacks of magazines stood at the foot of the bed: *The New*

Yorker, The New York Review of Books, The Nation. Singer's formidable rolltop desk was, at second glance, orderly. Papers, books, and manila folders were arranged in neat piles around a blank blue folder. To Boomfell, the family man, this looked like a lonely life.

Taking a leak in Singer's surprisingly bright and spacious bathroom, he was able to imagine—too easily—Wanda Gwertz up to her tits in the old deep tub. It stood on ball-and-claw feet.

Wearing an apron over his white tennis clothes, and rosy as an eighteenth-century English portrait, Eliot smiled handsomely as he carved a slab of steak and placed it on Boomfell's plate. Veins stood out on his tan capable hands. Yes, Boomfell saw, Singer was an attractive man. Wanda Gwertz must have noticed that. For dessert they had Singer's chocolate mousse, which was as good as Wanda Gwertz, under pressure of Boomfell's relentless questioning, had said it was: Fucking delicious, you bastard. He thoughtfully savored each spoonful as if seeking the secret of its subtle bittersweetness. They drank whiskey, wine, cognac, and at some point their mutual friend, the cellist, came up. Singer still laughed, he said, recalling the setting of his first intimacy with her (that was how Singer talked). It had been charged with danger and comedy.

"Don't make me guess," said Boomfell. He believed he already knew where the hard-to-believe trick had been turned. The White Horse Inn.

"The living room floor of the faculty club, following the May Day meeting of the Wine and Cheese Society." Flushed Singer sat back to laugh. "Behind the couch, Charles Boomfell, like thieves. *Behind* the couch—like furtive fresh-faced teenagers with nowhere to go. But you know what?"

Boomfell shook his head: he didn't know what.

"I wouldn't trade a week in a king-size bed for that sweet panting spontaneity."

She and Singer had been thick as thieves all afternoon,

swapping the wisecracks of schoolteachers, stuck in their muck of puns. In a wildly uncharacteristic gesture, Eliot had unbuttoned the top three buttons of his short-sleeved cotton shirt. In bare feet and her flimsy yellow sundress, Wanda had flaunted her well-being that day like a reckless ten-year-old. Boomfell, lurking at the edge of the party, had been blind as a spoiled old man to the sexual signals bandied between them as visibly as the shuttlecock they'd batted to one another at one point in the backyard. Fed up with the tipsy whine and wheeze society, he'd left the miserable gathering. Wanda would regret her refusal to leave with him, he had imagined, when he withheld himself from her for two or three punishing days.

"You were there that day, weren't you?" Singer asked. "Charles Boomfell wouldn't play in our game of volleyball. I guess you and Wanda had more or less had your fill of one another at that point."

"Wanda was a friend," Boomfell replied, "that's all."

But Singer was grinning. "She told me you became a bit of a nuisance. Something about sniffing around her house at night. Grand Avenue. Footprints under her window. That was it, the waffle footprints. Boomfell the runner. Vanity gave you away."

Boomfell guffawed his disbelief. She had seemed authentically frightened by those mysterious footprints under her bedroom window. No, there was no getting to the bottom of her—her twenty thousand leagues of deceit. To portray him as a skulking Peeping Tom to the likes of Singer! At last he felt betrayed.

"We had a card from her not long ago," Singer went on. "This spring she did the Elgar."

"You've heard from her?" asked Boomfell. He was unable to conceal his surprise. "I mean, you've stayed in touch?"

Singer leaned toward him over the small white table. "Haven't you?"

And Boomfell recognized the sudden sickening sensation

he had too often felt seated opposite Singer as he sought in vain, eyes scrambling, to find the move that would free his king, at least for a few more moves, from final mate.

Haven't you?

Now, as he lay in the dark beside his wife years later, following their vaguely disappointing dinner at Cyrano's, how well he remembered supper at Singer's—another surfeit of reveal-ings—right down to the apron over tennis shorts, the salad dressing, things said. To rerun that scene in light of Val's purported *thing* with the man—could Singer have been that bad? The behind-us past upon us again—and different than it had been. Unsettled, unknown. The way we're always on thin ice, liable to fall through the present at any moment without warning. Val's old news, chances were it never would have come up—her thing with Singer—it never would have hap-pened as far as Boomfell was concerned, had he not chosen Saturday night at Cyrano's, that particular time and place, for his surprise evening out.

You just sold your first house. He had taken her there to celebrate that unlikely accomplishment: his loath break with the past.

Now, on the other hand, what did any of it matter? These years later, other, graver concerns had come to the fore. Every-one had moved on to another world of worries. Their life together was becoming a lifetime. Times of their life together could be measured counting years by fives and tens. Roughly. You're a fortunate man. He reached under the covers for the hem of his wife's flannel nightgown and carefully drew it up over her legs. Fifteen and more years ago he could hardly believe his luck: slipping a hand into her silken underthings. Valerie Welsh! Desire survived intact in the same inside self. Sex became important—like sleep—when you weren't get-ting enough of it. Awake, unfold, want. Val groaned impatiently, drew down her nightgown, pulled up her heels, and turned her back to him.

Wanda Gwertz! From here they looked like a pair of innocents. Those days would have to amuse her now, if she ever thought about them: Charles Boomfell! Still there in the front row of the Atlantic Symphony Orchestra with your faithful cello? That seemed unlikely. Yet time passed. People got stuck. Ten years ago the Franklins went off to Maine to raise a house, have a garden, spin wool; they never came back.

Does Charles Boomfell exist now?

I believed in you.

Crickets sang under the stone steps below the window. Something sad about it. September. The harvest moon out there in their red maple. His lonely neighbor's lights were on. Holly Dean Lawson. The young woman never dreamed that marriage would mean someone never home—living alone in a strange house, circa 1830. You will find we adapt to our major disappointments pretty well as a rule.

So how have things turned out with you, Wanda Gwertz? In a sense he no longer cared. Are you married? Or working to save the planet? Are you still thin? Has fucking ever turned out to be thicker? In Boomfell's mind, she remained stubbornly out of fashion—her pants too loose or too tight, her skirts too long or too short, her colors too bright or too dull. She would never drive anything but an old Volvo a certain green. Consigned to the past as she was, he nevertheless made one definite assumption concerning Wanda Gwertz: she was thirty-three, thirty-four, thirty-five; she was all right; alive.

He never expected to see her again, any more than he expected to see Lantini, the Franklins, Eliot Singer, the woman from France. It took years to sort out the people you missed. That was no excuse. With a little effort he might have stayed in touch. An annual Christmas card, for example, might have kept things open. That was smart. Getting in touch no longer seemed possible. You assumed everyone was all right, going about their lives, and yet surely everyone wasn't all right. A mysterious symptom, a pain that got worse instead of better. A loneliness with no relief in sight. There were people he missed, awake on a September night, crickets outside, the new neighbor off to bed with every light in the house left on. With damned little effort he might have stayed in touch with them.

Leaning toward him across a small candlelit table, the serious face of Eliot Singer, perplexed and concerned, appeared somewhere behind Boomfell's closed eyes.

Haven't you?

Long silent Saturdays in deserted Lovejoy were among Boomfell's fondest memories of his short-lived teaching career. The classroom building, emptied of students, acquired a hallowed feel. Silence seemed to echo through the maze of darkened corridors. In the men's room the flush of the toilet would resound. Boomfell read bulletin boards and the office doors of colleagues papered with cartoons by Koren, Booth, Steig. He slid down banisters like a boy. From the plate-glass window on the third floor he surveyed the playing fields—two or three colors moving in clusters, breaking apart—like a reclusive monarch dreaming of future conquests. Once as he stood there an ovenbird flew into the glass wall and dropped to the concrete balcony, and didn't revive. In his office, a small windowless cell, he worked on his manuscript, or read, or maybe mused in undisturbed solitude. On Saturdays the building was a fortress in which time slowed down, and the secret life of Boomfell went forward.

In fact, he was seldom alone in silent Lovejoy. From the tall windows on the third floor, he would see a distant cyclist making his way up Amity Hill. Pump, man! This was also a newcomer, although Boomfell, who had missed the gala get-together in honor of newcomers, had not yet met him. Their offices were on different floors. Boomfell studied the course list. By process of elimination he concluded that the tall man who rode the white bike must be Singer. He was teaching a course in Freshman English like everyone else, but also a graduate seminar: "Swift." He looked older. Already he conveyed something of a world-weary professorial air as he walked from bike to building, briefcase in hand.

It might be a day of mist and drizzle and the cyclist would be a distant dab of yellow—Singer in slicker—on the bright blacktop, winding through the green fields of the campus. Asshole, smirked Boomfell. Yet he would be pleased, also pleased, to see the Saturday scholar of the second floor showing up after all. Indeed, Boomfell probably had been to the window several times already, wondering if Singer was going to make it this morning.

Or if Boomfell arrived as late as nine, he would likely find the soon familiar Plymouth—MOUTH—already parked out front, or the white Raleigh bicycle already chained to a young inflamed maple. Hurry! As he passed Singer's wing on the second floor he would look for the open door, a show of light in the dark corridor of closed doors. The rapid clatter and repeated ping of Eliot Singer's typewriter at that hour in the still building was an unsettling sound, urging Boomfell to his self-appointed task. What was this fellow Singer working on, Saturday after Saturday? Taking a leak, Boomfell occasionally heard the rumble of plumbing below him, reminding him that Singer was there, drinking coffee like himself.

One day, as he skipped downstairs to the vending machines, passionate voices, shattering the Saturday serenity of the second floor, drew him toward Singer's hallway. He approached cautiously and looked into the daylighted room. Singer was tipped back in his chair, his feet propped up on his tidy desk, one raised hand counting time with a pencil, deaf to the world. His knees, steep jagged peaks, hid his face. Boomfell retreated unseen. Each Saturday at the appointed hour, he soon learned, the radio broadcast of the opera went on in Singer's office.

Several times those first weeks, Boomfell passed him on the staircase or found the scholar, as he thought of him with friendly condescension, standing before the window on the second floor, smoking his pipe. Fall that first year was picture perfect, the playing fields bordered by an illuminated fringe of crimsons and golds. They might exchange a grunt by way of greeting, or merely nod, as preoccupied as big-time thinkers. What was Singer thinking? His presence was inspiring, contributing to the poet's dream of purpose and discipline. You developed a bond with the only other person in the building on Saturday. Did Singer feel the same way?

Dark rainy days heightened the sacrosanct feeling of the place. The ideal Saturday for Boomfell was a day of rain tapering off to clear sky by late afternoon as he emerged from Lovejoy—as if inner and outer weather were in tune. (In retrospect, such days didn't seem uncommon, yet how many could there have been?) At the end of one such day, showers gradually gave way to spangled sunshine. As he stood before the large west-facing window—lo and behold, he thought—a rainbow appeared. If you asked Boomfell, rainbows were right up there with visions. He could count all the rainbows he'd seen on one hand. To hell with his work in progress; life was full of surprises. Don't go away, he pleaded to the thin air, and bounded for the staircase, descending light as a goat.

Eliot Singer was already there, standing before the wall of glass on the second floor directly below the spot where Boomfell had been standing on the third. Arms folded, slumpshouldered. A broad swath of light, slanting into the hallway, just missed him. Boomfell stopped several feet behind him and silently stood by. The rainbow stood out there in all its colors, clear as a bell. There was Day-Glo green grass, westering sun, spectral mist arching overall like . . .

"Glorious," Boomfell burst out at last. "I was just coming to rap on your door, but here you are." He gestured to the indisputable fact of Singer's bodily presence.

"Glorious may not be the word," said Singer. He glanced at his watch, he couldn't talk, he had to get back to work.

The moment Boomfell returned to the third-floor landing he heard his phone, which continued ringing until he reached it.

"Where have you been?" Val asked impatiently. "I've been calling you for five minutes to go look outside. There was a rainbow, but now it's gone."

"I can't talk," said Boomfell. Before he could say so long, his wife socked him in the ear.

Glory be to God.

The day before Thanksgiving the poet found himself locked out of Lovejoy. He circled the building, pounding on doors. At the main entrance he threw his head back and hollered, his hands upraised claws. The steep face of the building, brick and reflecting glass, was silent.

"Sounds serious."

Boomfell started, turning to the speaker. Singer, still astride his bike, was ten feet behind him.

"The doors are locked," said Boomfell, still in the grip of his emotion. "I need to get in there. The doors are locked."

"And they call this a university," said Singer. He raised a hand to stop the flow of Boomfell's indignation. "I have a key. They lock up for holidays, but keys are available."

Wasn't that Singer for you: Sounds serious?

Wasn't that Boomfell: Locked out?

Singer suggested coffee. His office was spacious. More enviable, there was a window, which looked out on grass, trees. His desk was a bare surface, a blank pad of yellow lined paper in the center of it. Taped to the wall was a map of London's Underground and a large calendar. The blocked days were crammed with small tidy printing: the striving scholar's busy life. There were more books here than Boomfell owned—real cloth-bound books, not the sort of tawdry paperbacks Boomfell had been toting since he'd been a college sophomore. From his briefcase Singer brought out a bag of coffee, which he'd ground that morning at home.

"Smell, Charles Boomfell. How do you drink that rotgut from the machines?"

They became friends. Singer began to drop in on the Boomfells Friday nights. Saturdays they would meet in Singer's office for lunch. Occasionally, Eliot read to Boomfell from whatever was sticking out of his typewriter. Eventually, Boomfell let Singer hear a few lines from his work in progress. In contrast to the poet's long apprenticeship, however, it soon became clear that Singer's labors steadfastly advanced his career. He rarely put pen to paper unless he was assured that the result would appear in print. Everyone received copies. To my friend the poet and his faithful spouse. Best, Eliot. The fruits of Boomfell's labors invariably ended up in his drawer, doomed to go stale in time.

Singer told him, Try something possible.

Like real estate, he thought, swallowing lukewarm coffee from Arnie's next door, unable to face the phone calls he'd come here, to his Odyssey office, to make this clouded-over afternoon. Cold calls.

The name of the Humanities Division softball team they organized that first spring was the Myth (a lisped "mitts") of the Golden Age. Boomfell was in center. Stretch Singer was at first. They had Zilch with his bad back at second—every ball went through his legs—and another smallish man with a serious air, Bill Whipple, played a shaky third. Several times they persuaded Lantini to come out and pitch. He wore his tie loosened at the throat. His mitt, not much larger than a man's hand, went back to World War II. Singer wore a white handkerchief around his head. Boomfell bought a new glove from K mart for ten bucks, his first in fifteen years, and a hat with an *M* on it for two-fifty. During his edgy boyhood, baseball had never been so much fun. The thrill of batting a base hit on Saturday afternoon was more real to the poet than the temporary elation that might have accompanied the completion of a tricky passage earlier in the day. The Myth of the Golden Age never won a game in the university's intramural league.

The Monday morning following his one and only home run, he found a printed headline tacked to his office door: MYTH'S POET HOMERS.

Singer!

There's Boomfell in center, socking his fist into the pocket of his new glove, chanting to his chairman. Come on, Lanny! Lanny-anny-anny, put it in there! Be you, Lanny baby! Be you! They are ten runs behind in the second game of the season. He notices for the first time, written along the large thumb of his glove in black script indistinguishable from that of the manufacturer's labeling: BOOMFELL X-TRA. In black lettering along the wide last finger: CHUCK "THE GLOVE" BOOMFELL. And across the heel: CHARLES BOOMFELL SPECIAL. The day before he had unintentionally left his glove in Eliot's car.

Remarkable person! What winning wit and cunning sympathy it took to lightly toss Boomfell such subtle delight as he rather too seriously took to the field for the comedy of errors that this game, and every other, would prove to be. With that brilliant stroke Singer laid enduring claim to Boomfell's imagination. Every spring for years to come he would be reminded of the Myth's first baseman. Each time he dug out his ten-dollar K mart special to play catch with Ruth, and then later, with Ben, he had to smile with renewed warm feelings toward Eliot Singer.

His betrayer!

The friendship gradually fell off. Yet Boomfell would still see the bike in front of Lovejoy, hear the flush of the toilet in the men's room below. If he ventured downstairs in the afternoon, the opera was sure to be sounding from Singer's wing of the building. In a sense, the man remained his Saturday companion, but now it seemed they both took care to avoid each other. Along with lonely thousands, Boomfell took up the solitary sport of the long-distance runner. One late afternoon, from his third-floor window, he saw Eliot Singer—orange T-shirt, blue shorts, the white handkerchief around his head—setting off across the playing fields at a cross-country pace. He jogged down Amity until he reached the bike path, turned, and disappeared behind woods.

Glorious may not be the word!

That sort of annoying remark soon became amusing, even endearing, for what it said about the person you came to know. How far they'd come, Boomfell considered, from two strangers sharing a silent building on weekends. They'd become strangers again. From here—here and now—those Saturdays belonged to another life altogether. At best, maybe they shared some memories brought on, for example, by a face in a restaurant, a certain make of car, the light outside. And maybe not even that much. Who knew what Singer's mind had mysteriously selected to be played and replayed in memory? To Singer, the name Boomfell might mean Valerie more often than it meant her husband.

The Myth of the Golden Age.

He missed him.

Boomfell looked up from his Formica desk, from the hypothetical percentages he'd been idly calculating with half a brain. Does Eliot Singer exist now? The same Singer?

As he crossed the street from the liquor store, the on-and-off rain became cats and dogs, and Boomfell, holding his bottle of wine close to his chest, scuttled for shelter beneath Nibs's green-and-white-striped awning. The uninspired display window featured a female torso in a college sweatshirt, an easel, posters of O'Keeffe flowers, for example, poor luscious Marilyn Monroe turning herself inside out. Several illuminated globes hung from the ceiling. Motorists had turned their headlights on, it had become so prematurely dark. A red Toyota—Val?—stopped at the light in front of the bank. No, the young woman in the passenger seat was no one they knew. An unfamiliar bike protruded from the back end of the car, the trunk should have been tied down. The girl was laughing, sort of beautiful, friends, you figured, life was a lark, world on a string, nice for them. The voyeur, he thought, lurked under the awning. The car turned right, toward Boomfell, and he saw that the woman gaily gesticulating behind the wheel, hey, *was* his wife. In the next moment he spotted Ruth's old LET THEM LIVE sticker on the car's rear bumper. Since when was Val funny? Storyteller! So what about supper, Val, what's for supper? The dark-haired young woman might have been one of her girls, but Boomfell hadn't heard about anyone new. His sudden excitement was hardly warranted by this chance glimpse of Val in her everyday life, relax, yet he didn't look away until her red car, half his, was lost in the homebound traffic.

April

When I told Val I was in microbiology, bound for med school, she said she'd wanted to be a vet once as in once-upon-a-time. She was still a sucker for *All Creatures Great and Small* on public TV, the calving scenes where the actor actually stuffed himself into the cow up to his armpit. Do you call it a vagina? she said. Instead she became an anthropology major, drawn to vanishing peoples of the Amazon. She wanted to know about them, but she also wanted them to remain undiscovered, the way she felt about boys, she said, at twelve. We talked about the World Bank's disastrous Polonoroeste project, the wacko weather lately, the inevitable-seeming end of the world as we knew it. We'd met in the produce department, she gave me a ride home with my bike in the trunk, I asked her to put on her seat belt, it was raining, everything was a joke. At twenty-one she got pregnant, married, etc., instead of studying vanishing peoples she vanished from the world of options for a while to devote herself to motherhood. Do you call it a vagina? she said, laughing. I felt tense and close with the windshield wipers protecting us from the world, the four bags of groceries lined up on the backseat like very well-behaved children. She needed an income when they moved here so she and a friend started Houseworks, the friend went on to become an accountant and Val became the entrepreneur. The original idea was to free women from the housetrap, but of course you had to employ other women to do it, so drop the original idea. People needed to work, other people needed work done. At first it was just cleaning, still the bread-and-butter part of the business, then it gradually expanded to painting, even some remodeling, decorating, yard work, etc. With four full-time and half a dozen part-time associates, plus a network of subcontractors, she said as though doing an ad, Houseworks provided expert, conscientious, and creative help for all house and garden needs. Evidently half the people on her cleaning list wouldn't move their couches without first consulting Val, she was smart, she had taste, I guess, color sense, a lot of house and garden know-how, beautiful energy. She had blunt clean fingernails. Her smile was real or not at all. The job worked for me, I told her, because I could only handle twelve hours a week while I was in school, I'd rather vacuum floors than wait on tables, cleaning a bathtub was oddly satisfying, don't tell my more radical friends, who saw the whole house and garden family trip as the heart of the enslavement problem. She hadn't been sure about hiring me, she said, because I didn't quite look the part, her worst workers had been college students, the best were divorced women with at least one child and two jobs. She tried to match up employees and clients so that everyone was happy, sometimes she matched them up too well like the coed from Houseworks who began turning up Wednesday mornings to dust off some professor's dick rather than the Mission furniture, until they got caught red-handed. We were laughing, Val handily shifting and steering her red car through the dark shining puddled streets. I didn't think that would happen in my case with Miriam and Daniel, I said, the serious Gunthers, who got me from eight to eleven Tuesdays. Val laughed, she was relaxed and comfortable, I thought, She has a face, I thought, she has a smile. For smart people, why did the Gunthers seem so incompetent? Their place was always a chaotic jumble of kid's toys, take-out food containers, clothes everywhere, every glass and dish in the sink, newspapers and magazines piled up. Miriam was the perfect booked-solid all-purpose therapist at some outrageous dollars per hour with trips every month spreading the news about her hero, Alice Miller, always up to a million getting out of the house, little Norman off to day care, and Daniel pleading, But why, Miriam, why, Miriam, why, Miriam? Norman never cries, I said. As though he realizes there's no point, Val added. Daniel, the emergency room internist with quasi-punk haircut, was cute, we agreed, he went around as though astonished by everything, his eyes like half-dollars, nibbling whole-wheat pretzels, his ass flat in his baggy khaki pants. He could sew up wounds and influence heart attacks, but he couldn't cope with a dripping faucet, get the lawn mower started, even scrub his teeth, looked like. We laughed about Daniel Gunther's large yellow overcrowded teeth. He was a sweet man, generous with free samples of prescription painkillers and handy-to-have-around antibiotics. Last week I'd found Miriam's underpants twisted inside out at the foot of the bed, I said, which had to be a good sign, although it was hard to imagine them doing it, she was always going in four directions like a Picasso, while he always looked half-asleep. My favorites, though, were the two ancient ladies in the yellow saltbox on Sunset Avenue, the tangled vine growing over the front door, Marjorie, who was always in her garden talking to everything alive, and tiny Eleanor, who was always at her desk writing letters to strangers, smoking those damn cigarettes. They usually wanted me to join them for tea, I told her, and tell them all about my week, not to worry about the cleaning. Val thought they probably picked things up before I got there so they could enjoy my visit, eager for news of the world and just to be near me. We could all use that, don't you think, she said, a breath of fresh air every week? I said, Yes. My other two houses were less enjoyable. The insurance executive, James Gill, in the new Orchard condos, desperate without his wife, who had evidently left once their last child was safely in college, he couldn't bear to go grocery shopping, he said, his place felt hollow and unlived-in, like he felt apparently, he didn't flirt, though, which was a nice change. Val was sure men were all over me all day long, she said, did I have a boyfriend? I had a lover, Don, he was married, I told her, I felt like being honest, I wanted to see her reaction. She asked, Is that all right with you? Yeah, that's all I wanted right now, it was fine. I'd only met Mary Parker, the broker who specialized in environmentally sound investments, once. Her silent high school daughter was home half the time with the tube on, stoned I thought. When I asked once why she wasn't in school, the girl went into a weepy story about her mother never being there since the mother's new boyfriend, I tried to console her. That stupid woman, said Val, the poor kid, maybe Ruth knew her. Ruth: Val's daughter. I can relate, I said, because it was only me and Mom. So Val asked, Where was your father? driving through the rain, September rain. My mother was nineteen when she got pregnant with me, I told her, she didn't marry him because she didn't want to, according to her version. I had no memory of him except a few snapshots of a boy with a goofy haircut, taken in the days before hair was discovered, then he got drafted smack out of college, and was reported missing, that's all anybody knew, his name didn't appear on the black war memorial in D.C., I couldn't believe all those fresh-faced boys my age and younger, I said, all those sons and brothers, how could they let that happen. Suddenly everything wasn't a joke, Val was listening. Missing in action was spooky, I told her, my mother became a passionate peace activist for life, dragging me to marches, rallies, nuclear power plants for ten years. Val asked, What was that like? She's great was my pat answer. My grandfather offered to pay my college tuition, so I ended up coming East to college instead of staying in California, I wanted to check out the Eastern intellectual scene, quaint, clapboarded, dreary, but sort of liberating for me like being in a foreign country, my mother had gone to the same college for two years so there was that connection too, fall was great. We were parked outside my house on Crescent now, under the

50

wonderful old-world maple, with heavy romantic rain drumming on the roof. Here I am, I said. Tell me about your mother, she said. The year I graduated from high school she got her nursing degree after twenty years of various and sundry jobs, she worked with AIDS patients at San Francisco General, somebody had to do it. I started out as a psych major, I said, with a strong interest in dance, if you know what I mean, then I took a year off and came back to study microbiology. She asked me how old I was—twenty-three—and I asked her. Thirty-seven. She was wearing a khaki skirt, a baggy sweater, a wedding band, a man's wristwatch, those rubber boots with leather tops. I was wearing my checkered man's overcoat over my black jumper. A car swung its lights on us, pulling into the street, I asked her if she wanted to come up and have something like tea or wine. She had to get home, get supper, get the kids straightened out with homework, make her round of phone calls. The windows had fogged up with all this talk. She liked my name, she said, she'd never known an April, come to think of it. I rattled off the line, and she in thee calls back the lovely April of her prime, you know, Shakespeare, my mother was the poetic type. I had to wait two hours until it was late enough to reach her in California, she was out of breath getting the phone, she'd just finished a typically impossible day. I just wanted to say hi, I said. She asked me about school, my job, my housemates, the foliage, which she still missed along with the feeling in the air, my girlfriend Pauline in Boston. I told her Val had given me a ride home—the very together woman I worked for—and we'd had a good time talking, sitting in her car in the rain. I liked her, I thought she could be a friend.

II.

The closing on the Northfield property, in October, took less than an hour. Muler turned up at the bank in his overalls and his watch cap. He was hardly sociable. Boomfell's piece of the action, his percentage of Odyssey's percentage, came to a little over twenty-five hundred. That wasn't enough. He'd pay a lousy twenty-five hundred to avoid going through the whole thing again, phone call after phone call. To avoid the condescension of two-bit lawyers, Muler's hollow scorn, the chipper congratulations of Betsy Hart at the office. Twenty-five hundred would be cheap. By the end of the day he felt better; they needed the money.

The second week of October he sold one of the two listings he'd picked up from Marjorie Kenner, who had divvied up her clients amongst colleagues before moving to Florida. The house was a fake colonial in Echo Hill, and the buyer was a high school psychologist, recently divorced, with two sons. I'm probably making a mistake, she told Boomfell. I'm probably doing everything wrong. I'm only the realtor, he said pleasantly, all I can do is hold your hand. That's all I need, she snorted.

The phrase that had passed his lips haunted him: I'm only the realtor.

The same week he showed the Dickinson land, thirty partially wooded acres with a year-round stream, to Foley, the new owner of Greenstreet's. Foley signed a buy-sell agreement the following Tuesday. He had been given Boomfell's name by Lynch, the attorney who'd handled Muler's closing. Boomfell revised his hasty opinion of the modish lawyer.

53

He sold a retired couple from New Jersey on one of the new condominiums in the old Mulligan School building. They were moving to be nearer their grandchildren. We're so glad we called Odyssey, the woman told him, and we're so happy we met you. Blush, Boomfell.

Mavis, the owner of the Uncommon Kitchen, sent him Rodgers, an endodontist looking for a place where his wife could raise horses. Boomfell called Mavis and thanked him for the potentially handsome piece of business. Was this how the world worked? You joked, you small-talked, you did a favor for a favor. Smile, Boomfell, smile.

He inquired about a neglected mowing gone to birch and sumac and juniper. The land sloped to the south, there were old maple trees along the road. He had a possible buyer, he told Mrs. Hudson, if they were interested in selling. Hudson called back and gave him a price. Boomfell called Plum, the urologist eager for a site to make his passive solar dream house come true. The Plums returned to the Hudson field three times in four days and finally said they wanted it.

You hot dog, Val said. Maybe the Muler closing had been a turning point.

He took phone calls and made phone calls day and night, hustling from dawn to dusk, busy, busy, busy. One afternoon over a pitcher of beer he dared tell Weisman, I think I'm running lucky.

In November he fielded a tall couple in off the street. They'd been driving down the coast for three weeks, they said, looking for a place to live, burned out on city life, in their case Philadelphia. They worked at home and could live where they pleased. Boomfell spent the heart of the day showing Niki and David places they didn't like from the outside. How exasperating this soon became, driving in circles for the likes of these two in their jeans and boots and cableknit sweaters. Maybe they were thirty years old. She made stained glass, she said, and he designed furniture. At four Niki spotted the Odyssey sign in front of the Eldred Johnson Tavern, as it was known, on South Street—a place Boomfell had no intention of showing them. Circa 1770, it had a gracious center hall, five fireplaces, a large ell, original paneling, but it needed a lot of work, the realtor cautioned, and it was on the market for a lot of money. Niki, the assertive one, wanted to see it anyway. The building's tenant, a bearded young man who recognized Boomfell from Archangel's Bookshop, let them in. The next day Niki offered the full asking price. Inherited, he would learn eventually, was the answer to Boomfell's question about money. When the question of a local lawyer arose, he recommended Lynch.

Was this the way the world worked? Wasn't it high time Charles Boomfell found out?

By the middle of November he had a dozen new listings to his credit, a handful of prospective buyers, and four closings pending before the new year. He liked it, getting up in the morning with the day, a list of things to do, clearly before him. Straightforward tasks, which other people counted on you to perform. At the end of the day you had your checked-off list of accomplished goals, and the accompanying sense of day done. Was this how people lived?

It was easy. You get together, you talk about the roof, the heating system, the wallpaper upstairs, the room with the fireplace. You take a walk in the woods, or you walk around the yard, up to the attic, down to the cellar, say something about neighbors, schools, convenience, lasting value. You suggest changes, visions, financial alternatives, you go back to the office to fill in the blanks, write an ad maybe, make a few more calls. You have to stay in touch, stay on top of things, follow up, go to lunch. It was easy, he told Val. It wasn't like work. Work to Boomfell, the only thing he had ever considered work, was a solitary striving in the dark, dogged by doubt, with no reward in sight.

I'm making money, he told her. It's like stealing.

Val said, Steal it.

April

On my way home by bike, I'd seen Val carrying bags of groceries from the car, Val stooping to greet a cat on the sidewalk, Val awkwardly running after her son, Val greeting people at the front door. I'd seen her husband, Charlie, playing soccer with Ben on the stretch of lawn between the maple trees and the sidewalk, I'd seen him tackle the boy to the ground, rolling in leaves. Driving past her house at night after class, I'd often seen someone in one of the lighted front rooms behind the multipaned windows. The house on the long town common was an old squat brown-black cape from so-called colonial days, snug amongst its lilac and laurel, backed by two straight tall spruce and a dramatically towering white pine, three middle-aged sugar maples, orange-gold this fall, out front. The only New England trees I knew for sure were the ones in Val's yard, Mac named them for me one afternoon as we drove by. The afternoon I coasted into the gravel driveway I sensed no one home, I walked around to the back door, the orange cat appeared, leaves blowing around, my heartbeat as rapid and almost as loud as my halfhearted knock. It was a solid plank door of vertical boards with a large black heart-shaped thumb latch, it opened, I stood in the low-ceilinged kitchen, Val, I called, the dark wood floor and the beams overhead made the room feel heavy, warm, cave-like. Outside on the sidewalk, two skinny girls maybe twelve years old, beautiful, walked by as briskly as cadets, You're sick, the taller was saying to her friend, *sick*, she shouted, *sick*, she shouted as I pedaled hard down the street, *sick*.

Monday night, the week of Thanksgiving, Boomfell was wrenched from sleep by a frightful ringing across the room. He groped in the darkness for the phone.

"Charles Boomfell. Hi." The man paused with the expectation, evidently, that his voice identified him, but Boomfell couldn't imagine who this could be. "How are you?" Then he felt the tug of this voice, someone from somewhere, and when the caller said, "Can you hear me? Are you there?" he realized who this was. The phone rings in the middle of the night, he would tell Weisman, you lift the receiver: past is present.

The conceit of the man not to have given his name at once, testing Boomfell's ear.

"Eliot Singer!" And he attempted to lend a heartiness to his surprise. "How good to hear your voice again."

"Is it? I woke you. Sorry about that."

"I was reading," Boomfell told him. "Don't worry about it."

"You sound like you've been sleeping. You must be surprised."

"Where are you?" Boomfell asked. "What's up?" His former colleague must be in the area, he guessed, guest-speaking at one of the colleges. Out on the town, the town where Boomfell lived, following a jolly meeting of minds. Spare me, thought Boomfell.

"What's up? Singer's up. Singer's down. I'm in Toronto, my second year here. Didn't you get my card last Christmas?

57

Listen, forget all that. That's not why I called. This isn't a reunion, all right? This isn't for old times' sake."

Silence surrounded Singer wherever he was, and the telephone connection was remarkably clear, which brought his voice close. He spoke quietly, yet with crisp impatience. It was not the reserved and somewhat aloof tone that Boomfell associated with him. "Listen, one question, it's very simple, I want to see you, I want to talk. Can you come up?" He waited for an answer.

Boomfell said, "Sounds like fun, Eliot. I don't know. It would take some planning. How do you like Toronto?"

"No, I mean, can you come up right now? Like immediately, Charles Boomfell, tonight, tomorrow morning. We need to have long talks."

"What's going on, Eliot? I don't understand."

"Of course you don't understand. Take it from me, Charles Boomfell, it's important. You're the only person I can talk to right now."

Did Singer imagine he was in a position to drop everything—the list of appointments on his desk, the upcoming school night in which Ruth was to play her violin and Ben was to be a pilgrim—and fly to Toronto? That evening they had fashioned from construction paper and aluminum foil the tall black hat with its silver buckle. Did Singer imagine that Boomfell could afford the fare?

"Are you there?" Singer asked.

"Can't we talk right now? Over the phone?" Singer was disapprovingly silent, and Boomfell hastened to add, "Let me see what I can do. Can I call you back?" Surely, there was nothing he could do.

Singer gave him two numbers; he would be at one place or the other. "I'll hear from you tonight, won't I? Don't let me wait too long. Thank you, Charles." Without giving Boomfell a chance to reply, he hung up.

The man appealed to a loyalty and concern that their relationship had never warranted as far as Boomfell was concerned. Least of all now, years later, out of the blue. Eliot Singer would be the last man in the world Boomfell would think to call, needing to talk. Needing to talk about what? Meet me in Toronto, don't ask why! The imperious tenor of Singer's demand was ridiculous. Now and then you received phone calls from half-forgotten friends steeped in booze and all blown up with sentiment. Yet Singer sounded anything but drunk. He sounded intense, anxious. Standing in the bedroom wearing nothing, Boomfell now felt chilled. He crossed the room and took his clothes from the Windsor chair by the window. Such urgency was contagious.

The light behind the pulled shade in his neighbor's window, visible through the leafless branches of their red maple, went out. Our newlyweds, he called them. They'd bought the place a year ago and had nailed the date of the house, circa 1830, to the front door. The new husband was away more than he was home. His young wife left the lights downstairs burning all night.

There had to have been many people Singer might have called. These years later, did Eliot Singer imagine Charles Boomfell was a friend? He felt both dupe and deceiver. Singer had the nerve to call. Did you say no?

"Charlie, who was that? What time is it?" Not quite awake, Val only wanted to hear it was all right to go on sleeping.

"I'll tell you in the morning. It's midnight." He pulled the covers over his vacated side of the bed.

Downstairs in the kitchen he called the airlines and was relieved to learn there was no seating available on a Tuesday flight to Toronto. Then he recalled the basic consideration that, in his excitement, he had overlooked: they were going to his sister-in-law's for the holiday. In two days it was Thanksgiving. The situation was beyond his control.

Let Singer come to Boomfell if he needed to talk. At least let the matter rest until the sane light of day. Yet now it was

Boomfell who couldn't wait until morning. He dialed the first number Eliot had given him, fishing a beer from the refrigerator with his free hand.

He imagined a phone ringing in a dark empty room—five long rings—but before he gave up, a woman answered, and Boomfell asked for Eliot Singer.

"Who is calling please? Eliot is not here." She spoke with an accent he couldn't identify for sure. He had awakened her.

With apologies, he identified himself—a friend in the States, a former colleague—and explained that Eliot had given him her number. "Frankly, I don't know what's going on. I haven't spoken to him in years. He sounded troubled."

"Your name is not familiar," she said. "Did he say he would be here tonight? I haven't seen Eliot since Friday."

"May I ask who I'm speaking to?"

"Astrid, Eliot's wife, but no, he is not living here now. You don't know anything?" she asked.

He didn't.

"Well, he must tell you himself. Eliot is going through something. Friday he was like a stranger." Abruptly, she added, "It's late, isn't it? If he comes here, I'll tell him you called."

"He gave me another number as well. Maybe I should try there."

"Yes, why not?"

"Sorry I disturbed you."

"Could you give me your number?" she asked. "Do you mind? And your name, how do you spell that?"

Enamored of voices, Boomfell imagined a sturdy handsome woman with dark thick hair. While she worried, Singer was out making crank phone calls to distant acquaintances in the middle of the night.

"I'd heard Eliot had gotten married," he said, "but our conversation makes it conclusive."

"No, we are no longer married. I'm sorry, I assumed you knew that."

"As I was saying, I haven't actually spoken to him in years."

"Thank you for calling, Mr. Boomfell."

Wide-awake with intrigue, he rang up the second number. Singer was right there.

"Charles Boomfell, you called back."

"It doesn't look good, Eliot. Flying is out, for openers. And, of course, we have plans for Thursday. It's that time of year again."

"Thursday?"

"Thanksgiving."

"Oh, for God's sake. Forgive me, Charles. It's different here. Thanksgiving in Canada is over. You see, Singer is out of touch. Of course you couldn't do it this week. I understand completely."

"I was thinking, if you could get away, we'd be happy to have you here. That would make a lot more sense for us. We have plenty of room," he lied.

"Let's do that, let's plan on it." The promptness of his reply suggested that an invitation was what he'd been after in the first place. They decided on the following week. He would arrive on Thursday and stay through Saturday. He was sure he could find someone to take over his seminar Friday afternoon. He would book a flight immediately.

Boomfell asked, "What's going on, Eliot? I just talked to— is it Astrid? The first number."

"What's going on? This story, Charles Boomfell, will keep you busy at the typewriter all morning. What happened? She kicked me out is what happened, she never wants to see me again. She leaves her husband, she takes her little girl and comes to live with Eliot—"

"You mean Astrid?"

"Astrid? I'm not talking about Astrid. She comes to live

with Eliot, she loves me. What do I do? I'm crazy about her, but I treat her like shit. What happened? She wised up. She's young, beautiful, she has her whole life ahead of her. She sucked cock for a year, then woke up and said, Eliot, get lost. Just a month ago we both got divorces and promised to live together forevermore. I'm supposed to marry this girl tomorrow and tomorrow and tomorrow. She's gone. Listen, I have messed her up so badly, she doesn't know whether she wants to go back to school or kill herself. Her husband, her ex-husband, makes threats. He wants custody of the kid because he can't have the mother. What happens next? I knock her up like we're in high school. I can't believe that happened. Can you? Have I ruined her life? Must life be ruined?"

Was this the story? Boomfell was disappointed, yet relieved, and curious.

"Who is this person?"

"Her name? Her name is Lucky. Charles, I'm such a mess myself. I'm living in a hovel, I have no money, no furniture, I have debts, I owe and owe and owe. Why am I going through all this? You're an epic poet, Charles, tell me what's going on. People say forget her, take a trip. I don't want to travel, I don't want money, I don't want to be famous in my field. I want this woman, I want her hands and mouth and tits, I want her cunt. The best fuck of my life, Charles, I hope you don't mind if I say so. It's almost that simple. I know what I want. How do I get her back? I'm forty, she's twenty-five. When I found her she was a baby, she knew nothing, she learned fast. She sat at my feet and learned about art and life and ecstasy. She grew up in one year, and now she doesn't want Eliot anymore. She wants an abortion. Eliot's baby, Charles Boomfell. I'm going to commit suicide one day and the next day I'm Ben Hur. My psychiatrist says I have a very high affective level. Do you know what that is? I get excited, very excited. Since all this happened, I've been going to Edward the psychiatrist. Astrid insisted. I'm not going to kill myself. For one thing, I'm crazy in love with Alex. I love life, Charles. I do. I don't know why."

"Alex?"

"My son, Alex. He's becoming a big person. He has beautiful hands. He has beautiful legs and eyes and hair, a fanny like a loaf of bread you could eat, everything. You told me no one understood about children until they had their own. I remember you saying that and, Charles, I agree wholeheartedly. I had no idea."

Boomfell didn't remember ever making such a remark to Singer.

"What about Astrid?" he asked. "You weren't married that long, were you?"

"How long? Astrid is an angel, a tall strong angel. God knows what I would do without Astrid. Right now she is my only friend. In fact I should go there. If I knew what was good for me, I would go there. Five years, more, a long time."

"It all sounds rather intense."

"Intense? Charles Boomfell, intense? I know Lucky. I know and know and know. She can't take it anymore, she wants out, she won't talk to me, she never wants to see me again. Fine, I understand. But what she says and what she feels aren't the same thing, are they? Of course not. Don't talk, I told her for one year, just suck. She woke up. Today I sent her three letters by pony express. Three incredible letters. No answer. And yet two days ago she called me. I hung up on her. It was so upsetting to talk to her. She wants, she doesn't want. She tells me her life is too confused, she needs to take a deep breath, sort things out. Sort things out like this is a Laundromat. She feels everything slipping through her fingers. In a few months she lost a husband, maybe a daughter, plus her pathetic family—a father, a mother, two sisters. Total rejection is what she gets from her family since she left this schmuck the antique-collecting husband, who makes her head spin with hate. Since Singer, she is Kafka's bug as far as her family is concerned. Her mother told her if she never sees her again it won't be too soon. How's that for support? She's lost everyone as though a 747 had crashed into a mountain, only worse because nobody's dead. Everyone is alive. Even aunts and grandmothers turn their backs. The poor girl! And what has she gained, Charles? Eliot Singer. You see? A family of monsters. Soulless, heartless monsters, who eat at McDonald's. Because of them, she suffers. I suffer. Here I am suffering, I say to myself, because of these pieces of shit. And what if she doesn't come back? But then I think she must be thinking the same thing. What if I don't come back? What if Eliot doesn't come back? She doesn't want that either."

Of the many questions that came to mind as he listened, Boomfell decided, in the ensuing pause, to settle for a question of fact. He asked, "How long has she been gone?"

"A week. One week. Eternity, that's all. I cry, Charles Boomfell. Big Eliot Singer cries in his pillow like a baby. A student has been staying with me, today she had to go somewhere. Do you understand? You can't go, I said. She had to. She promises to be back Thursday. These young women, Charles, they love to hear the ins and outs of their flesh described by a forty-year-old English teacher. It's horrible. She's beautiful, but Eliot can't get it up in the morning. She tries, nothing happens. While she's taking a shower, wondering what's going on here, I jerk off with a picture of Lucky in my head. That can't be healthy, can it? I must get her back. Charles Boomfell, you're an epic poet. How? She's going nuts with her daughter, her abortion, her mother, who eats french fries, her husband, who is a dangerous anti-Semitic fascist. Before their divorce he sent me a list of places on his wife's body that I was forbidden to touch. Like some ancient Canadian tribal law, Charles. That's funny. I'm the only one who can help her, she won't let me see her. Tell me what you think."

Boomfell thought he should take it easy, wait and see.

What was a week? "Give her time, if that's what she wants," he suggested.

"What's a week?" The question baffled him. "What's an hour, Charles Boomfell? What was from three to five today? Eternity."

"You seem to have survived."

"Do I? I think I'm a mess, life is a disaster, but then I think maybe I'm not, maybe I'm not a mess. Do you know what I mean? What runs I've had lately, the adrenaline is so great, ten, twelve miles without taking a breath. Today twelve. I could have gone on all afternoon."

"That's important."

"Essential. Life-giving."

"You sound like you're doing all right, Eliot."

He sounded strung out, definitely that, but also aware that the predicament he described to Boomfell, while it pained him, also entertained. Here he was in the middle of the night pouring himself out to someone he hadn't spoken to in years, who had every reason to be annoyed if not indifferent to his sad story, yet Singer was aware of just how well he held his listener's attention. Coming from Singer, it was a good story, an irresistible story. His straight-faced sense of humor had remained intact, the hint of smiling irony at the bottom of everything, even his announced suffering. Boomfell considered such self-awareness a powerful and protective weapon. "It will be good to see you again," he ventured.

"When I come down, let's meet someone. Tell her you have an interesting friend with a high affective level, an exciting vocabulary, and intensity to burn. Tell her he's coming with charm and cross-country skis. Will there be snow?"

Boomfell didn't expect snow for some time.

"Let's not talk anymore tonight, Charles. I'm exhausted."

"Take care until you get here," Boomfell told him.

65

"I'll try."

"Let me know about the flight."

"Yes. I'll call you early next week. How is Valerie? And the children? I haven't even asked."

"She's well. Everyone's fine."

"And you?"

"I'm all right."

"We'll talk," said Singer. "Thanks for calling, Charles Boomfell, I mean it."

"Good night, Eliot."

Whether Val was curious or even momentarily alarmed by Singer's story, she kept it to herself.

"What's going on?" asked Boomfell. "Wherever you turn, people are going to pieces."

"But you've got it all together, right, Charlie?"

That evening he overheard her say to Laura Weisman over the phone, "That poor girl. She's in love with him, and she has to get away from him."

Singer's story, he knew, would enliven a round of cocktails later in the week. A stranger's enactment of everyone's desire. Unreal as fiction, yet real: the friend of a friend.

Later, propped up with her book in bed—Val had been reading *Middlemarch* since summer—she asked, "You don't think he's actually going to come down here?"

Boomfell doubted it. Chances were they'd never hear from him again. In his transformation from family man to madman lover, Singer had probably alienated everyone in his present life. So he rang up a sympathetic listener from the safe past.

"I used to think he was such a great guy," Val said thoughtfully. She closed her book and switched out the light. "Now he sounds like just another jerk."

. . . .

To Weisman he said the midnight phone call was like being stopped on Main Street by a drummer draped in white sheets, barefoot, his head shaved, and realizing, as he called you by name, that the deep-set eyes in this pale skull were familiar, the smile was vaguely familiar from somewhere, and then recognizing in the guise of a Krishna convert none other than the eighteenth-century scholar Eliot Singer.

Weisman trotted out the tiresome phrase "mid-life crisis" and smirked. Short confident Weisman with his clichés and his cowboy boots from Santa Fe. Boomfell didn't think the glib slogans of the day quite applied to Singer's case.

"Hey, Charlie, maybe we should all run into a girl named Lucky and get divorced and feel alive again. Everyone wants to live in the garden of delights with rakes and pitchforks sticking out of their assholes. Lovesick tantrum-prone professors of the humanities in their headbands and running shorts, their only topic is themselves, otherwise they've got nothing to say."

April

Val used to operate out of her kitchen, but that got too crazy, she wanted to keep home and work separate, so once she could swing it she rented a room in the renovated Stallman Building, which has been taken over by women of all kinds going into business: antique jewelry, used clothing, the rug dealer specializing in kilims, picture framing with gallery, toy store, stringed instrument repair, Sasha's, which sold crystals, beads, Indian bedspreads, old and new kimonos, a quasi-gym space for aerobic and dance classes, a resident masseuse. Val checked in for an hour or two mornings and afternoons to get messages, make calls, manage the scheduling and money routine, she's made the little second-story corner room cozy, striped couch, well-worn Oriental rug, house and garden books and magazines, big mirror, Pierre Deux curtains—who's Pierre Deux? I asked. Two Frenchmen—vase of flowers, the entrepreneur with a room of her own. The view is the Catholic church, the Virgin Mary out front. She could get along without it, she said, but it was more convenient for everyone to touch bases, she liked having a fully deductible place to go, she was worth it. Wednesday, two older women were leaving when I turned up at four or so, Val said, Let's go to Angelica's for something like cappuccino and carrot cake, Ben was at a friend's, Ruth had a rehearsal, and she had an hour to kill. That was perfect because I was meeting my friend Pauline at the Peter Pan bus station right across the street at such and such a time. I was flattered and eager, wished I wasn't still wearing rolled-up baggy jeans and my piss-colored cotton sweater. Val said, You could go around in a feed bag and look better than the rest of us, she had on her fall colors, a knitted nubby jacket with silk scarf, her taupe skirt, a black tam. Our walk to the café was windy and cold, which made getting inside that much better. We both ordered gooey wedges of cherry chocolate something as it turned out. I admired her new laced-up boots, she was really happy about them, she explained, because she always had a rotten time finding shoes that fit her vast feet, she called them, which, just nerves probably, led me to that ancient Chinese foot-binding business from Dworkin's wild book. Women crippled and enslaved for life in the name of beauty and sex appeal, hobbling around deformed, on canes if they were aristocrats, while only discardable working women, peasants, had feet that functioned. Men, according to the writer's source, believed tiny mummified bent-up feet in jeweled slippers made for exciting new vaginal folds and layers that afforded them otherworldly fucking, I laughed. You know, the truth is I've always had a hang-up about my long feet, she said seriously, you mean that comes from China too. I told her I liked her hands. Looking at them, long-fingered, veined, she said, They're a wreck. So what about this lover? she asked at some point. I told how we'd met in the perennial gardens across from the pond last August, just before I'd started working for her, his wife was away, he was pretty appealing in his Patagonian shorts, surprisingly well informed about trees and various thymes, with funny anecdotes concerning his recent twenty-five-year high school reunion, and a trip to Poland and Hungary, he was our Eastern European man on campus, he loved to cook, he swept me away to Nantucket for my major romantic event of last summer. I thought when his wife came home that would be the fitting end of our little fling, but he only became more needy and intense, so lately he was driving me a little crazy. Val was watching me carefully, I thought, as if to catch the truth of the matter. We had a mutually okay Thursday-night routine worked out, but lately he'd been dropping by every other night, he needed to talk about his article on Poland's future, his wife's moods, a stomachache that had him worried, he should probably leave her now rather than prolong the pain, etc. I had too much work to do, I couldn't have him around whenever he felt like it, he was also getting on my housemates' nerves. Mac, the nicest man on earth, absolutely devoted fifth and sixth grade teacher, owned the place, Don treated him like the help. Sue was a therapist who ran discussion groups at a women's shelter, Ellen was a social worker who handled Medicaid cases, they weren't Don's idea of women, all right, and he made no effort to conceal that, just the opposite. Val made an earnest speech about the perils and impossible unfairness of Don situations, who gets hurt, where it leads, etc. Don't let him screw you up, you don't need him for anything, you're you, you're beautiful. I wanted to reach across the table and take her hand. I told her about the time in September I stretched out on the bench near the pond for five minutes with my eyes shut, the sun felt good, and when I opened them this basket case was standing directly over me with his pants around his ankles, jerking off, I ran and screamed, men had been showing me their pricks since I was a little girl, that type worried me a lot more than Don situations, I said. She was off to her sister's in Connecticut for Thanksgiving, we were planning a feast with everybody we knew coming to our house, including Ellen's mother from Michigan or Minnesota, and the father of Mac's oldest friend, who had nowhere to go apparently since his son died, an AIDS casualty in New York City. Val didn't know a single soul who had died of AIDS, she said, not a close friend anyway, she could forget it was happening until it came up on *All Things Considered*. A gay man in his forties, Mac had lost many friends, I said. Like hunger, she said, she didn't know people who were hungry but most of the world was hungry. She'd never been sexually assaulted, she'd never had an abortion, she'd never broken a bone, she said, people suffered and died constantly, but no one nearest her had yet died, for example, except grandparents, which was different. She didn't think she knew anyone who abused their children, for example, but evidently the abuse of children was rampant. She'd been lucky, I told her. She could get scared, she said, thinking about how lucky she'd been. We agreed that one piece of the chocolate triple-layer extravaganza would have been more than enough for both of us. A tall thin girl, long strawberry-blond hair, a blue down vest, approached our table with her index finger held to her lips. Before Val could turn around to see what had seized my attention, the girl clasped her thin reddened hands over Val's eyes, Val grabbed the hands and pulled the girl down around her, pulling the smiling face against her own, Ruth had left her rehearsal early and come looking for her mother. I was excited, I was jealous of them both, I think, I couldn't think of what to say. Pauline came running when she got off the bus, gallivanting, half skipping in black leather shoes, white socks, her Rasta black hair wildly everywhere, a bulky gaudy paint-splattered Peruvian wool sweater over her black dress, she grabbed me into a hug, we hadn't seen each other in three weeks, I was afraid Val's car would pass by, and kissed me on the mouth, laughing my name. Why did you do that? I said impatiently, the stunned paranoid weirdo weekend host. Because I felt like it. She was rosy, sparkling eyes and earrings, happy, she smelled like the can of sardines she'd eaten on the bus, the wrapped flowers in her hand turned out to be one bird of paradise.

The Sunday after Thanksgiving was unseasonably mild, a break for Boomfell, who was hardly prepared for winter yet. The last of the leaves might have been left on the ground if it was not for this pleasant pause in the march of seasons. He might have been juggling storm windows in bitter wind with numb hands. Cordwood, dumped in the driveway two months before, might have been under snow already. The *Farmer's Almanac* said snow.

Following a breakfast of buttermilk waffles, four Boomfells went to work, united by a rare sailing mood of family feeling. Ruth was gorgeous, each time Boomfell looked, raking leaves like there was no tomorrow. Red-gold braids, sky blue vest, pink skin. Guard your life! Val cleaned windows as if in contest with squat industrious Mrs. Synczk down the street. Her rag squeaked. Boomfell goosed her in her secondhand sailor pants while she wobbled on the stepladder, wagging her behind. As tirelessly and thoughtfully as he built spaceships with Legos, Ben stacked wood in the shed at the rear of the ell, proving himself equal to the task.

"I couldn't have done it without you," Boomfell told him.

Ben looked up with his goofy grin, his face masked with dirt, picking his nose. "I know."

The woodpile was a work of art. Folk art by father and son.

With a Boomfell at each corner of the canvas drop cloth, they carted the last pile of leaves to the narrow border of woods

72

behind the house. It was the end of the day. Ben took a running dive into their impressive heap. Ruth jumped feet first.

"Come on, Mom."

Smiling wearily, happy just now, Val sat down in leaves, faded gold, like an elderly lady at the beach dunking her old behind. "We did it."

Such tasks, Boomfell considered, gave a reason to live. The palms of his worthwhile hands pleasantly stung. Through clean windowpanes the scene outside his living room—the swept lawn with its dark bare trees, the silhouettes of houses across the way, the horizon just now, a luminous backdrop the length of the street, consisting of broad bands of lavender, salmon, pink—was as complete and satisfying as a work of art.

"When it's like this, I can't even think about moving," Val said, coming up behind him. A new place, more space, new faces, was a constant topic between them. "I wouldn't want to be anywhere else."

Thrilled with the light coming across his front lawn, Boomfell said, "Life is frightening."

The pizza for supper—onions, peppers, and mushrooms— was pop art. They ate it in fifteen minutes. Later, while Val and Ben cuddled on the couch before the television, wrapped up in *Nature*, the inside scoop on ants or apes or desert life, and while Ruth settled down to her homework with stoic resignation, Boomfell settled himself in the small front room with a fire, a little whiskey, and "The Death of Ivan Ilych," warm inside and out with well-being. Relax.

The phone went off on the other side of the wall, and he heard his daughter impatiently push her chair back from the kitchen table. In a moment she opened the door behind him. "Are you home?" Since her father had gone into real estate, she had learned to tell expedient lies to strangers on the phone. It was a woman with an accent. He went upstairs to take the call. Who with an accent knew him?

. . . .

"Mr. Boomfell, this is Astrid Singer. We spoke last week. I'm sorry to disturb you."

By his welcoming hello, gracious Mr. Boomfell intended to put himself at her service and anxious Astrid Singer at ease. "I was wondering when I'd be hearing from Eliot. We had a long talk . . . was it Monday?"

Yes, she knew they had talked. "I'm sorry to disturb you," she repeated. "I thought you might have heard from him today, but I see, no, you haven't. I had your telephone number. I thought, I will try there? But forgive me, I feel foolish."

"Do you know if he's still planning to come down Thursday? We're looking forward to seeing him." When she didn't answer, he said, "It's been a long time. It should be quite interesting."

"It's very bad," she said flatly. "Eliot, he has tried to kill himself."

He snorted disbelief. "What?"

"And now, you see, I don't know where he is. This is the problem. Today she took him out of the hospital. Lucky, the girl. They let him go with her, if you can believe that. He has not come back. The way he is now, he is a danger to himself. Sitting here, waiting to hear something, it is very hard. I thought he might call you. Maybe he wanted to go there. To Massachusetts. I thought I should try anyway."

Lucky the girl.

"You don't know where he is?" Boomfell asked.

"The police say wait and see. This is how they think."

"Is he all right? I mean, was it serious?"

"Serious?" The words bewildered her. "First pills, many pills. Then he cut his wrists. To the bone," she said emphatically. "Both wrists have been put in casts. One hand is without

74

feeling. He may lose the use of certain fingers. They don't know yet. Serious, yes."

"Good Lord."

"Of course now, he is in despair. With Eliot, his precious body is so important. His skiing, his hiking, his piano. He has hurt himself badly, he is not well, and now, like this, they let him leave with the girl. You see what I'm saying? It's so frustrating."

He found it difficult to concentrate on what she was saying. The woman's accent interfered. Questions crowded. What questions were allowed? If Eliot Singer had tried to kill himself—and meant it—why was he alive? He asked, "Who found him?"

"Eliot called someone—a colleague—who called me and said Eliot sounded very bad. I told him to take another person and go to Eliot's apartment immediately. I couldn't do that. They found him unconscious. One arm had stopped bleeding. He didn't remember calling anyone. That amazed him later, that he had called someone."

"When did it happen?" he asked, but that made suicide sound like an accident. "When did Eliot do this?"

"Wednesday night. No one knows what to do, that is what's frightening. You know, Eliot, he is charming and he is used to getting his way. I know him. The hospital people, his psychiatrist, Eliot manipulates them. He appears bright and witty and in control, but his feelings, inside, he is not in control. He is out of his tree. They think he has made such a recovery, that's how intelligent they are. This turmoil with Lucky has been going on for months, Mr. Boomfell. On-and-off craziness. He is happy like a child, then despair. She is like him." Astrid said this as if the idea amazed her. "She is also out of her tree. Together . . . it's too much, believe me. His ecstasy. He shouldn't see her now. Don't they know this is the problem? Isn't it wrong?" she asked.

"I understand what you're saying," he said. "No, it doesn't make sense." What did she want from Boomfell?

"He must remain in the hospital. But now . . . No one will take charge to do something, it's unbelievable."

"What does his doctor say?"

"The psychiatrist? I can't talk to him. He doesn't listen. That man, I am sorry, he is simply good-for-nothing."

"You know, I haven't heard from Eliot in years. He's the last person I would have thought—"

"Yes."

"Monday, when I talked to him, he seemed fine. He was excitable, I thought, but there was nothing to suggest—"

"Of course."

"We were laughing," said Boomfell. "Eliot can be very funny."

"Do you think so?"

"He asked me to come up, that's why he called."

"I know that. You were unable to come."

"We decided he would come here instead. Thursday. That was the plan. By the time we hung up he seemed just fine. If I'd thought for a moment that anything like this—"

"Yes, I know."

Wednesday, he realized, had been the day before Thanksgiving. He'd shown the house on Pleasant Street to the fat couple from Connecticut, the Martulas. In the afternoon he'd taken the Byrons through Beech's and had gotten home before Val. That's right. Wednesday was the day he'd started on the woodpile, Val had made stir-fried chicken for supper, and that night they'd all gone to the school play. Ben onstage, grinning in his pilgrim's hat, his hands stuck in his pockets.

"What happened between Monday and Wednesday?" he asked. "He fell apart?"

"Eliot is out of his tree," she repeated patiently. "At the hospital they think he is marvelous, but I know what he is going through. He is happy—unbelievably happy—then he is

76

dying. Monday she was gone, it was over, Tuesday she had her abortion, Wednesday Eliot does this to himself, today, Sunday, they let her take him out of the hospital. What does it mean? She is frightened too, of course. She didn't plan on this . . . chaos. She doesn't know what to do either. But Eliot needs to be in the hospital."

"I didn't realize she was about to have an abortion."

"Yes."

"There's no one there who can have some influence?"

"This is the problem."

"Eliot's from New York, isn't he? His family must be concerned. Can they help?"

"I wanted to call them, I'm afraid that would only create more difficulties. Eliot's parents, they are old, the father is weak, the mother has asthma. She would have an attack. All last year they were sick because Eliot left us. No, I couldn't do this to them."

Parents of Eliot Singer—figments to Boomfell. Old, asthmatic, spare them. Singer had married a saint. Who are you? he thought. What do you look like? Suddenly, the phone was an exasperating encumbrance. And yet face to face, he considered, she wouldn't speak so freely.

"Don't you think they would want to know?" he asked.

"That has always been a problem, Eliot and his family. He has a brother, older, but they haven't spoken in years. I don't think he would come, I don't think Eliot would want to see him—not like this."

"A friend," said Boomfell. "He has friends up there."

"Since Lucky, he has nothing to do with friends. Oh, now there are visitors, of course, his colleagues, you know, who haven't spoken to him for months, now they flock to the hospital. And Eliot, sitting there, he is Superman. But it's not true." She added, "We have been here one year. You don't have friends so soon."

"How about your family?" he asked. "What do they think?"

"Impossible. They are fond of Eliot. Switzerland is far away. They aren't involved in this. They would worry," she explained. "It is better this way."

"Listen," he said decisively. "Eliot's family should be notified. They're entitled to know what's happened, they'd want to know, I'm sure."

"Do you think so?"

"Contact the brother. Tell him the story and let him take it from there. Toss him the ball," said Boomfell, "and see what he does with it."

"The ball?" she asked.

"You can't be expected to deal with the whole thing yourself. They would expect you to contact them. His brother will want to help, that's what families are for."

"Do you think so? I should call him?"

"Right now," he told her. "Tonight. In the meantime, if I hear from Eliot, I'll call you immediately." On the cover of an old *New Yorker*—a vacant beach with one lonely seashell in the foreground—Boomfell took down her number again. Just in case.

"Thank you, Mr. Boomfell. It has been helpful, talking to you."

"Charles," he said. "I'm glad you called. When you hear from him, let me know, okay? I want to know what's going on."

"Yes?"

"Yes, by all means."

"That's very generous."

"The whole thing is hard to believe. I don't think it's sunk in."

"I know."

Almost as an afterthought he said, "How are you doing? You seem to be holding up well."

His question surprised her. "Me?"

"Chances are he's fine," Boomfell suggested.

"You depend on these people, but they don't know what they're doing. That's what is so disturbing."

"Call the brother, then you should try to relax," he told Astrid Singer. "Don't sit up all night worrying."

The woman laughed skeptically. "We will see."

Take care until you get here.

I'll try.

"Who was that, Dad?"

"No one you know."

He stepped outside into welcome cold air. The smell of the wood fire, for instance. The moon there between the lateral boughs of the white pine, rent by ice storms, was unreal. The giant pumpkin in the middle of Val's herb garden had a cartoon charm. Bittersweet formed a tangled arbor over the weathered gate. The picket fence had weathered to a dark silvery gray. Beautiful, you know—so fucking charming it was hard to believe.

From the farthest corner of the backyard, he was able to see the smoke issuing from the stout chimney of their house, a light in every window. Their home! How had Singer blocked out everything? His son, for example. Sleep tight, see you in the morning. The importance of school tomorrow, for example. Your kid trusted you to see him through.

I'll try. I run ten, twelve miles a day.

Singer had sounded all right to Boomfell. Was he now, in fact, different, someone different than the person Boomfell had known? The composed face that came to mind from years before did not belong to a man who might slash his wrists. The melodrama of that phrase! To the bone, Mr. Boomfell. He could be dead, for Christ's sake, had he thought of that? Was it an almost careful, deliberate act, you wondered, or a hazardous hysterical slashing? Alone in a room, a hopeless mess on your hands, your athlete's heart spilling blood onto the floor, not at the resting pulse rate of the long-distance runner, but too quickly. Good-bye. Then waking up in a hospital bed, a basket case. The look of the room. The look of the people, for instance, the nurse or doctor, his Lucky, approaching the bed. Hi, how are you today?

His hiking, his skiing, his piano. You took up the piano?

His ecstasy. You took up ecstasy?

In the shed at the end of the one-story ell, something darted as he switched on the light. Too swift and light-footed to be a marauding cat. The odor of newly stacked wood was a fresh live scent. Here was what he had done with his day to make life worth living.

Take care.

I'll try, Charles Boomfell. I love life, I don't know why.

That's important.

With more force than was necessary he drove his maul into a piece of oak, which split neatly. Like a clean base hit. He set another piece of oak on the chopping block and cracked it in half, shouting as he brought the ax down. To the bone.

He had failed to hear what Eliot Singer had been saying less than a week before because he was Charles Boomfell—the same Boomfell—and in the mind of Boomfell, Singer was still Singer.

Astrid Singer called back just before eleven. Eliot had been reached at Lucky's, at last, and was now back in the hospital. She thought Boomfell would like to know. She had tried to reach Eliot's brother, as he suggested, but David was in Europe. His wife would give him the message tomorrow. It was better not to depend on them. Eliot had laughed when she told him she was going to call his brother. "This is his attitude. With the brother, everything is money. The family has always been rich, that is not Eliot's interest." She had also called the psychiatrist, who refused to speak to her. "These intelligent men, they don't like to be scolded when they make mistakes."

When he asked her how Eliot seemed tonight, she said, "Wildly happy, like a teenager now that he has his Lucky back again."

Astrid, he could hear as they talked, began to relax. Another full day's anxiety over Singer had ended. Her initial reserve gradually gave way under the influence of his do-gooder's eagerness. They were in cahoots, speaking quietly long-distance, the anonymous disembodied voices of strangers. Singer's breakdown was shipwreck; they had washed up on this tiny island—the telephone—at eleven o'clock at night.

"What is it about Lucky anyway?" he ventured. "Do you understand Eliot's fixation on her?"

"She is merely young and beautiful. Nothing more."

He pressed further. "You don't sound angry."

"The anger is over. Eliot, he was not so easy to live with, you know, even before Lucky. His order, this perfection, that was not easy. Your orderly life, I asked him, where has it gone? But my goodness, his yogurt, his Mozart, his books and papers, his running shoes lined up in the hallway—pairs and pairs all colors."

Boomfell laughed. Already laughter was possible.

"Thinness, I think, became his ambition. Eliot, where are you running? He would not sit and have dinner with us. Eliot, what is it? Astrid, please. He would come home and lie down in the middle of the day. Even the children couldn't help in these moods. Keep them away. Life was too much. The university, he couldn't bear another day of that. Then what are you doing there? I asked. Astrid, please. Run run run. Then suddenly there is Lucky. Eliot was running on the bike path, he simply ran past her, they talked, who knows what? Eliot comes home and tells me something important has happened. His happiness was simply ridiculous, I laughed at him. In one week he has moved out, he is gone. Is it true? You couldn't talk to him. Lucky took her little girl and left home as well. They took separate apartments in the same building. Is it true? I asked. It happened."

"You don't do that," said Boomfell. "Throw your life away at the drop of a hat."

"Eliot, you know, he hates ambiguity, he couldn't be here and there. Everything must be clear."

"As though that were possible."

"He left everything, he didn't even take his whale tooth from the bookcase, his treasures, things he couldn't live without. The week before we were to have our holiday in the mountains, that's when he left. I had been walking miles and miles all summer to prepare. Then something would go wrong in his perfect happiness with Lucky, and he would need to tell me everything. His anguish. He would call, and silence. Eliot, what is it? Speak to me, what's the matter? That was not Eliot."

It didn't sound like him to Boomfell.

"I believed he would come back. Then I began to think maybe I don't want him to come back. The divorce was a relief, believe me. Then they were going to get married. Good, I thought. Now you see where we are. Today was like a bad dream. If he wants to destroy himself, they can't stop him, this is how they think now. Yet I can no longer take responsibility for him. After all, I am no longer his wife."

"You know where he is tonight," he reassured her. "He's all right." Comforter!

"You've been very patient. It's late. The children have school."

"Eliot mentioned his son. Are there other children?"

"My daughter, Nicole. The children adore him, they don't know why he's in the hospital, they will have to be told. I'm not thinking about that tonight. Eliot doesn't want them to see him like this."

Offering platitudes about the resilience of children, Boom-fell shrunk from the unthinkable: Ruth and Ben facing their father in shreds, their bewildered eyes posing questions that would never be spoken, never answered.

"You have been very kind. It has been good to talk."

Her voice was calm, close. Hanging up, he felt suddenly, was like letting go, letting the woman sink back into her bad dream, all her worries, like phantoms, gathering around her again, nothing changed.

"Listen, I'd be happy to come up there if you think it would help."

"That's too much trouble."

"I'd like to see Eliot. I mean it," said Boomfell. "My schedule is fairly flexible these days."

"Really? You would come?"

"I'll tell you what," he suggested, "why don't you ask him? We'll leave it up to him."

"Are you sure?"

If Eliot wanted to see him, Boomfell wanted to be there.

"That's very generous."

"Let me know," said Boomfell the Generous. They decided she would call in a day or two, after she had spoken to Eliot. As they said good night he thought she sounded almost cheerful.

And yet what, he wondered the moment he hung up the phone, would be the point of going there now? Whether Singer was wildly happy with his Lucky or wildly hopeless without her, what would Boomfell represent, standing in his necktie at the foot of the bed, but another duped well-wisher chortling about his flight, his family, his life lately, as though Singer had just had his appendix out. As he imagined it, any such reunion scene would be an unendurable fraud. Astrid might be naive enough to ask him, but no, it wasn't likely that Singer would prove similarly naive enough to believe that Boomfell could do him any good at this point. What was Boomfell to Singer—after all!—or Singer to Boomfell?

On the kitchen counter the brown paper bag with its beautiful black letters—BEN B—struck him with the force and resonance of art. The lunch bag was a glimpse of another busy day in his son's merry life. How had Singer blocked all that out?

Ben B. was asleep on his back, a small person in a large bed. At the foot of the bed he had laid out his clothes for tomorrow, khaki pants and a plaid flannel shirt. Boomfell stepped across the hallway to look into Ruth's room. Above her bed, a sperm whale spectacularly breached. Blubbered tons of doomed glory.

His whale tooth! His treasures, his rich family, his brother, his anguish, his Alex and Nicole, his piano, his mountains. Who was Eliot Singer?

Val lay on her side, facing the window. "Were you on the phone?"

When he'd reported to her the substance of Astrid's earlier call, she hadn't said anything. She'd disappeared upstairs, ostensibly to tuck Ben into bed. Boomfell hadn't followed her, and she hadn't come back down. "I thought you were asleep."

"I was—almost."

"Astrid Singer called back. He was at the girlfriend's, now he's back in the hospital."

"Is he all right?" Her tone was neutral.

"Wildly happy, she said, now that he has his Lucky again. Who knows?"

She turned onto her back. "I've been lying here thinking about him. Suicide." Her voice roller-coastered over the unreal word. "What happens to people?"

"I should have gone to see him when he called last week."

"What would anyone have done with a phone call like that?"

84

"Responded."

"He probably called a whole bunch of people."

"Not according to Astrid. She never would have called me otherwise."

"Charlie, what could you have done?"

"Been there."

Unexpectedly, she rolled onto his back, grabbing him around the chest, a hard hug. When he didn't respond she let go.

"I told her I could go up there if Singer wanted to see me. That seems reasonable, don't you think?"

"Do what you want."

Awakening later, he turned onto his left side and edged into his wife's sphere of warmth, fitting his body snugly against her backside. They had settled down to sleep this way for five, ten, fifteen years. Creature comfort. She permitted his hand, a curious scout, to make its way between her legs, and when she moved, a moment later, it was to get comfortable, rather than to pull away. They knew what they were doing and expertly drew out their creature comfort until the quickening moment, with its familiar whispered warnings, had come.

"We really got things done today, didn't we? We're good at that grunt stuff. Ruth and Ben were great. We never would have finished the leaves. Now it can snow."

He thought, Are you happy?

With his eyes closed, he saw Singer swinging his leg over the tall seat of his graceful touring bicycle, gliding off. The complacent bachelor. The setting of his attempted suicide seemed to be a small bare room with a mattress on the floor: a cliché.

Long after he thought Val had fallen asleep again, she moved to his side of the bed and snuggled against him in spooning fashion. Behind his back she said, "I hope I die before you do."

. . . . . .

Keenly anticipating Astrid Singer's next call, he felt inwardly
poised, as if before an adventure charged with unknowns.

Monday morning he fielded a phone call from a man in
White Plains. He and his wife were intrigued by the center-
chimney colonial Odyssey had advertised in *The New York
Times Magazine*. They intended to be in the area Wednesday
or Thursday. Boomfell, with more important things to think
about, passed the call on to Weisman.

Monday afternoon he reserved a seat, just in case, on the
Wednesday-evening flight to Toronto—a city he had never
visited.

By Tuesday night, impatient to hear what part he was to
play in Singer's story, he called Astrid's number. The woman
who answered the phone spoke with the gay breathlessness of
a hostess in the midst of a busy party. When he gave his name
and asked if Astrid was there, the woman laughed. "Oh, Mr.
Boomfell, please hang on."

"That was David's wife," Astrid explained. She and Eliot's
brother had come the night before. The brother had spent
most of the day at the hospital.

"You must be relieved."

"Yes. David came at once, you were right. And Eliot has
greeted him warmly. It's quite interesting." Eliot had also
agreed to see the children, and she had told them what he had
been through. "Of course it was worse for Nicole. Alex is only
five. Eliot, you know, is like a god to him. Nothing can destroy
that."

"He couldn't have been thinking about them when he
did it."

"Everyone would be better off without him—even the
children, that's how he was thinking. Eliot blames himself for
everything, he is completely worthless, he has ruined everything. That was despair."

Loss of self-esteem had not entered Boomfell's mind where Singer was concerned, not even under the present extreme circumstances.

"What are they doing for him in the hospital now?" he asked.

"What more can they do? It's up to Eliot."

He came to the point of his phone call: he had reserved a seat on a Wednesday flight to Toronto.

"I asked him if he would like you to come. No! That's all he said. No! Like that. He's angry with me now, he doesn't want me to interfere. Anything I suggest is wrong."

"I understand." Yet that had not occurred to him either, that Singer might read his long-distance relationship with Astrid as meddlesome conspiracy, rather than selfless concern.

She thanked him for calling, for being a friend to Eliot, for being so kind.

"If he changes his mind," Boomfell told her, "I'll be happy to come up." As he told her to stay in touch, to keep him informed, to take care, all in all assuring her that Charles Boomfell was to be counted on, Astrid repeated the words "thank you" several times. Thank you, thank you, thank you.

Singer's tall strong angel didn't expect much from people.

"Well?" Val asked.

"No, he doesn't want to see me now. It's not surprising, it would have been an awkward reunion." Yet the abrupt retort with which Singer had scrapped his Samaritan adventure—no!—stung. Leave him to his brother.

"Good," Val said with finality, as if putting an end to Eliot Singer's brief unsettling reemergence in their lives.

The people from White Plains, Louis Weisman informed him on Friday, intended to make an offer on the center-chimney colonial. "What can I say, Charlie, you threw it in my lap?"

Puppy! Dumbbell! That was money in his pocket. Vanity, boredom, sentimentality, a woman's accent, an unknown city, all that—it had lured him from responsibility, common sense, the here and now. Learn, he pleaded with himself. First things first.

April

Val smacked the phone down, as in a movie, and swore, Fuck, shoving her hair off her face, as I came in. My mother, she said. The whole impending holiday bit made her feel trapped and hateful, it didn't help that everyone felt the same way. Val's mother, I thought. Her father could be seriously ill, yet her mother obsessed about who was to get what for Christmas, they didn't know what was wrong with him, something to do with his insides, she felt terrible, torn, she should be there but couldn't be there, but why did she feel that way, damnit, the last time she'd actually talked to him about anything of consequence to either of them was never. I stood there smiling. If she thought about it very hard, she couldn't remember him ever giving her one blessed word of encouragement, praise, advice, you name it. Just now, five minutes into the conversation with her mother, she'd heard the other phone in their house being quietly hung up, her father listening in without so much as hello or good-bye. What does that mean? Val asked. It wasn't worth discussing. He must have had a life she didn't know about. It was just too bad, she didn't even have time for her children lately, which was supposed to be the point. Her mother never stopped with her list of complaints. Val was supposed to offer endless sympathy, but if she presumed to share difficult feelings of her own, her mother changed the tune and told her to count her blessings. Her mother didn't want to know what was really going on, she didn't want to hear about money, marriage, what Ruth was going through, real feelings, she only wanted to know that everything was all right, no one was sick. For years now her mother no longer knew who Val was, and Val couldn't tell her, it was too late. Sometimes I feel no one knows who I am, what my life is like, she said, and I can't tell them. I was a smart kid, she said, I was as smart as anybody. Houseworks! Everyone became numb around the edges, dark and lonely inside, almighty family life boiled down to a few stressful holidays each year. So what's going on? I said. So who are you? I said. Tell me, I said. That made her smile—don't be a wise guy—but I was serious, I meant it. She didn't have time for coffee, she had a hundred things to do. I wanted to say, What? What's more important than telling me who you are?

He arrived at eleven, as scheduled, to take the Pocaris through the Salters' split-level house.

"Give me a minute," Eileen Salter called from a second-story bedroom.

Boomfell and his clients toured the frozen unkempt yard for ten minutes. They returned to the front just as the woman of the house, arm in arm with someone bearded, was leaving.

"Sorry," she called, as she and her friend hurried along the flagstone steps, leaning into the wind, laughing the exclusive laughter, he thought, of lovers. They were both wrapped up in long scarves. "Make yourselves at home," she called.

The scent of dope lingered in the master bedroom. Ted Pocari seemed shyly amused. His wife said the bedroom smelled like a dump burning and marched back downstairs.

Was this why the Salters were selling—their life together was unraveling? We'll try to have the place in order, Jim Salter had assured him when Boomfell called to arrange the showing. He was a soft-spoken astronomer with a special interest in sun flares. Boomfell recalled the cheerful speech he'd made to them concerning the importance of appearances—how fatuous. Disorder had taken root in their lives. Eileen Salter's gutsy laughter as she skipped off, clinging to her boyfriend's arm, gave the lie to the realtor's skin-deep relationship to reality. A year ago he would have read the Salters' marital trouble at a glance.

Purveyor of dreams! Harbinger of happiness! He dealt with

the deceptive surface of people's lives. Real estate was turning a buck. More and more he saw himself, if he stepped back to look, viewing daily life—reality!—as a deal, real or imagined. Boomfell, who had always savored the human comedy for itself—the greatest show on earth. He had been blind to what the Salters' messy kitchen meant because he'd wanted the Pocaris to make an offer. People had become clients, the landscape had been reduced to property, and language, the life of language, beloved English, was dying on the lips of Boomfell. Every day now he could hear himself—if he stopped to listen—wallowing in the general corruption of words, mouthing the glib jargon of the business.

Gracious custom-built classic contemporary . . . he'd written to describe the Eichenbergs' flimsy hodgepodge of a house. Not one word of that blurb was true. New colonial with tennis court . . . *New* colonial! With customers Boomfell heard himself—if he listened—using words like elegant, homey, special, as though those words had no meaning. Spacious could be a ten-by-ten screened porch in the morning and a dirt cellar in the afternoon. Unique, one day, was someone's dated conversation pit with a piano in the middle of it. Tasteful could be off-white paint. Enduring was an exposed beam. Your own dream house could be a split-level ranch with a clothesline in the backyard. Boomfell, who had once lovingly used language to unlock mysteries and discover new territory, now peddled clichés like a car salesman. Closing the deal was what counted. Tell them what they wanted to hear—sell them.

He remembered a question Val had posed not long after he started with Odyssey—does Charles Boomfell exist now?—and the look in her eyes as she asked it.

All those years they'd hardly had a pot to piss in, they'd had everything they needed as far as he was concerned. Youth was only part of it. Absorbed in his work, for better or worse, he had freed himself from wanting what other people wanted. The Odyssey job represented stepping out of this trance as out of a trench coat, proceeding through daily life stripped of his protective gear, on an equal footing with everyone out there. The new motive became money—the meager store-bought success money could buy. That was the rat race. On his best days he could persuade himself to go for it. On bad days he knew the rat race wasn't going to work for him. There was no substitute for the charmed life of self-sufficiency in which, caring not a hoot for brand-name pleasures, he was mostly content—connected. To the Boomfell of before, who never went anywhere, daily life had been adventure. On bad days, such as the week following the Salter incident, he knew his new life was a serious mistake. He'd been better off at the bottom, hustling temporary jobs, casing Main Street like a Martian grinning in his disguise, getting a kick out of the earthlings.

For days he shrank from his realtor's routine respon-sibilities. The numerous pink slips awaiting him at the office shrewishly nagged: call, call, call. If you didn't return the call, they were ready to drop you, and if you called back to report what they didn't want to hear, they let you hear their thinly veiled resentment. Boomfell had the likes of Rice giving him ultimatums, for the love of God. Munsen asked for favors—feed the dog—as though giving orders. Eichenberg hung up on him with impunity when an appointment was canceled at the last minute. One morning Myers scolded him, a petulant whine, for failing to reset the alarm system. The realtor was at everyone's beck and call night and day seven days a week as if, in this whore's business, he had sold body and soul. At the closing on Hartley's land, buyer and seller cozied up to one another with jokes, the chirping attorneys read the simple documents aloud as though presiding over a disarmament agreement. Boomfell, the lowly agent of the transaction, sat off to one side, invisible to the others in the room. Invisible! There were days these days when his growing file of names and numbers—his be-all leads and contacts—read to Boomfell like a list of enemies.

April

Mary Parker's slightly chunky daughter, Cindy, was out like a light in her sunny pink bedroom, which reeked of vomit and whiskey, the bottle of scotch just about empty. She moaned when I shook her, I took her pulse, I knew she'd be all right, having evidently thrown her guts up. I wiped off her face with a warm face towel, I called Val who came over right away, black pants, a turtleneck, rosy cheeks, and called the girl's mother at work. She didn't want me to clean it up, she wanted Mary Parker to see it. Twenty minutes later the woman arrived in her environmental stockbroker's gray suit, her shocked dismay quickly turned to ugly impatience, didn't know what she was going to do with the little pain in the ass, Cindy had been making her life miserable for months, as if she, the mother, had nothing to do with what had happened here. Cindy would just have to sleep it off, just please clean it up and skip the rest of the house if necessary, she had an appointment with a client that she'd canceled twice already and couldn't possibly miss. Val said no, this was her mess, she'd damned well better wake up concerning her daughter, the girl needed help, needed her mother, she was going to have to cancel her damned appointment. Yay! People surprise you. The environmentally sound investment whiz wasn't going to stand there and be scolded by someone, etc. She left. We lugged the girl to the guest bedroom, her butt half dragging on the floor, took off her stone-washed jeans, tucked her into bed, threw open the windows in her stinking bedroom. Like the Hardy boys we looked through their personal address book and found another Parker who lived in town, turned out to be Cindy's father, whose wife luckily happened to be home, came right over with a graduated series of three little towheaded kids, and said she'd take care of it, they'd been worried about Cindy, who had refused to have much to do with her father for years, etc. We'd love to know how that story came out, Val and I agreed, but we probably never would because we wouldn't be going back to clean that place again, period. School was getting pretty intense for me anyway, I could use the time, I could manage on my three other houses. We went to Jacob's for lunch, her idea, thick onion soup and French bread with a glass of California chardonnay. Terrific day so far, I told her, dusting James Gill's bookcases, the Great Books, Ariel and what's-his-name's *Story of Civilization*, I stumbled upon his cache of hard-core pornography hidden behind Churchill's *History of the English-speaking Peoples*, I didn't have time to get into it, I said. Val didn't laugh, she hated that crap. It was funny, I said, because James Gill was the tall, graying, middle-aged distinguished type who treated me like a kindly Abraham Lincoln father figure and here were these glossies of pretty girls with fantastic tons of hair trying to swallow pricks as thick as their wrists. Val said everybody needed to cope with that nagging issue somehow, she and Charlie watched *George's Cherry Tree* on the VCR one muggy night last summer, children absent, just to see what would happen. She didn't like the wormy low-life aftertaste. A long-ago friend of theirs, they'd heard, had recently put himself in the hospital over some lucky girl, people were nuts, life was crazy. Is that Charlie? she said, looking out the window at busy Main Street with pronounced interest, as though sighting Charlie was highly unusual. Where? It is, she said, pointing, across the street, there, the red wool thingy, his tam-o'-shanter, what's he up to, she smiled, Christ, he looks miserable, she almost laughed. Corduroy jacket with a tie, hands sunk in his pockets, he stood switching his head from left to right, clearly frowning, like a person trying to get his bearings in a strange city, the afternoon college crowd streaming past. Val was smiling. He set off up the street at a determined pace then, head down as against a wind, Val sat back, clapping her hands together once, laughing. I thought, She loves him. What's he do? I asked, he looks like a teacher. He used to be, he was selling real estate at the moment, she said, at least trying, ever since September, not what he'd choose. My mother sold houses for a while in San Francisco, I told her. What would he rather do? Val wasn't sure anymore, she said, Let's not get into that. Life doesn't get easier as you get older, she said, or have you figured that out already. She only figured that out when she was thirty or so, she used to think you got to know a few things, you actually got wiser as in older and wiser, but it got harder, more mixed up, uncertain, she didn't mean to get dreary and stupid on me all of a sudden, she smiled. I said, I think you can get what you want, I intend to get what I want, live the way I want to. Big speech! Val smiled with closed lips, reached across the table, That's the only way to be, she said, she wanted her children to feel that way, You're right, she said. I've seen Charlie playing soccer out front with Ben, I said, he's pretty attractive, he seems like a good father. Charlie was a wonderful father, according to Val. Soup was served, she asked me about Don these days. He was really an okay guy, but still a nuisance, frankly, spooking around at midnight when my head was swimming with biochemistry, my microbial genetics course, etc., creeping under my clothes, you know, while I was at my desk looking like shit, I was sure, and feeling about as sexy as a sanitary napkin. Get rid of him, Val said, if that's how you feel. Other times I liked to have him around, I confided, he was tender, passionate about Poland's problems, his wife sounded awful bitchy, most of the time she seemed to have a urinary tract infection. It's none of my business, Val said, I just hate to hear about these older married parasites wasting . . . I was touched by her genuine-seeming concern. Maybe the wine pushed me over the edge, this seemed as good a time as any, I thought, in the context of all this girl-to-girl talk, to let a little light into the conversation. Maybe you're right, I said, I'd always leveled with him about Pauline, for instance, he never seemed to mind, but lately he was becoming possessive, pushy about that, which was way over his head. Pauline had been in Europe all summer, I told Val, and we'd both been too busy this fall to connect more than once a month, so I didn't mind having Don down the street to cope with the nagging issue, as Val put it, but the last time she was here, he kept turning up on the sidewalk, the phone, wouldn't leave us alone, and that definitely wasn't going to work. Val looked funny, a long string of melted cheese from the soup stretching out of control. Wait a minute, did I miss something, she said, do I know about Pauline? We're girlfriends, I smiled, and let it go at that. Seconds passed while she dealt with the cheese, looking up at me with her head down over the bowl, Jesus, she said, do you know the Heimlich . . . her favorite niece, her sister's oldest, was probably a lesbian although no one in the family had yet let it be known, as though pretending not to know meant it might not be so. The niece's father was straight and narrow, with a lethal dose of old-fashioned Catholicism, and needed to be protected, he'd probably prefer to see his daughter locked up in a hopeless marriage than liberated in a tender loving . . . She said, We didn't have that in Connecticut when I was growing up so I don't know much about it. I said, What do you want to know about it? She asked, Does Pauline have boy-friends too? Not anymore, Pauline will tell you she was born to love women. She asked, And Don is all right with Pauline? I'm all right with Pauline, I answered, she doesn't sweat the small stuff. You make me feel like a developing country, Val said. She asked me what I thought she should do with her hair, which was always . . . Get it cut was my advice. It was Friday after-noon, our table was by the window, the day had turned cloudy and gray, the street was full of healthy people, everyone's breath in the air, I wanted it to last, I wanted the light to last, growing dark very slowly, unnoticeably, I felt full, I wanted the fullness to last, I wanted Val, sitting across from me, to last. It was Friday afternoon, she had to get back to her one-room office, she had to get Ruth, had to get Ben, she had to go to the grocery store for supper, she needed liver tonight, whenever she had her period she wanted liver, she wanted to have me over sometime, she said, if I thought I could stomach an old-fashioned family meal. The answer was yes.

Following an uneventful morning he drove into the hill towns, letting the road lead him. Christmas shopping deserved to be ignored a little longer. His list of loved ones: name and question mark. He hadn't driven into the country, its narrow roads lined with stone walls and rock maples, since before Thanksgiving. That holiday already seemed long gone. The midnight phone call he had received before Thanksgiving now belonged to another season. Eliot Singer had again receded into the opaque past from which his troubled and unsettling voice had momentarily intruded. The episode was relegated to the harmless unknown—like a disturbing sound in the middle of the night that, by morning, seems more imagined than real. The man's difficulties, whatever was happening to him, had become as remote as . . . pumpkin pie, falling leaves. Singer's subsequent silence, now that Boomfell was no use to him, was typical. Unless the poor bastard, he considered, driving through winter woods, had really come apart at the seams. Out of his tree.

If Singer's troubles had faded, Astrid remained present— her voice—and Boomfell found himself, as now, stubbornly attempting to conjure her, the person behind the accent. That is very generous, Charles. Thank you, thank you, thank you. Chances were he would never lay eyes on her—a relationship lived first to last long-distance. The phrase "tall strong angel" didn't give birth in Boomfell's mind to a flesh-and-blood image.

Smoke rose, a vertical plume, from Muler's stout chimney.

Douglas Hobbie

Cordwood was stacked six feet high on the front porch. No, the unbeholden artisan wouldn't welcome a friendly call from the realtor. The place looked lonely at the end of its long drive, backed by gray woods. The smoke was the only sign of life. Good luck to you, Muler.

On Creamery Road, canopied by bare branches, an old man in bib overalls, a faded hip-length denim jacket, and peaked cap gathered sticks into a bundle. He straightened up as Boomfell's car approached, and slowly raised an arm in greeting. Boomfell waved back, waved hard, as if the farmer were hard-of-seeing. The man continued to look after the car, Boomfell saw in his mirror, his arm still raised. Old codger. He didn't see enough people in a week to let someone pass without a hello. In town, people looked the other way—a smile was suspect, a wave an unwanted pressure.

West of Northfield he turned onto a dirt road, following a hunch as to where it led. Less than an hour later he was lost somewhere in woods. The road narrowed to two ruts, the woods rising on either side. The light at the end of it was a small farm: house, barn, two or three outbuildings all weathered dark gray. The road blocked by guinea hens. Two large mongrel dogs bounded toward the car, raising a racket. Geese appeared, honking. He turned around in the barnyard, careful not to hit one of the hens. The dogs ran alongside the car, barking, for half a mile. Who the hell lived like this anymore? Who were these people?

By three-thirty it had begun to snow in large wet globs. Kinda beautiful. He crossed a stream on a wooden bridge. An abandoned one-story building there had to be one of the old schoolhouses from back when the woods had been pastureland. He passed a neglected apple orchard, the trees fallen to nature. The deciduous woods became hemlock. They held the snow and gave Boomfell that wonderland feeling, you know, for the first time again. Winter again. The road soon became a white untraveled path. He stared through the onslaught of

100

falling snow, hoping the road wouldn't become a ditch suddenly, or a dead end. As he downshifted into a corner, a branch sideswiped the car, and an animal—*the* animal as it became in the retelling—sprang across the road from right to left not ten feet before him. He watched it clear the stone wall and disappear into the evergreen undergrowth. Brownish with dark spots, a squarish head, small ears, no tail. Although he'd never seen a bobcat before, he knew that's what it was. He got out of the car to take a good look at the clear imprint of the wildcat's paw, three fingers in diameter. Snow fell into the silent woods, his pulse raced. Through a hard-on fit for a king—or a boy—he pissed a full stream halfway to the wall, his daily dose of vitamins yellow as a crayon. What a day, what a hell of a day this dreary Friday had become.

By dusk he came to a three-way intersection and chose the paved road, which led to Sally's Corner. He knew where he was. Then, to top things off, the moment he turned on the radio he heard an old song, an old Boomfell favorite about leavin' on a jet plane, to sing along with.

He tuned to public radio for the evening news and caught the local station's "Community Calendar"—upcoming events in Boomfell's corner of the world. There were wall-to-wall holiday vespers, potluck dinners, a pair of Bach concerts back-to-back, contredanses, an evening of Corelli, Pachelbel, and Friends, Handel's *Messiah* somewhere, the *Nutcracker* again, a reading of Dickens at the library, a puppet show. In the swift recitation of all this scheduled hullabaloo, Boomfell, only half listening, heard a name—*the* name—that caused his pulse to bump double-time. His foot went for the brake. A trio, but he didn't get the name of it, and of course he didn't get the names of the other two members, but it was a trio, the something trio, and he heard Wanda, he heard Gwertz, he heard cello. He didn't hear where or when. How many Wandas with the name Gwertz could there be playing cello? The wild animal had caused only a mild rush of adrenaline compared to the excitement he felt now. And he felt exposed somehow, nakedly exposed, as if the radio announcer had been speaking directly to Charles Boomfell, whose reaction to this piece of news as he drove through snow in the dark, bent over the wheel, was being simulcast nationwide.

At dinner, exhilarated by his afternoon of endangered species, as he described it to his family, he drank a bottle of zinfandel single-handedly. Later, after everyone had gone to bed, he began a letter to Astrid Singer—just wondering, he wrote, how Eliot was doing these weeks later—but soon threw the page on the fire. That was over. It was still snowing when he went to bed—the first real snow of the season. In the morning, he decided, he would take Ben cross-country skiing, rather than go to the office to return the phone calls he had missed that afternoon.

"Nice of you to call, Charles Boomfell."

He recognized the voice immediately, from the first disparaging word, despite the unlikely hour, seven-fifteen on a Tuesday morning, despite the unexpectedness of the call.

"I was just saying to Val we'll probably never hear from him again. How are you? Naturally, we've been wondering—"

"That might have been true, you might never have heard from me again. Evidently that possibility hardly disturbed you."

"So what's happening? Where are you?"

"Where were you, Charles Boomfell, that's what I was thinking. A phone call didn't seem too much to ask under the dire circumstances. A few minutes on the phone for Eliot locked up in the loony bin."

"I did call, as a matter of fact. Astrid . . . we had several discussions about you, as a matter of fact."

"How exciting for the two of you. Please don't mention Astrid."

"I was all set to go to Canada, Eliot. Astrid told me that you said no, you didn't want to see me. I could understand your unwillingness—"

"You see, I don't remember. I have no recollection of Astrid asking, of saying no. Eliot was out of it—absent. For days and days I was absent, playing hooky from daily life, and for every day I was absent, I received another detention. I haven't been well, Charles Boomfell. I have been detained for the first time in my life. I never received a detention in high school, for example—my lonely perfect years of high school. I was never suspended, expelled, even scolded. Little Eliot Singer, they loved me, I was so industrious, Charles, so motivated, so smart, so tall for my age. Eight hundreds on my College Boards, math and verbal. What am I doing here, that's what I asked myself repeatedly, what am I doing locked up in a psychiatric ward in Toronto? How did a handsome boy who got sixteen hundreds on his SATs become confined to this ward with crazy people—moaning, staring, bed-wetting crazy people—thinking Lucky Lucky Lucky? What happened, Charles Boomfell?"

"Listen, where are you? It's seven o'clock in the morning, I'm standing here trying to tie my tie. Are you still in the hospital?"

He had already tied it once and now, the second time around, it came out wrong again, the narrow part damn near down to his fly. He pulled at the knot, the phone held between jaw and shoulder, almost seven-thirty already. Val looked into the bedroom from the hallway and silently formed the words with her lips, Who is it? He waved her away impatiently. Who? she demanded without speaking.

"I'm out, I was released last week. I've been up. Sleep is not one of my strengths these days. I'm up. What have I been doing all night? I go to the kitchen, back to the living room, sit down, get up. I peek into the bedroom where the girl sleeps like a baby, I return to the kitchen where I hate the color of the

walls. The place is a hovel. My hated hovel. Open the refrigerator, there's nothing to eat. Take a shit, there's no toilet
paper. Sit down, get up. I go to the window, there's Eliot in the
window—a fool in the window. I lie down to close my eyes for
two minutes, and two seconds later I open them again, jump-
ing up like the doorbell has just rung. How did this happen? I
ask myself. How did I become an insomniac? I need to sleep. A
few nights like this, Charles Boomfell, you could go out of your
mind, I'm not kidding."

"You're at your apartment? There's a girl in the bedroom?
Just a second." He covered the phone with his hand. "You
won't believe this," he told Val. "I'll talk to you later."

She was already late. Ruth had a rehearsal after school, she
reminded him, and Ben had gymnastics, so they probably
wouldn't eat until . . . Nodding, he waved good-bye, go.

"One hundred and sixteen stitches, Charles Boomfell. I
keep thinking, one hundred and sixteen stitches. Why? How
can this be? Charles, you have to come up, we have to talk.
Everything was fine. Lucky and I, we're doing it like bandits at
every opportunity, we're in love. I'm in the loony bin, I'm
stitched up like a football, but we're happy, everything's going
to be all right. For the past four weeks we're getting married,
making plans, maybe a honeymoon in Paris after New Year's.
Honeymoon, Charles, isn't it a marvelous word? I never used
to like it. You get the picture. She gave me a sweatshirt, white
with big red letters. Lucky loves Eliot. She insisted that I be
wearing her present whenever she turned up. I wore it every
day. Extra extra large. Lucky loves Eliot. At last it's time to go
home. Eliot can go home and resume life, try to get back to his
wonderful life, Charles, so Saturday comes, I walk out into
winter sunshine, carrying my creepy belongings, and what
happens? What happens?" he cried, almost cried, his voice
breaking on the first syllable of the second word.

"You all right? Eliot?"

"Lucky checks in. She books herself onto the very same

floor—floor eleven—while Eliot is leaving, and now—are you ready, Charles Boomfell?—and now she won't let me see her. She's suffering from nervous exhaustion, or depression, or I don't give a shit. She's suffering? Her doctor won't let me near her. Charles, can you imagine? We're about to get married, except the minute I'm out she can never see me again. I hate her. Eliot hates Lucky. I look at myself, these self-inflicted wounds. I think, Look what she's done to you. I've been locked up for a month. I return to the ward and my fellow crazies are yelling, Hey, Lucky loves Eliot, Lucky loves Eliot. She can't see me, she says, but the truth is I never want to see her again. I can live without her. Believe it or not, I can live without her."

Singer paused and in the momentary silence a question arose, seemed to arise, from his last statement, which led Boomfell to mutter reassuringly, "Of course you can."

"Charles, can you come up? You told Astrid you wanted to come up. Would I be calling you at seven in the morning if it wasn't important? I'm very tired, I'm exhausted. I'm going to New York on the twenty-second. My brother sent me a ticket. He insisted. Christmas in New York, which I loathe, frankly, although I used to love New York. When I was a kid I loved New York. I didn't want to live anywhere else. I couldn't imagine living anywhere else. But what's the date? I looked at a calendar, the twenty-second, that's a long time—days and nights from now."

"Goddamnit, Eliot, right now I'm trying to get my goddamn tie on, you know. I'm supposed to meet the Pocaris at nine—I mean, I've got appointments all day long, I've got to get Ben over to gymnastics after school. You know? Tonight we're supposed to go shopping again—chasing through stores for the perfect elusive gift for people we only see twice a year, right. It's the worst possible time. Listen, can I call you later today? Do I have your number?"

"Appointments all day long? What are you, Charles, a dentist?"

"I'll tell you about it when I see you. I don't have time to go into it this morning, you know—"

"We bought a house together—our little nest—months ago. Her money, but we both signed the papers. Now she wants to sell. I get a call from some moron who says he's representing Mrs. Lafrenier. No, Mr. Singer is not going to cooperate. If I can help it, she'll never see her money again. Am I supposed to be nice? Nice to someone I hate? Christmas shopping? Charles, we have to talk. The girl in the next room—she's still sleeping, she sleeps like a baby—she's a lovely girl, but talking to her is like talking to a child, a small child."

"You're still with a therapist, aren't you? Maybe you should give him a ring. That's why he's there, right? I mean, are you all right? You sound pretty good, but that's what I said the last time, isn't it?"

"No, I'm better now. I'm better now. But it takes time, that's what they say." In a quieter, more confiding tone, he added, "The whole thing has been shattering, Charles Boomfell. It's been quite shattering."

"I'd like to come up, Eliot, I just have to work out the details. Let me work on it."

"I'll call you in a day or two. Charles, I appreciate this. Bring your running shoes. How have you been anyway? How's everything?"

"I'm a monument of stability. We manage."

"That's what I thought I was. If nothing else, Charles—stable."

"I'll talk to you soon."

"But maybe I am. It occurs to me, maybe I am."

His day did not go well. Lisa Pocari, a purple gnome in her quilted down-stuffed coat, couldn't conceal—didn't wish to—her impatience toward Boomfell for dragging them out to a nondescript contemporary stuck in dark cold pine woods without a lawn. Eichenberg, spurred on, Boomfell knew, by his mousy wife, called at noon to say they would not be renewing their contract with Odyssey if Boomfell wasn't prepared to run an ad in *The New York Times Magazine*. One of his afternoon appointments was canceled just as he was leaving the office to get to it, and the other appointment, at three, proved more depressing than promising—a dairy farmer in Everett at the end of his rope. Ben came home from gymnastics with a headache that made his eyes look vacant. There was yelling between Ruth and her mother over a pair of Val's shoes that had been misplaced, it seemed, permanently. They drove to town, halfheartedly searched three or four shops for nothing in particular that might make a Christmas gift for Val's mother or her sister or her niece, and gave up in a sour mood. On the way home their ongoing discussion of Singer's morning phone call became an argument.

"It's not your problem, Charlie. It's not your responsibility. He needs professional help, he doesn't need someone to drink beer with. We can't afford a round-trip ticket to Canada right now. You can't afford to take time out to go playing the friend."

"A hundred and sixteen stitches, Val. All right? 'Shattering' was the word he used. Singer? Shattering? I don't know any more about it than you do, but if I hear from him again and he sounds like he did this morning, I'm going."

"Aren't you magnanimous? Aren't you heroic?"

It was just after six the next morning, just minutes since the awful alarm on his digital watch had gone off, when the phone rang. Val had already picked it up in the kitchen by the time Boomfell got to it in the bedroom. There was a giddy nervousness in her voice as she said good morning. Her greeting was too bright, absurdly chipper, thought Boomfell, insofar as it couldn't possibly be a good morning for the man on the other end.

"How lovely to hear your voice again," Singer said wearily. "You sound wide awake. You're an early riser, aren't you?"

"Eliot, I was so sorry to hear about what you've been going through. Charlie has told me—"

"I'd love to talk, Valerie, but I'm afraid I'm not up to it. I wanted to be sure I reached Charles before he went out. I had to be sure I reached him. Is he there?"

"I'm right here."

"Charles Boomfell, I had this idea you wouldn't be there. For some reason you wouldn't be there."

"It's just after six, Eliot."

"I couldn't wait until seven. As soon as I began to think you wouldn't be there, I had to call, that's all there is to it. Sleeplessness, it's like a drug."

"You haven't slept?"

"I'm getting off, Charlie. Good-bye, Eliot." She hung up.

"You have a wife, you have children, you go to sleep at night, you get up in the morning. How, Charles Boomfell, how is it possible? Remember our friend Macbeth? Singer has murdered sleep. Blanchard and Sontag and Wassong came by last night to see how I was doing—they'd formed a committee to see how their colleague fresh from the loony bin was doing. They must do things in numbers. The Singer commission. There they were at the door of my hovel. They figure they hired me with tenure, they're looking after their investment. I tried to look at it from their point of view. You really hired a live wire this time, gentlemen. Hit the jackpot. Blanchard has been doing my Milton course. He's practically holding hands with Wassong as if I might swallow him whole if he gets too close. Maybe I look frightening, I can't tell. Sontag brought a casserole from his Austrian wife. She made Teutonic stew for Eliot. I don't want to eat. We just wanted to see how you were coming along, Eliot. We wondered if there was anything we could do. Blanchard and Sontag were pulling their beards. They just thought they'd stop by on their way home from tennis. When I first arrived here I played doubles with them twice a week. I can't believe I ever did that. Do you know what they look like in the shower, these aging men padding on tiles in their old bare feet, with their soft limbs and their softer white bellies, their academic asses and sagging wad of genitalia—they look like extraterrestrials. But, Charles, that's what I feel like."

"I know what you mean."

"Do you? The look of them. Blanchard, the Milton scholar, in his turtleneck and his tweed jacket. I suppose he's been going around like that for twenty-five years. Nothing in the past twenty-five years has compelled him to change his clothes. Sontag wouldn't shut up about how to heat up the Teutonic casserole. I haven't slept in days, I'm sick with worry, Lucky's in the hospital, I don't even know what I'm doing here—alive, I mean—and Sontag won't shut up about his wife's stew from the old country, from the ancient mother who lives in the mountains where Sontag goes hiking every summer with his Teutonic binoculars. Million-dollar binoculars. He teaches American literature, Charles Boomfell, he hasn't read anything since Ernest Hemingway. Wassong is our writer, a pathetic cross between vanity and vodka—moody with big dark moody eyes. He married an old cunt from the old country so he could go hiking every summer. Sontag, I mean. I was not sociable. I put the burden of the visit entirely on them. I gave them my last three beers. There were long minutes of silence. Wassong sat with his head in his hands, looking like a nut from floor eleven. Sontag started describing a movie he saw. Imagine telling me about a movie? Wassong didn't like it, he informed us. Imagine? Blanchard recalled a marvelous point at net. Eliot wanted to scream. I couldn't sit still. The beards got on my nerves. Why don't they go home and shave off the goddamn beards, let their miserable wives and little assorted brats see what they look like, let their little chins into the world. I didn't say it, of course, but I began to fear I would say it if they sat there any longer. I was afraid I'd tell them what I thought of them. Blanchard is actually afraid to stand at net, up close to net. He has never read the *Areopagitica* in its entirety. A Milton scholar! You really ought to see it if you get a chance, Sontag says. I don't think you missed anything, Wassong pipes up. My God, Charles, they've come to tell me I should go to the movies, I should play tennis, I should eat stew from Austria. I'm sitting there waiting for them to drink my last three beers. I haven't said a word, hardly a word, and then I was unable to suppress my emotion any longer. It was horrible. I told them I wished they hadn't come, their chatter was driving me crazy. I told Wassong he was the most depressing sight I'd seen in weeks. His moods repelled me. I told Sontag to please take the stew back to his wife, or I'd throw it out. I told Blanchard . . . Never mind what I told them. It was horrible. They looked at each other as if to say, Yes, gentlemen, I'm afraid he's out of his mind. But then—guess, Charles Boomfell. Guess what!"

"What?"

"The moment they left I wished they were still there. I missed them. I wanted to apologize, I wanted to eat Austrian stew and talk about tennis and movies, I wanted to tell them how much I appreciated their concern. Blanchard in his turtleneck, Charles, he came to visit me every other day in the hospital. Imagine. He brought books, magazines. Last week Wassong brought in a cocktail hour for us—whiskey. That was nice of him. When we moved here he was instrumental in finding us a place to live. Sontag was the first to have us to dinner—a big wonderful dinner from Austria. After I told them to please leave, I wished they were still there so I could tell them what nice people they were, how helpful they had been, how fortunate I felt to have friends. But I don't feel that fortunate. If they were still here, they'd drive me crazy and I'd ask them to leave all over again. I'd insult them, then I'd miss them. I'm exhausted, Charles. But you were home, you're there. What if you hadn't been home for some reason?"

"You sound tired, Eliot."

"I'm supposed to teach a class today. That was part of the commission's purpose—to see if I was up to it. I'm supposed to discuss *Paradise Lost* for two hours. I'm an expert. Charles, you were planning to come up, weren't you? This weekend. Did you say this weekend?"

"I said a couple of days. I might be able to make it this weekend."

"I was thinking—I have plenty of time to think—perhaps it would be better if I came down. It might be useful to get away. I can't bear to think about her in the hospital, but I can't think about anything else while I'm here in my hovel. It's not good. She's alone, she has no one. Her family, you know, her cretinous, thick-skinned, heartless family, they have rejected her completely. They don't know her anymore. She doesn't exist. That's a family for you. I feel so sorry for her, Charles— alone, locked up, paranoid. And she refused to see me, the only person in the world who can help her. She should be begging to see me, she needs me."

"She's in good hands, Eliot, she'll be taken care of. Leave her alone for a while. I think it's more important for you to get some rest, get back on your feet. You aren't any good to anyone in your present state."

"I'm inclined to agree with you. If I could get away for the weekend. I think I'll be all right as long as I know I'm getting out of here for the weekend. I'll teach my seminar, take a long run, leave Lucky alone, fly to the States on Friday. How's that sound?"

"Are you sure you're up to it? Should you check with anyone?"

"Should I ask Edward the psychiatrist if I can visit Charles Boomfell? I'm not dangerous, Charles. Of course I'm up to it."

"Good."

"I need to detach myself. I need to sleep. I can't pace back and forth in my hovel thinking Lucky Lucky Lucky. The poor girl, Charles, she's locked up on floor eleven, she sees no one."

"Call the airlines, book a flight, then let me know when you'll be getting in. And do me a favor."

"Of course."

"Forget about Lucky for the next few days. Don't think about her."

"You have a sense of humor, Charles, that's what I like about you."

"And you do me a favor," Val said. She had come into the room as his conversation with Singer was ending. "When he calls back, tell him I'm sorry that I'll miss him. I have to be at my mother's this weekend. I'll take Ruth and Ben with me."

"He's coming to enjoy the warmth and security of a family snug in their house, Valerie. The whole family. What the hell would I do with him alone around here? He sounds nuts."

"You wait on him, Charlie. I'll be damned if I'm going to make a meal or change a bed or wash a towel. . . ." She stood before her closet door in pantyhose, naked to the waist, hugging herself with both arms. "Christ, I'm freezing. Do we have to freeze all winter?"

"I'm not going to tell him you won't be here. I'm going to say we're all looking forward—"

"I won't be here." She took a gray wool dress from the closet, held it at arm's length, and as quickly stuffed it back on the rack. "I'm sick to death of my clothes. I have a lunch date today, I just wanted to look nice for a change."

"You always look fine."

She pulled on her white cashmere sweater, and stepped into her paisley skirt of earthy colors—her best skirt. "This is the only decent thing I own," she said, moving to the mirror above the chest of drawers. "Every time I want to make myself presentable I have to drag it out. God, I look dreadful."

"You're going to be here, Val. It's imperative."

"This is your party, Charlie, not mine. Look at my face this morning—it's ghastly. Who has hair like this? Will you look at my hair. What goddamn genes."

"People in your family live forever."

"It's not fair."

Within the hour, as they were about to leave the house, the phone startled him again.

"Charles Boomfell, I've been thinking. I'll only take a minute. Listen, I called the airline. I can get a flight tomorrow, arriving midday. I think that's better. The girl who's been staying with me, Rachel, she has to be away for a while. She just left yesterday afternoon. I urged her to stay. She couldn't."

"The weekend would be a lot better for us, Eliot. We're working, the kids have a dozen things going on. . . . You already have a flight?"

"These next few days are a bad time for me, Charles. I urged Rachel to stay just until Friday. She went home for the break, she couldn't change her flight. I think about Lucky alone in the hospital. She's surrounded by crazy people, Charles. These next few days, it's not a good time for me."

Boomfell took down the flight number, the time of arrival. He would be there.

"Charles Boomfell, I knew I could count on you. Now I'll arrange a ride to the airport, I'll do some laundry, I'll pack. Like a holiday, Charles. Eliot on holiday."

"Are you okay? Everything's under control?"

"Yes. Much better."

If he had been ambivalent, at best, about Singer's proposed visit, now he hoped the man would get there.

April

No, this is her daughter, Ruth said, I immediately felt calling was a mistake, I wasn't her friend, I just worked for her, I was probably interrupting dinner, but she sounded fine when she came to the phone, as if she didn't mind. Stage fright. I started talking about Marjorie and Eleanor, they were usually so lively and fun, I said, but Marjorie hadn't been outside for weeks, too cold, of course, and this morning she seemed downright depressed, I felt helpless. The place was usually so neat, but today it needed to be cleaned, the beds needed to be changed. They sat cooped up in the kitchen with the thermostat on eighty, the place smelled of stale cigarette smoke, I couldn't imagine what they did all day. Someone from the church took them grocery shopping twice a week, apparently, because Marjorie refused to drive in the cold weather, their black-and-white tube was always on with the sound turned off, except for basketball, the pair of them were fanatic basketball fans. Eleanor had her letters to everyone, carefully written in her shaky arthritic hand, today a letter of congratulations to the paperboy, whose name appeared on the honor roll, she read the *Enquirer* faithfully with its GIVES BIRTH TO CYCLOPS, UFO KIDNAPPING, CANCER CURE, but Marjorie was lost without being able to get out and putter around. Today she'd been working on a Sierra Club puzzle, the Grand Tetons, on the card table in the corner. Puzzles are for idiots, she said. Is that all I'm good for, I wonder. I guess I'm not good for much else, am I? This winter will probably be the end of me, she said, she felt it in her tired old bones, she didn't mind, except she'd never see her garden again, that was her only regret. Would I have someone look after the garden, she said, because Eleanor never cared a thing about the garden, she'd always done the garden alone, it was the garden that had kept her alive until now. Eleanor said dying this winter would suit her just fine, she'd lived far too long for anybody's good already. Val laughed, You sound exactly like them, she said, you're perfect, she said. Eleanor never missed anything, but Marjorie's hearing was terrible, she was blind in one eye. She complained she never slept anymore, which got worse in the winter. What good are you if you can't sleep? she said. Eleanor said, If you aren't sleeping in there, what are you snoring for? I was washing the kitchen floor on my hands and knees, Stop that tiresome wiping, Eleanor said, and sit down with us for five minutes, life is too short. I made tea, I'd brought them scones from Normand's, I wanted to make lunch, there was nothing in the refrigerator. I'm sure we'll both be better off dead and gone, Eleanor said, puffing on her Marlboro, she must smoke half a pack a day. The vitamins I'd brought them weeks ago were unopened, just vitamin C, beta-carotene, calcium/ magnesium. We're far beyond vitamins, Eleanor said, she didn't want to end up in the hospital hooked up to machines because she'd started taking vitamins at the last minute. She'd had so much done to her already there was nothing left to take, half her insides were missing, she said, she'd had a hip replaced years ago, she'd never let them touch her again, she just hoped it would be something simple like a massive stroke, wasn't that what they called them, massive? If she came down with that Alzheimer's they've come up with, she said, shoot her. Eleanor was only four feet tall, I said to Val, but she was all there. I told them their morbid talk had to stop, it was very unbecoming, it was upsetting. Marjorie said, You get tired of being alive, but the good Lord won't take you. I don't know what he wants with keeping an old lady like me alive, He must have His reasons and not for us to know. Your good Lord doesn't have reasons for anything, Eleanor said, don't you read the papers? Val was laughing, really laughing, as though I'd only called to entertain her. Don't you just love them? she said. Marjorie came down with pneumonia every year, apparently, I'd asked them if they'd had their flu shots. Who would bother with a flu shot at our age? I asked Daniel Gunther if he'd go over and give them each a flu shot, but he was too chicken-shit. Everyone's gone now, Marjorie said, I don't know why we aren't. Eleanor had been married to Marjorie's brother, I'd learned, both husbands had been dead for years. The house belonged to Marjorie. She'd lost a son in the Second World War, she had a daughter, who was in her sixties, Marjorie hadn't seen her for thirty years, she should have been used to it by now, she said, but every year at this time she got upset all over again. Evidently Eleanor had no family left anywhere, she'd never mentioned children. Eleanor was the one who wanted to know what the greenhouse business was all about, what the Russians were up to now, what the world was coming to with everyone lying and stealing and doped up and murdering each other just as they pleased, that poor fool in the White House smiling at the camera without a thought in his head, etc. Eleanor was amazing, we agreed, with her nail polish and her smeared lipstick. Marjorie didn't have her sparkle. They both asked for you, I told Val, they think you're wonderful, you've been so good to them, so I had an idea, they seemed so bored and in the doldrums, how about we take them out to lunch or maybe a Christmas concert somewhere. . . . Val said lovely idea, but she couldn't possibly fit that in. I'd felt badly about leaving them today, I said, they seemed sad and lonely. Val became impatient, Those two live wires managed very well for themselves for women well into their eighties, in fact Eleanor might be ninety already, they were doing better than plenty of people many years younger, she said, they were survivors. It wasn't at all surprising for them to become a little depressed, especially this time of year, she was always amazed at how brave and cheerful and interested Marjorie and Eleanor generally were, she hoped she'd have their guts, Val said, when she was old. I just needed to talk about it for five minutes, I said, I hoped she didn't mind. She said, Of course I don't mind. The other thing was I wondered if she'd like to go swimming sometime at the school for an hour, she'd been talking about getting winterish and out of shape. She hadn't been swimming in an indoor pool since Ben probably, Call me next time you're going, she said, maybe she'd try it once. Don Candy meanwhile had let himself into my room with surprises, a white poinsettia, large pizza, six-pack of Polish beer, whistling two turtledoves and a partridge in a pear tree, corny, lovable.

III.

He arrived at the airport twenty minutes early only to learn
that the plane, Singer's plane, was half an hour late. He stood
before the plate-glass window and watched planes arrive and
depart—to Spain, for example, Greece, the Caribbean. He
was a fool to have allowed himself to be roped into an egomaniac's crisis—now of all times of the year. He was a fool. But
when the arrival of the flight from Toronto was announced,
Boomfell hurried anxiously to the gate, more excited than he
wished to seem. He scrutinized each disembarking passenger
filing past as if any one of them, man or woman, might have
been Singer in disguise. Incredibly, Singer didn't appear.
Boomfell had blown the entire day going to the airport, and
now . . . Stoop-shouldered, glum, a head taller than anyone
else, Singer stepped from the connecting ramp and made his
way to the wide carpeted corridor of the concourse. He
wouldn't have left his seat on the plane, Boomfell realized,
until all the other passengers had already left. Of course not!
Frowning, pouting, unhurried. Boomfell was reminded that
life was short. Seven years was not a long time. Singer wore a
black wool sweater, rather than the tweed jacket, the shirt and
tie, that his former colleague had expected to see. Otherwise,
this was unmistakably Singer. He didn't appear to be insane.
Despite himself—everything today was despite himself—
Boomfell smiled broadly, and raised his arm in a big wave.
Singer walked heavily, as if he'd been on his feet all day. An
overnight bag was slung over one shoulder. He didn't wave in

return, no sign of recognition for Boomfell, and although he appeared to be looking directly at his friend of years before, he didn't smile. No smile for Boomfell seven years later, no involuntary show of emotion, say, although Boomfell couldn't wipe the grin off his face.

"Eliot Singer!"

"Have I made a mistake? That's the question I've been asking myself. Maybe this is a mistake. If I'd spent another five minutes on that plane, I would have gone out of my mind. I would shake hands, Charles, but, you see, it's cumbersome."

Both Singer's wrists were in casts that started just above the knuckles, leaving his fingers free, and extended partway up his forearms, noticeable beneath the sleeves of the sweater. Handwriting in several colors, both faint and bold, embellished the visible portions of the casts.

"You look well, Eliot. You're looking very well."

"Another five minutes on the plane would have destroyed me. The person beside me, Charles, I wanted to take him by the throat and squeeze every bit of breath out of him. I would have been happy to have a speechless drooling idiot or a moody terrorist sitting beside me, I'm not joking. This was a monster. I had to hear about his company, his travels, his children, his wife, his planned holiday. His father died last year—I know what his last words were. I don't want to know them. His nephew is dying of a brain tumor, he'll probably be dead before Christmas. I know everything, Charles."

"Now you're here, right? Forget the plane ride."

"He interrogated me. What did I do for a living? Where was I going? What happened to my arms? I told him I was a clown who had fallen off my stilts. He believed me. Five minutes more and I wouldn't have been responsible for my actions. The people behind me were laughing and eating peanuts, the person in front of me had his seat so far back he was snoring in my lap. The flight attendant with his stainless-steel cart of garbage, he insisted that I take peanuts and soda. Charles, I don't know what I was thinking. I shouldn't have come."

"This is new, isn't it?" Boomfell asked, touching his own face.

Singer raised his hand to the closely trimmed beard that outlined his jaw. "No. Years ago. When I got married. Let's get out of here, Charles."

"Shall we have a drink first? I'll buy you a drink."

"Impossible. We must leave immediately. Airports! Look! Look at mankind in a hurry on his jet planes. It's terrifying. There, you see him? There he is." Singer pointed to a distinguished-looking man in a gray suit just then being embraced on all sides by no less than five or six people of various ages—a welcoming family.

"What?"

"That's him, the man who sat next to me."

"The monster?"

"Please, quickly." In the car he said, "We must talk, Charles, we must have long talks, but not now. Now we need silence."

Val extended her hand to greet him, but Singer rather impetuously lumbered into a hug, his armored arms closing around the small of her back. Momentarily her heels left the floor, and in that brief embrace, Boomfell noticed, taking in each nuance of their reunion, the eyes of his wife closed.

"Valerie of Boomfell," said Singer, his amusing name for her from years before. He held her at arm's length as if to inspect her from head to toe. "Time hasn't touched you."

"Like hell it hasn't."

Lately, as she shuffled before the sink in her soiled suede slippers at the end of the day, Val often looked worn-out. Tonight, in her broad-shouldered sweater and the pleated corduroy pants that tapered to tidy laced boots, she was downright rosy-cheeked, bright-eyed, invigorated, as if she'd taken a wonder drug reserved for such reunions. In the glow of the kitchen light her clean hair, glinting dark, had a frizzy halo. Boomfell was—and the thought surprised him—proud of her.

His children had also cleaned up their act for the occasion. Ruth, shyly advancing into the room, might have been going out on a date. When Boomfell hugged his son hello, he smelled, of all things, toothpaste.

"Is this Ruth?" Singer asked, amazed. "Is this Benjamin?" For a moment he engaged them with questions about themselves. He remembered that Ruth was a violinist. He admired Ben's digital watch and asked the boy for permission to sleep in his room. Singer was irresistible. The children returned to their homework flushed with surprise at his admiring interest in their lives.

"They're smitten," Val told him. "How do you do that?"

But Singer was frowning. "I miss Nicole and Alex. I miss them constantly."

As he led their guest through the dining room and into the living room, Boomfell saw that the house had been picked up and set to rights. At the least, their life appeared orderly and prosperous. Their prized Welsh cupboard, laden with Val's precious china, the old gateleg table, their Windsor chairs and worn Orientals—here was a tasteful and substantial home. Reviewing the place afresh through Singer's eyes, in a manner of speaking, Boomfell wouldn't have changed a thing. Val had already started a fire in the living room, which lent the evening, the instant they stepped into the room, an inviting and festive glow.

"We were lucky to find this place when we did," Boomfell volunteered. "It was a steal." The entire paneled wall, he explained, Rumford fireplace and all, had been walled up. The clapboards had been covered with asbestos siding. The roof had been tin when they bought the house, and the floorboards, the wonderful old wide pine boards, had been covered with linoleum. "This is what we've been doing for the last five years," he said, "restoring an old house. I wouldn't have thought it could be so satisfying."

Singer sat heavily in the wing chair by the hearth and looked into the fire. "I don't think I can deal with this."

"Let me get you a scotch. Is scotch all right?"

Singer drew his hand over his face. "What am I doing here?" he asked. "I wonder if I could be alone for a few minutes. I need to think, Charles. The plane was impossible. And now this—children, dinner, a fire. I have to think. If I could just sit here for a minute."

In the kitchen Boomfell told his wife, "I don't think this is going to work."

"He's so thin, Charlie. What's he doing? Did you take him up to Ben's room?"

"He's thinking. He asked me to leave him alone so he could think."

"Oh great."

Singer

Nicole, she is as tall and thin and handsome as a Masai warrior. She calls me Dad, but she was already signed, sealed, and delivered by Astrid before I appeared on the scene. She was almost ten when Astrid and I got married. She's out of patience with Eliot these days. I'll probably lose Nicole completely, which is painful. I imagined that I would be useful to her on her lonely journey into the hopelessness of grown-up life. During the years we lived together I rarely helped her with anything except an occasional homework assignment, and then I probably did more harm than good. I was too blocked and clogged and dead. I wasn't living my own life, Charles Boomfell, how could I help a young girl live hers?

Two years ago we were hiking on the Jungfrau, just the two of us, while Astrid and Alex visited Astrid's perfect family. They were so clean, Charles, so clean and good-natured and considerate I couldn't breathe. I kept stepping outside to take big breaths of Swiss air. Nicole and I, we went on our big adventure, and Eliot the make-believe father fell down a cliff and couldn't get back up. The solid-seeming snowy ledge I was standing on collapsed. I was hanging on with hands and feet. I will fall all the way to my probable death, or Nicole will hike back to the cabin we passed a half hour earlier and get help. Alone at fourteen on this frightening mountain, Nicole flies with long braids to the rescue and brings two men on a snowmobile with rope to save Singer's bitterly cold ass. At fourteen Astrid's skinny daughter saves my life, and in return I burden her broad skinny shoulders with misery, knowing full well that her father's death has made it all the more imperative that I be there to help her rather than to hurt her. I didn't know I was incapable of helping anyone.

I had all the answers. I presented myself as a possible answer to Astrid's loneliness only to end up making the woman more unhappy than ever. Tragic loss didn't prepare her for the drudgery of everyday discontent that I introduced her to. Nicole has to hate me for that. Astrid doesn't hate me. To Astrid, I'm pathetic and crazy and pitiable. But Nicole . . . Evidently, they had been a perfect family—ex-husband and ex-father had been tops in both departments. He was an architect. One day he visited a building site and a plate-glass wall fell from five stories, crushing him. Isn't that perfect? A forty-nine-year-old French architect. Nicole keeps his drawing tools in her desk. She has models of some of the buildings he's designed. He was a genius, that's the first thing I learned about him, and that is the reason I took an immediate dislike to him, even though he was dead. I've always been offended when someone wants to tell me about his friend the genius—as though I were being personally insulted. It wasn't smart to get killed by a sheet of glass.

Nicole and Astrid seemed so sad and beautiful when I met them. A tall woman and her dark-eyed daughter with braids. They were living in Rome because Astrid couldn't bear to stay in Switzerland. They had a tiny apartment with a hot plate for a kitchen. It was a sad story, but there was really nothing sad about either of them. Astrid wouldn't sacrifice the child's happiness to her own misfortune. I was attracted to her inner strength—as well as her nice face and long fingers. Also, I was lonely in my creepy pretentious life as a fellow at the American Academy. Doesn't that have a nice ring to it—the American Academy in Rome? It proved to be an insular club of well-mannered self-seeking academics, playacting at their earnest life of the mind and living like poor graduate students. Astrid and her daughter seemed real by contrast. They were having coffee in the café I went to every morning.

Nicole was already formed, a person. At ten she addressed her mother as an equal practically. But Alex . . . I didn't want him, Charles. I urged Astrid to get an abortion. It will be very confusing for Nicole, I argued. I meant that it would be very confusing for Eliot. It would be inconvenient. Destroy the fetus, I insisted. Astrid was too smart and good to be persuaded. And, of course, Nicole absolutely adored him from the moment he was born. Alex is the best thing that's happened to her. Naturally, I adore him. I adore him, Valerie, yet all my love for Alex has not been enough to prevent me from sacrificing his happiness to my needs. Now he's a wounded child. Last spring I went to the house to play the Tooth Fairy. Astrid won't play. They didn't have tooth fairies in the Switzerland of her childhood. I reached my hand under the pillow, under his peaceful sleeping head. In the envelope, with his perfect white baby tooth, was a note that his big sister had helped him write. Dear Tooth Fairy, can you please bring my Dad back to live with us? Thank you, Alex. There was a pencil in the envelope for the Tooth Fairy to reply. I wrote, Your father loves you, and put a dollar in the envelope. Downstairs I wanted to pull Astrid limb from limb for letting this happen, but of course Astrid didn't know anything about it. Nicole was just trying to be nice to her little half-brother.

How can we do this, Valerie? How can we bring innocent children into the world in order to wound them for the rest of their lives by the time they're three, and in most cases before they're born? In most cases the genetic blueprint is a one-way ticket to destruction—infants implanted with our insanities and sicknesses the way bats are born blind. I was as beautiful as the next kid. My parents couldn't help destroying me any more than I can help making Alex's life as difficult as possible. I came home from school in my blue blazer with straight A's for over twenty years. I couldn't wait to have my snack and practice the piano for two hours. I would have been miserable if I'd been prevented from doing everything they wanted me to do. I did everything in my power to make my mother smile at me and to make my father tousle my dark hair affectionately. I did everything in my power to be the person they wanted me to be. Every word out of our mouths slays the child in the interests of our longings and fears. It's happening to Alex right before my eyes even though I'm aware of it, perfectly aware, and don't want it to happen.

I remind him to do well in kindergarten. Kindergarten, Valerie! I urge him to make friends and play all the games other kids play and practice *his* piano every afternoon. I want him to go to Yale like his father. Terrifying. This is all in the interest of his happiness, and it will all contribute to the volcano of unhappiness that began to mass itself in the pit of his tiny being from the moment he was conceived in our ancient tiny apartment in Rome. It may remain dormant for years and decades— disguised or avoided or ignored—but its bitter eruption is inevitable, Charles Boomfell. I am so anxious for his happiness, he can't fail to be unhappy. The poor kid.

On the other hand, I haven't seen him for weeks. It was difficult for him to face me in the hospital, a shrunken, defeated father, with tears on my face, surrounded by an assortment of scary basket cases. Does my innocent little boy deserve this? Of course not. He is well on his way to becoming just as fucked up as everyone else. What can anyone do about it? I want the Tooth Fairy to come through, but there is no Tooth Fairy. The Tooth Fairy doesn't exist.

I lived for my parents' approval and esteem, and I was a little master at securing it. It would have been unbearable if either of them had left home. I'm sure the black thought never crossed my light-filled mind. Eliot's precocious mind couldn't think a thing so simple and likely. And yet, look what has happened because my parents provided a comfortable and secure home for us, and remained married to one another for over fifty years. Half a century, Charles Boomfell. People say, Wonderful, way to go. How sad and insane. Does fifty years of marriage represent love, or wisdom, or success? They love each other the way two white mice locked in a cage for fifty years love each other. They spend most of each day in a stupor of boredom, or in silent and exhausting rage with one another over absolutely nothing of consequence to anyone—not even them. In order to sleep they curl up instinctually. Fifty years of that, Valerie of Boomfell. It is a form of sickness the society fosters to maintain order.

I was a beautiful child. My cherubic face in old photographs breaks me up. At my first concert, in my dark blue suit, I was not much taller than the piano. That child was buried beneath layers and layers of garbage heaped on him by his unhappy pretending parents. What I didn't know, Charles— they didn't like me. You laugh. It sounds crazy because it is crazy—crazy of them. They should have loved the little kid I was. Instead, they loved my accomplishments, my eagerness to please them, my perfections as their son. The moment I departed from their conception of me, the moment I stopped being their little boy and began to emerge from my warm cocoon of delusion into the cold nakedness of adolescence—it sounds like a horror story, doesn't it?—they couldn't conceal their disappointment. The summer I refused to return to music camp my mother cried, and my father withdrew from me. I was a murderer. At the bottom of my dresser drawer they discovered a magazine featuring tits and asses, and they wanted me to talk to their friend Dr. Kline. The idea of their little Eliot whacking off in his room was too much in conflict with the Eliot they had created and raised in their minds. If I was in a bad mood, they hated me for it. It was vital to them that I always seem happy. I was to become one of two things— a doctor or a musician. Have you heard that one before? I could be one or the other provided I was successful at what I chose.

They were concerned with their happiness—just as I'm concerned with my happiness, not Alex's.

I didn't have to go into my father's investment business and make millions and millions of dollars by the time I was thirty because my big brother was already playing that role to the hilt. David has always hated me for that. I got to pretend to be myself, whoever that was, while he toed the line. When he visited me in the hospital in Toronto, the anger in his face was overwhelming. Even dying I was outdoing him. I get to kill myself, while he has to hang in there as responsible businessman, father, son—kiss ass with clients, nurse his old sick parents, visit his brother in the loony bin. He makes millions upon millions of dollars each year, Charles. He flies around in chartered planes, drives around Toronto in a limo, he wears diamonds and furs, nail polish and transplanted hair. But my big brother is locked in. He reminds me to remember my parents' wedding anniversary. It would mean something to them, he tells me, if I sent flowers. But to me their anniversary is not to be celebrated. Look what they and their fifty years have done to you, I tell him, sitting there in his million-dollar suit.

I didn't want to be a doctor or a musician. Imagine? Instead of pursuing medicine or music after I graduated from college, I went to Israel and lived on a kibbutz for a year. I wanted to relate to the legendary Jewish half of me, which had nothing to do with religion because there was never any religion at our house. My mother was brought up Anglican Church English. I've never told you this story, have I? Of course not. Never reveal anything, that was the first commandment of my personal code. I fled to Israel, I wore shorts and studied Hebrew, I rejected their plans for me. I knew that my survival meant escaping from those plans. I didn't see them again for years. I tramped around Europe with my knapsack. I took courses at Cambridge and acquired a quasi-Anglo accent. Was that Eliot Singer? I returned to the States and got—God love us,

Charles—a Ph.D. in you-know-what. I was still at pains to somehow please my parents. Why else would I have gone to the waste and nuisance of acquiring that meaningless degree? Anyway, they've never forgiven me for it.

By the time I started teaching, I'd lost faith in my work. Remember our first jobs, Charles? You were there, I don't have to tell you about it. I escaped to Italy, but the American Academy—the self-perpetuating ambition, the fatuous self-congratulation—proved unbearable. At the lowest point of my year in Italy, I met Astrid. The two of them sitting in the café, mother and daughter, I couldn't take my eyes off them. I escaped into Astrid. Astrid spread open her long legs for Eliot, and I burrowed into her warmth and goodness. She was a wonderful homemaker, clean and neat like her mother. But when she became pregnant and I urged her to destroy the fetus, I knew it was just a question of time. I couldn't possibly go on living with Astrid in her state of goodness and perfection and sanity. I love Alex, Charles, but my lovable son's whole life is not enough to make me give up . . . what?

I urged her to have an abortion—Astrid—because a child would have been a terrific inconvenience for me. Astrid insisted on having the child. On the other hand, when I forbid Lucky to kill my possible child, when I insist that another helpless child be brought into the world, what does she do? She walks into an ugly brick building and gets Eliot's beautiful child sucked out of her by some arrogant young man with a little vacuum cleaner—a moron with a medical degree like Eliot's parents wanted him to have. That man thinks he knows what he's doing. A complete stranger with a surgical mask over his face, hiding behind a surgical mask, sticks his plastic tube into Lucky, into my Lucky, and vacuums out this helpless living . . . I'm sorry. Forgive me, Charles. Valerie, forgive me. I can't talk about it. I think of this masked stranger in an antiseptic room, and Lucky in those stirrups . . . How could she do that to me?

She doesn't deserve my attention, does she? She doesn't deserve my suffering. This is the woman I can't give up for my son's happiness. Instead, I've decided that he'll be better off without me oppressing him on a daily basis. He'll survive like everyone else who survives, a prisoner of the misery, the generations of misery that brought him into being. But the miserable woman to whom I have sacrificed his happiness, she never wants to see me again. Lucky loves Eliot forever, Charles, but now that I'm on my feet again, prepared to resume my wonderful life, I am forbidden to go near her for a month.

Thirty days the doctor has prescribed, as though that number of days had meaning. These ridiculous doctors, who present themselves in control of every situation, who imagine they're living their lives, when they are merely going through the paces laid down for them by the striving little world they were raised in. My shrink, Edward, is one of the most insecure men I've ever met. He wants me to approve of the way he's handling my case. It's funny, but also crazy. Thirty days, this make-believe Freud suggests, as though thirty days of not seeing her were possible. He might as well have said, Hold your breath for thirty days. She won't even speak to me on the phone. That's stupid of her, isn't it? She can't help it. At this point I don't even like the woman. I hate her. Eliot hates Lucky. Except I can't get her out of my mind. What can I do? One day I went to hug her, but I grabbed her neck instead, I could feel her invisible Adam's apple under my thumbs. I let go before something irreversible happened. Valerie, is this Eliot Singer? I don't want to behave like a hysterical escaped lunatic. That's not what I want.

Life with Astrid, for a while it was so orderly and sane, I couldn't believe it. I regained faith in my work. Reading and writing, Charles Boomfell, there was no other work worth doing. Discipline was my creed. We had breakfast, I went off to my book-lined office in one of the oldest buildings on campus, where I enjoyed another typically productive day as scholar and teacher. At four o'clock I might enjoy a satisfying game of tennis with witty cheerful colleagues in the humanities. Back home we would have a nice supper, the three of us. I would read in the evening. In bed I would place my ear against Astrid's growing belly and listen to the stir of our growing fetus. If we felt like it, we fucked in an orderly, sane, and satisfying manner. It wasn't love, but it was livable. We had a couch, a color TV, a happy young girl who called me Dad, a new little car. Astrid was a new world to me—a caring orderly world. French toast, you wouldn't believe such French toast in the morning. Pregnant, she was so happy, a radiant woman focusing her energy, gathering Swiss strength, to give birth. Her skin glowed from within. The arrival of Alex was . . . You have two children—you know. I loved my life at that time. For months, for almost two years maybe, I loved my life— although of course I didn't know that as well as I know it now.

Now, being alone, for instance, it's impossible. Alone, I feel nonexistent. Like there is no point, Charles, no point whatsoever to sit at the table and eat, sit at my desk and work, sit on the toilet and shit—no point to go from the table to the toilet, from the toilet to the desk, then back to the window to look out of my hovel at the people in the street. It's as though I were performing these hollow practices invisibly, if you see what I mean—as if I didn't really exist outside of my mind. I frequently look in the mirror, for example. The girl who'd been staying with me, the first girl, she was useful as a witness, so to speak. She lent a sense of dimension to my pacing and prowling. After I did this to myself it was as though I had AIDS. She was gone. The other girl, Rachel, I'm her adventure this year. Instead of going to India to see starvation and death, she moves in with Eliot. She's not as interesting to have around the house as Nicole, that's the truth. In any case, she's gone too. Being alone, I begin to feel myself ceasing to exist. It's disturbing. The family, you see, Astrid and Nicole and Alex, in their eyes, I existed. I played my part. Husband, make-believe father, father. At the breakfast table you must look alive. You ask questions about school, you help with homework, you plan what you're going to have for supper. There's everyone at supper to talk about everything that happened today. You have to look alive, Charles. The pressure of their lives warmed me. Astrid and Nicole and Alex . . . That world is gone. I must put it out of my mind.

What I can't get out of my mind is Lucky Lucky Lucky. I hate her. There is the house she wants to sell, but I'm sorry, Eliot is not cooperating. She's going to have to buy me out—reparation, Charles Boomfell, for my blood. Thirty days! The make-believe Freud arbitrarily declares thirty days without knowing what it's like for me to live one day without being able to speak to her on the phone for two minutes. I feel so sorry for her, Valerie, locked up in Eliot's alma mater nuthouse with women who wet their beds and pull out their hair and burn holes in their flesh with cigarettes—women who kill themselves all day long. Beautiful young Lucky harassed and sexually threatened by women of all ages who are out of their minds—and she won't let me help her! You could go crazy in a place like that, Charles. She could suffer permanent damage before she gets out of there.

I tried to see her, but I couldn't get past the thick stubborn people on floor eleven who have their orders to protect the patients from unwanted visitors. Maybe it was just as well. What would I have done if I'd gotten inside and found her lying in her narrow bed with her pale face looking up at me from the pillow, and her eyes telling me that she didn't want to see me? Would I have attempted to strangle her again? The eyes, you know, saying, Oh shit. She would have looked at me as if I were a hopeless little boy who had been naughty again, and I might very well have tried to strangle her again. Or she might have looked at me in a nice way and allowed me to lie down on top of the bed and comfort her. . . . You see, the fantasies, they come to the surface spontaneously. My mind is a sewer of fantasies. I lie on top of the hospital bed and Lucky permits me to put my hand under the covers and under the pale green nightshirt issued to her by the hospital, and allows me to transport her to a lonely orgasm while crazy women whimper and stare and fret around us. Forgive me, Valerie, I can't help it.

Believe me, I want to get this garbage out of my mind. I want to return to normal life and appear as a normal man going about his business. The other day I observed a man get out of his car and walk into a drugstore. A moment later he came out of the drugstore with a newspaper under his arm, unwrapping a candy bar—a beautiful chocolate candy bar. He took a bite as he got back into his car. I thought, That is a normal person. I was filled with envy and loathing. Here was someone whose mind was not a sewer of longing and hate preventing him from experiencing the simplest everyday pleasures such as a candy bar, or buying a newspaper and enjoying all the violent insanity and self-destructive stupidity happening all over the world. How about the world these days, Charles Boomfell, doesn't it make you proud to be a human being?

Of course, I was beside myself when I left the hospital, having failed to see her at all. I couldn't return to my hovel. Rachel, the girl staying with me, I knew she was leaving on Tuesday afternoon and I couldn't bear to look at her. It was so ludicrous of her to be holed up with me in the first place, making her eggplant parmigiana, or her lasagna, or her salad dressing. She was particularly proud of a blue-cheese salad dressing, which I admired every time we sat down. She didn't know what she'd gotten herself into, she shouldn't have been there at all. I begged her not to leave, but she had to go home for Christmas. I couldn't return to the hovel and look at her face.

I thought I'd drop in on Blanchard, the fellow who'd been doing my Milton seminar, but when I imagined his face as he opened the door and saw who was there, or worse, when I imagined his wife's blank face if she was the one who came to the door . . . No, I couldn't go to Blanchard's. The thought of his kitchen with his super-duper new custom-made cabinets, or his living room with the new chintz-covered couch he was so excited to get on sale—honest to God, Charles, it made my skin crawl. I would be interrupting their favorite Sunday-night TV shows and I knew they would not be able to conceal their displeasure. They would be seething inside, but they would never have the nerve to tell me they didn't care about Eliot Singer's fucking problems and only wanted to enjoy the ordinary safe and sane evening they had planned for themselves, sitting before their television with a bowl of popcorn. Sitting on the new chintz-covered couch. They would be polite, as always. What am I doing with friends like Blanchard? Why do I know people like Blanchard, who can't possibly be there when you need them to be there because everything between you is so polite and hollow and unreal? Blanchard was the one Astrid sent over the night I did this stupidity to myself. Blanchard and Sontag and Wassong, the committee. I was unconscious, but it must not have been pretty. We have that between us, although it has never been mentioned—the room, the blood, the body, the ambulance, all that, never mentioned.

I thought of dropping in on Sontag, but then I remembered his wife. I couldn't possibly deal with her bustling efficiency tonight, her determined cheerfulness. Ever since she had one breast removed and took up yoga, she has been happier, Sontag told me, than ever before.

Without a thought in my head except Lucky Lucky Lucky—like my pulse throbbing at my temples—I entered a church along with a flock of people just then going inside. I simply fell in step as if this was the reason I was out on the street tonight. I popped up the church steps just as if I knew what I was doing. It was a vespers service. Imagine, Charles. Given my state of mind at the time, it was a reckless thing to do. I had nowhere to go, I simply wanted to get off the street where I felt I didn't exist, where I felt invisible and nonexistent. I wanted to be near other people. I would have followed them into a burning building. It just happened to be vespers. The organ is playing, everyone is all dressed up, greeting one another with hellos and smiles and waves. In the men's room— I went directly to the men's room—the fellow I'm pissing next to wishes me a merry Christmas. He's delighted with the occasion. The thought hadn't even occurred to me—Christmas. I can't even piss, of course. I need to, but I can't. The organ is playing, there's all kinds of perfume coming in with the cold air. I could have left at any moment, but I stayed. I wanted to be near other people, that's all there is to it.

Girls appeared in white blouses to light the candles, live candles all around the church. In the balcony, a handbell choir of old-timers began playing carols. Each one ringing his or her bell at the right time—the precise instant. It was so nice of them, I thought, these old folks going to all this fuss—all the practicing, you know, in order to play Christmas carols for us. All I could think about was my old parents alone in New York waiting to die, and Eliot sitting in his pew shoulder to shoulder with all these worshipers—a complete impostor—and Lucky back in the loony bin when she could have been here with me getting turned on by the candles and the handbells. Charles Boomfell, it was horrible. Lucky Lucky Lucky, I'm thinking, with these white-haired people up in the balcony ringing those bells, concentrating as if our lives—all our lives—depended on their performance. Then the processional—O come, O come, Emmanuel. The voices, everyone's voices, it was very moving. The choir, you know, advancing like onward Christian soldiers. It must have been a college glee club from somewhere, young men and women in white and black. They sounded wonderful. The whole thing—the beautiful young people, the voices and music, the candles, all the people holding up their earnest faces like this meant something to them— it broke me up.

This is normal life, I thought. These are normal people

gathered together to raise their voices and hopes for an hour or so, then go home to their normal lives and feel better, have some popcorn and watch TV before getting into their normal beds for a normal night's sleep. There were prayers and readings of the scriptures and more singing. I couldn't get Lucky in her narrow bed, with her pale face, out of my mind. Or her body under the covers of her narrow bed, her hands under the covers, and her head on the pillow maybe thinking about Eliot while she slips a lady's finger into her perfect orchid with crazy women moaning and grinding their teeth nearby—while these beautiful young people are singing, *Ave Maria, gratia plena . . . Sancta Maria Mater Dei!* Pray for us, sinners, now and at the hour of our deaths, Charles Boomfell. Amen.

There's a family right in front of me, a perfect little family a lot like yours—mother, father, sister, brother—the grown-ups smiling as if they had gone to heaven, the daughter as composed for the occasion as an angel—perfect except the little fellow has a problem with his sweater. The church is blazing hot, I'm sweating in my turtleneck, and the little guy wants to get his damn sweater off, but he can't. He gets caught in it, he's thrashing around, and now the mother's trying to help him, and I'm thinking of Alex. Naturally, I should be there with Alex and Nicole and Astrid. I had this whole family, Momma, Poppa, Sister, and Baby Bear, the whole perfect normal thing with breakfast, off to school, home for supper. We had the drive in the country on Sunday, the annual visit to Grandmother's house, although my mother could never understand a word Astrid said. We had a master bath, a cookie sheet that didn't burn cookies, we had Blanchard and his family over for pizza on Saturday. We had everything. A Christmas tree? Did we have a Christmas tree, Valerie? Of course—with Alex's homemade star on top, and chains of popcorn, and Astrid's ornaments from the old country.

Here's the kid trapped in his sweater, starting to panic in his sweater, and the mother is frowning now, and the father is frowning at the mother. *Sancta Maria Mater Dei!* On the one hand, it's funny and wonderful, and on the other hand, you know that this boy will be devastated, or has already been devastated, and now I'm thinking my place is with Alex to help him and protect him from all the stupidities and countless threats to his well-being—although so far I've only contributed to screwing him up beyond anyone's expectation—so I reach over, finally, because he's right in front of me, and pull off the sweater. The mother smiles at me and the minute she smiles at me I want to go home with her and fuck her. That's pathetic, Valerie, isn't it? I don't know. Charles, is that how you think? Does everyone think like that? Lucky Lucky Lucky, I'm thinking, then Astrid, Nicole, Alex, but right now I want to grab this young mother. The little father turns to me to smile gratefully. I smile back like Superman who has just saved the day.

In fact, I'm going to pieces, I'm about to burst into tears at any minute. I want to throw my arms around the mother. Lucky should be here with me, Astrid should be here, Alex and Nicole should be here. I shouldn't be alone like an escaped monster, Lucky shouldn't be locked up like a nut, Astrid shouldn't be trying to get the tree into its red-and-green stand, setting it straight—all that!—without Eliot to help her. But all these things were happening. I was there alone—invisible and nonexistent. *Ora pro nobis, precatoribus,* these babies are singing at the top of their voices. Pray for us, sinners. . . . It was overwhelming, Charles Boomfell.

When we started with "The First Nowell," I was unable to join the singing. I wanted to, but I couldn't open my mouth. My head was throbbing. Sweat is running down my back. If I stop chewing my bottom lip, I'm going to start crying in front of everyone, but I didn't run out, I stayed. I pulled myself together. Then they began Bach's Mass in B Minor. This is really why we're here—to listen to Bach's Mass in B Minor. *Kyrie eleison. Christe eleison.* It's extraordinary. I needed Lucky to be with me to hear this because I knew if she was there listening, hearing what I was hearing, our problems would be over. No more craziness, no more loony bins, no more strangling and suicide. *Kyrie eleison. Christe eleison.* Lord have mercy upon us. Christ have mercy upon us. Lucky Lucky Lucky. Astrid, Nicole, Alex.

I notice an exquisite girl in the chorus. What's exquisite? I mean striking to Eliot. Disturbing to Eliot. She has longish dark hair held back from her face in that typical way. I can hardly see her, to tell you the truth. There are a hundred girls up there in white blouses. She's just one more right in the middle of the pack, but I notice her. She opens her mouth wide when she sings—really sings—and her eyes are dark, but I don't really know why I've singled her out. I'm invisible and nonexistent in the middle of the church, but I'm looking at this girl, I've focused on her, and I get the idea that she's looking at me. It's ridiculous, she can't even see me, yet I'm convinced that she's looking right at me while she sings her heart out. *Kyrie eleison. Christe eleison.*

I have to meet her, that's all there is to it. Bach's extraordinary mass is going on, Lucky is masturbating herself to sleep on floor eleven, Astrid is setting up the Christmas tree for Alex without my help, and Eliot is now sitting in his pew with an erection, surrounded by normal people, thinking about this girl's hands and mouth and her schoolgirl body under her white blouse and black skirt. Her parents could be sitting right behind me. Suddenly the girl is the possible answer for me. Rachel is leaving soon, despite everything, and suddenly . . . There is something about this girl in the chorus that is very important. I'm looking at her, directly into her eyes, and she's looking directly at me while she sings like an angel in Bach's Mass in B Minor. She sees and knows and understands, you see. *Gloria in excelsis Deo.* The moment the service is over I will rush up to the stage, and she will agree to come home with me, home to Eliot's hovel, and . . . How can the mind even conceive this garbage, Charles Boomfell?

I had every intention of going up to this poor innocent girl just as I'd gone up to Rachel in the grocery store. I intended to involve her in my life—just because Lucky wouldn't see me, or even talk to me on the phone. The recessional was "Adeste Fideles," which I sang at the top of my lungs. My buddy who'd gotten lost in his sweater turned around with a big grin on his face to see what was going on. *Adeste fideles, laeti triumphantes.* It was very wonderful, Charles Boomfell, and here comes the next love of my life, this poor ignorant stranger, this baby in her blouse and skirt, with her singing mouth wide open. I haven't taken my eyes off her. Honestly, Charles, I'm about to jump out of my skin as she walks by, singing away with her chin up. And guess what? She doesn't stare into Eliot's eyes, she doesn't smile or blush or frown. She doesn't even glance at me. She doesn't know I'm there. Invisible and nonexistent. I was astonished.

Darkness gradually engulfed us. A half dozen boys and girls with their long brass snuffers silently extinguished one candle at a time, candle after candle, and while this was going on, a single lovely female voice sings "Silent Night." *Stille Nacht*, Valerie. I swooned in the pew, next to the stout smelly woman beside me. I wanted to live, and I wanted to die.

And now we come to the final moment of the extraordinary Sunday-evening service. The lights come up, everybody stands to leave. Eliot and a few sentimental old ladies need to blow their noses. Who should I see stand in their pew and begin to shuffle toward the aisle about six rows before me? Who but Astrid and Nicole and Alex. *Kyrie eleison*, Charles Boomfell. *Christe eleison*. Astrid like a tall strong angel in her beautiful white wool dress with the big collar, Nicole as thin and handsome and straight as a Masai warrior in her jumper, Alex, my perfect Alex, in his beautiful blue sweater with the snowflakes. Take me home, I wanted to cry. You are my family. I want to be normal, I want to stop this shit in my head. Take me home where we can all get into bed and sleep together all night long. Astrid looked beautiful, immediately casting out of mind the image of the girl in the chorus. I'm coming home, I saw myself blubbering to them as I thrust myself into the aisle and fell on them with kisses and hugs. I saw Alex swinging off my neck, and Nicole grinning in her happy way, and Astrid calmly placing her hand on my face and quietly speaking my name as she had done so often. Imagine this stuff in my mind, flooding my mind? Where does it come from, Charles Boomfell? Instead, I turned the other way and fled to the outer aisle. I fled the church while everyone was nodding and smiling and wishing one another God bless and good night. I fled directly back to Rachel for better or worse. But Rachel had gone out to see friends—friends! Always friends!—said the unbelievable note she'd left in her big handwriting on the kitchen table. And on Tuesday, of course, Rachel left to fly home for the holiday, to meet her father at the airport and return to her childhood home, and I was left pacing my three rooms, a maniac in his hovel, Charles, thinking Lucky Lucky Lucky.

"He strangled her? Isn't that what he said, he tried to strangle her?"

"It's sad. But if I hear another word about Lucky . . ." Val pulled her flannel nightgown—fire-engine red—over her head, let it fall over her pale body. Reaching under the hem of it, she stepped out of her underpants, which she left, a salmon-colored wad, by the side of the bed. "I just want to get it out of my mind, Charles Boomfell. I just want it to end."

"Ssh," he cautioned, "he'll hear you."

"Did he go to bed, or is he still downstairs?"

"I think he's still sitting down there."

"I hope he doesn't murder us in our sleep."

The wine tonight, glass after glass of it, put him to sleep, but also woke him later, it felt like two or three. On his way to the bathroom he saw that a light had been left on downstairs. He'd asked Singer to turn the lights out behind him, damnit. Halfway downstairs, naked except for boxer shorts, he heard muted metallic sounds, Singer poking at the fireplace in the living room. By the time he and Val had gone upstairs, the fire had been reduced to glowing embers. From the sounds of things, Eliot had gotten it going again. Boomfell resisted the impulse to continue downstairs, and quietly returned to the bedroom. You had to assume the man was responsible, sane. This wasn't a halfway house, Boomfell wasn't a fucking male nurse. What were his chances of getting back to sleep now?

He reached for his wife's body. He lightly ran his hand

between her slightly parted legs—a habitual wee-hour inquiry, knowing that his chances of finding her open to his suggestion this night of the Singer invasion were hardly fifty-fifty—and found that her hand, Val's hand, was already there. He guided her blunt fingers and felt her arch her wrist, reaching. She wasn't content tonight with the fairly utilitarian sex that typically occurred between them. Impatiently, she got on top, straddling him broncobuster style, and discarded her nightgown. Reaching for his prick, momentarily shrunken by all the commotion, she demanded, "Where is it?" Her urgency would have been funny, if it wasn't so . . . serious. He opened his eyes to observe her altered state. Briefly, the person who towered above him, supporting herself with her hands on his shins, hardly seemed his wife at all. The long muscles of her thighs were visibly stressed. Her ribs, aligned in their herringbone V, were clearly delineated. The tendons and arteries of her neck stood out like those of an athlete under pressure. Her nostrils, shaped like denuded cloves of garlic, flared. Easy, Val, easy does it. As she labored toward orgasm, she murmured, "Fuck me," several times, which was not like her either, head back-tilted as though the self-arousing command were addressed more to something above than to the instrumental person below her. As they pulled up the covers and resettled themselves for sleep, neither one of them said a word, not even good night.

Half listening for their guest's step on the narrow staircase, Boomfell had difficulty falling asleep even now. Singer's step on the stairs didn't come.

Tall baby-faced Simpson in his vile fur coat, that was the realtor's morning. He had come to Boomfell through Lynch, who turned out to be a collector of old maps. Simpson was looking for a country place in a picture-book setting to restore. He followed the rich and feeble to Florida to be on hand when they began to rid themselves of the treasured art and antiques they could no longer accommodate as they shuffled, cards and feet, toward the end of their prosperous lives. He went around in a silver-gray Mercedes with a phone in the front seat. The tufted interior of the car looked like the inside of a coffin. At Reed's Simpson sauntered through the old farmhouse—scuffing heels on the floorboards, roughhousing the cabinets and closets, twisting water faucets—as though inspecting a kennel. Old Reed, who had sold his cows to the federal government the year before under the auspices of the Whole-Herd Buyout Program, stood in faded denim overalls before his enamel sink, staring out the kitchen window toward his empty weathered barn, and wouldn't respond to Boomfell's small talk concerning the weather. The farm had been in his family for four generations.

"How can these people let such lovely old places stand and rot," the art thief brayed, as though the old man couldn't hear.

Later, when Boomfell returned to the kitchen to thank Reed for his time, the old man said, "Get that bastard out of here."

Simpson stood on the porch and looked across the road to the gray wooded hillside of maple, birch, oak, and beech. "This place could be what I'm after," he said. He'd take down the wall between the kitchen and the dining room, gut the upstairs, pop in skylights, build a deck off the west side. "I could dismantle the small barn in back and use the stone foundation for a sunken garden, couldn't I? That would be charming. Incidentally, the cupboard in the dining room—did you see that old pine cupboard? Those things are worth a fortune today. Ask him if that goes with the place, will you? Offer him a few hundred dollars if necessary." Simpson buttoned his fur coat, grinning at the prospect of easy gain. Vile.

Heat came into Boomfell's face. "You were pretty fucking rude in there, you know it?"

"I beg your pardon?"

"You don't get what's going on here, do you? That old man's great-grandfather built this house. Can you grasp that?"

"I want that cupboard," Simpson said. "Don't let it leave the house."

"You repel me," Boomfell told him. "I don't want to do business with you."

The art dealer sneered. "What on earth are you talking about? I didn't think you could afford to be so touchy about old farmers."

That was his morning. He spent his lunch hour attempting to help Andrea Sarti install an automatic garage-door opener, and failed. Damn thing wasn't as simple as it looked. At one o'clock he turned up, as promised, to take Mrs. Hill through the Huntington house, a sprawling place she would never buy, for the third time. Then he stole an hour to stop at the Golden Bowl on Green Street and succeeded, eventually, in choosing a gold pendant for Ruth's Christmas, along with a pair of earrings for Val. While one young woman wrapped his gifts, the other called to clear his credit card. It was declined.

"That's impossible," said Boomfell.

"I'm sorry. I tried it twice." She placed his piece of plastic on the glass case as though, it seemed to him, she wished she'd never touched it.

"Would you take a personal check?" he asked.

"I'm afraid I can't do that." Her thin face was a mask of makeup. Her fingernails were the color of blood. She turned her back to him.

"Listen, I'll return with cash tomorrow. Could you just set them aside for me? I can be here by noon."

"I'm sorry. We can't do that during the height of the shopping season."

In her eyes, he had lost all credibility. "You won't set aside a goddamn pair of earrings for one day?"

"Only if the owner okayed it. He's not in today."

"This is unbelievable."

"Maybe they'll still be here tomorrow."

"I never intend to set foot in this store again," he swore.

"Oh, what a shame."

Instead of taking the girl by her skinny throat, he left the shop, slamming the door behind him. When he glanced back she stood primly behind the counter, her expression deadpan, giving him the finger—a thin white finger with a crimson tip.

At three, when he was supposed to be back at the office meeting someone named Simon, he was stuck behind a yellow school bus on Elm Street. Released in small colorful groups at frequent intervals, gorgeous kids laughed and ran, happy for Friday.

Where was he racing? There was no way around it. He reached for the lumps of tension in his shoulders and pressed down hard, massaging. Relax. The pain, rising from behind his ear to the top of his skull, momentarily subsided. The nauseating headache, present from the time he'd awakened that morning, had been gaining on him since he'd parted from Simpson at Reed's. Simpson the art thief, Simpson the pig in his fur coat, the sleaze-bag in his silver Mercedes—he had represented a significant future sale. The touchy realtor, he had bills to pay.

Simon, whoever he was, never showed, never called, nothing. The bastard, whoever he was.

April

She said I sounded like a storm trooper coming down the hall
in my clogs. Clog-hopper. Aren't your feet cold in those things,
they make you look six feet tall. She was wearing jeans, her
L. L. Bean boots because it might rain or snow, a cableknit
sweater her mother had made her ten years ago, she said, she
looked pretty terrific. She was racing today, she'd gotten a late
start, it was already noon, she had tons of shit to do. I immediately launched into the Japanese documentary Mac had
come home with last night, trying to decide if he should show
it to his sixth graders or not, we were all glued to the set,
stunned, I couldn't get the images out of my mind, everyone
needed to see this. Val couldn't remember the last time she'd
been stunned by a movie, she didn't look up from her calcula-
tor, her weekly planner. Last night she felt like she was in a
movie, she said, a bit part in a psychological thriller, she didn't
have time to go into it. The name of the film was *Hopi Prophecy*, all about government uranium mining in the South-
west. . . . The phone rang, something about wallpaper, she
faked a little tantrum, gave firm clear instructions, and hung
up. Idiots! This ancient Hopi prophecy in hieroglyphics over
the door of a kiva described the path of doom, basically, and
the way to salvation. Practically everything on the doom side
had already happened in one way or another, thanks to the
fucking white man. . . . The phone rang again, Just do it, Val
said, and hung up, pushed her hair out of her face, bending
over her desk. A Japanese film about Hopi Indians? she asked.

147

The movie started with Hiroshima and Nagasaki. I felt like someone from another planet, I said, witnessing this incredibly stupid earthling madness. The government just moved the Indians out of the way, took their land and turned it into a uranium mine. Naturally, the only people who worked in the mines were Native Americans; hundreds, probably thousands of young men had died of lung cancer. They stole their land, then sent them into the mines to get cancer. It took tons and tons of earth to come up with a tiny almighty amount of uranium, but the tons left over were radioactive too, radioactive dust everywhere, they showed open truckloads of radioactive material moving across the land without warning. . . . They let the impoverished ripped-off Indians dig the foundations of their houses in radioactive earth so they ended up with whole communities of children screwed up with birth defects. The people who lived in harmony with the sacred land—have you ever seen a picture, for instance, of one of the original adobe Hopi towns, you can hardly tell it's there, a totally organic extension of the landscape—the land and its people get destroyed in order to build bombs and fuel the Four Corners power plant to keep L.A. lit up. Save the land and bomb L.A., as far as I'm concerned. Did you ever hear about this? I asked. Val? She looked up. The land was dead as far as you could see, cattle contaminated from the poison grasses and water, beautiful rivers poisoned because holding tanks containing radioactive sludge from the power plant had burst. Can you believe this? They destroy the land and the completely innocent men, women, and children, I pleaded, in order to make bombs intended to destroy some other land and people. Remember Chernobyl, which everyone has forgotten about already, this is the same thing, but we've never heard about it. Have you ever heard about it? Young men with cancer, children born deformed and sick, the pristine land spoiled forever so they can build wacko bombs and L.A. can keep polluting people's minds and the air with its garbage. The film ended with the Hopi declaration of peace, the Hopi have the power to change it, to show us the path to salvation, they have the power, that made me laugh and cry at the same time. We don't even know about it, nobody even knows this has happened. Where is fucking smiling Dan Rather and his millions of dollars a year to give us the news? This is the government doing this to Native Americans, our democratic government of the people. Val was looking at me, she was frowning, she was busy. Of course we didn't know what the hell was happening half the time, she was trying to get out of there early today, what was I getting myself into a state about, was she supposed to do something about the Hopi? I felt violent, I gathered up my coat and knapsack of books, I felt stupid, I clattered down the wood staircase, fighting tears probably, hating myself. She caught up with me on the sidewalk, What is it, are you all right? she asked. I had to go, had to . . . What are you so upset about, April?

When Boomfell returned home, soon after five, the house was in darkness—the only dark house on the street. The kitchen, as he stepped inside, hitting the light switch, felt desolate.

"Val?"

No note on the kitchen counter, for example. Two coffee mugs in the sink. Upstairs, there was nothing to indicate that Ruth had returned to her room this afternoon—no knapsack of books, no violin, no clothes flung onto the bed. He heard a sound, some sound, come from the master bedroom.

"Val? Are you home?"

Their bedroom was empty, the bed unmade, her pink bathrobe in a pile at the foot of it. In Ben's room, a giant exercise suit of synthetic material was laid out on the floor like the cutout clothes for a gigantic paper doll, along with a black turtleneck jersey and white socks—laid out to dry. The cool room had acquired a damp locker-room odor. He could see Singer thumping through the narrow streets of the neighborhood in the black-and-metallic-gray sweat suit—a scary gaunt alien. Ben's bed looked as though the family guest had slept on top of the plaid comforter, if he had slept at all.

"Where the hell is everybody?"

As he descended the stairs, his mind was already dreaming up unlikely misfortune—an accident involving the whole family, or Singer going to pieces again, or Ben with something broken at gymnastics. The way they twirl around on that high bar, hoping to land on their feet.

150

Their intended meal, a roast of lamb, was still in the refrigerator. He called Val's office at the Stallman Building, but received no answer. He called Ruth's friend Gretta, who hadn't seen his daughter since school. It wasn't like Val not to let him know what was going on—to let him come home to a dark house to wonder what was wrong. He rarely returned to an empty house.

"Goddamnit, Valerie."

He took three aspirin and poured himself a stiff scotch. There was no point in starting the damn lamb if there was no one around to eat it.

The phone startled him.

"Hi, it's Holly next door." She sounded as if she were calling from the next room. "Is Eliot there?"

"Eliot?"

"I saw the lights go on, I thought he might be back."

"I don't know where anyone is. Have you seen my kids this afternoon?"

"Tell him I found the book I was telling him about. I couldn't find it when he was here. Tell him I really think he should read it."

"You've met Singer?"

"Eliot? Yeah. He's only here for the weekend, isn't he?"

"I think so. Listen, have you seen Val or the kids?"

"Oh, somebody's pulling in right now. I bet that's them. Talk to you later, Charlie."

Talk to you later? He almost never spoke to his neighbor, Holly Dean Lawson. He rarely laid eyes on her from one day to the next. She appeared briefly on her back porch to call home her wayward dog, or he might catch a glimpse of her in a window, or hurrying from car to house with an armload of books or groceries. She only ventured outdoors, it seemed, when her husband was around, and her husband was seldom home. Jeff, the young company man on the make, evidently didn't mind being on the road five days a week at all. His young wife, meanwhile, rattled around in their partially insulated house, circa 1830, in her down vest, worked toward her degree in clinical psychology, and went to bed with the lights on. The Lawsons and Boomfells had enjoyed dinner together twice, soon after they'd become neighbors, once at each house, but those obligatory occasions hadn't blossomed into friendship. Talk to you later about what? He had never heard that friendliness—that "Charlie"—in her voice before.

Val stumbled through the back door unsteadily, as though the several oversize red-and-green plastic bags she held in her arms were attacking her.

"Oh good, you're home," she said.

"Jesus, Val, I come home, it's dark, no one's here—"

"Check it out, Charlie. For Ben I got two flannel shirts, two pairs of Levi's, and the skis. We have to pick up the skis at some point. I picked up a white cotton sweater for Dad. He doesn't care what I give him. He'll love it. And guess what, Vivian and Peter are getting a very nice big salad bowl like ours. So they're done, Charlie. Peter and Vivian are done! Wait till you see what I found for Ruth." She rummaged through her packages, her black beret plunk on her head like a hat out of Brueghel. She had not quite looked at him yet.

"I thought there'd been an accident or something. Where are the kids? Where's Singer? Where is everybody?"

"Here it is." She held up a long black-and-white garment of wool, a sweater large enough to be a dress. "Isn't she going to love it?"

"Our Visa was declined today. I went to buy something, the goddamn little snippity—"

"I could have told you that. You're an old fart tonight, aren't you? I had a wonderful burst of energy. I even got my mother something. Mother is finished, Charlie. An outfit. It's so nice to go Christmas shopping and actually get something accomplished. Ruth and Ben are overnight for the weekend. I thought it was a good idea under the circumstances."

"What circumstances?"

"Ben is at Noah's and Ruth is staying with Jenny. With Eliot here, I thought it was a good idea."

"Are we going to have an orgy?"

"I thought maybe we could go out for dinner tonight—the three of us. God, I need a shower. Those stores . . ."

A busy person, she bustled from the room with her packages. Boomfell topped up his whiskey and followed.

"What time did you get out of here this morning? How was Eliot?"

"We talked for a while." She stuffed the large bags under their bed, shoving them with her stockinged foot. "I got a late start, but I made up for it."

"So you sat around having coffee with Singer, talking about Lucky—"

"You didn't even notice. Don't I look different?"

"No."

"Of course not, I still have my dumb hat on." Val snatched off the beret and fluffed her hair with one hand, shaking her head. "There, what do you think?"

"A haircut?"

"Thanks a lot, Charlie."

"It's fine. I think you look younger maybe. It's cute. How much?"

"Don't worry about how much. A lot more than cute. I hate cute."

"Holly next door just called and said she had a book for Eliot. What's that about? When did he meet our neighbor?"

Val undressed quickly and left her clothes in an inside-out bundle before her open closet door. "Christ, it's freezing. I'm always cold in this room. I'm all goose bumps, Charlie. Look!" He observed her bumpy backbone as she suddenly crouched—like the spine of an island they had been to once. Her bush was matted flat, and dull. Her breasts were small empty sacks. In the long ago, which was not so long ago, she had been all soft, plumpish, ripe. Just now, she didn't walk to the bathroom like a naked woman being watched by a man. She scuttled, crouching, like a creature that was cold. "He met Holly? I don't know a thing about it."

"Good Lord."

"Jeff will whip her for that, won't he?"

"I'm her neighbor, I've never gone over and visited her in the afternoon. You know what I mean?"

"Oh, what a shame." While the shower warmed she squatted over the toilet and peed. "Eliot's too much, honestly. He's different than he used to be . . ."

"How perceptive of you."

She stepped into the tub and pulled the shower curtain closed. "Hmm, that feels good. He's different," she continued, loud enough to be heard over the water, "he's so goddamn candid and naked and open about everything—it's almost embarrassing—but he's also the same."

"How do you mean?"

"I mean he's also the same as he ever was. He drives you nuts, he's an egomaniac, and yet people climb all over each other to do things for him. He's so damned appealing."

"Where is he now?"

"Exactly. That's exactly it. He called up a woman, a friend of Astrid's, I think. She teaches here—at the college. I got the impression she couldn't see him, or didn't want to be bothered. Eliot insisted. He was only here for a day, he had to see her this afternoon. He told her to cancel whatever else she was doing. You know? And evidently she did. She was going to pick him up after he went running, after he took his shower, and whatever the hell he does."

Steam billowed from her shower. In the humid warmth of the small room, his chilled whiskey tasted sweet.

"So is he coming back tonight or what? I've been busting my ass all day. I'm tired, I'm hungry."

Val peeked around the shower curtain. "Poor baby. I told you, we're going out to dinner."

"Do you have the money? I'm broke."

"They'll take a check."

"So how about it, is the old fire still alive? Have you talked about the old days?"

"He treats me like . . . I don't know—a chum. I'm sore from last night, you bastard. Charlie, I forgot a towel, damnit."

He chose a large soft yellow towel for her, newish and nubby, rather than one of the worn coarser ones. When he returned to the bathroom he placed it on the warm radiator for her.

"Are you there?" she asked. "What do you know about the Hopi Indians?"

"What do you want to know about them?"

"Anything."

"They're a branch of the Pueblo in Arizona or New Mexico, I think. There can't be too many of them left."

"How do you know that?"

"I know they've had the shit kicked out of them like every Native American group all over the country, like all Indians everywhere. What do you mean, how do I know?"

"Uranium mining, what do you know about uranium mining."

"It's bad for you. Why?"

"Nothing."

"What's that got to do with Hopi Indians, they're mining uranium on the reservation or something?"

"Someone was talking about it today, the fate of the Hopi."

"What are you doing in there?"

"What?"

"What are you moaning about?"

"This hot water feels so good. I'm being reborn. So how was your day?"

He sipped, observing himself in the mirror through a thickening film of steam. "Impossible."

"What happened?"

"Nothing. What could happen?"

"Then what was impossible?"

"Everything was impossible. It was one impossible thing after another. I did something stupid, just to spite myself, I suppose."

"Oh, Charlie, what now?"

"I had a sale, and I threw it away. Remember Simpson, the art thief, he's standing there in his fucking fur coat looking down his nose at noble old Reed, who is like poetry, for Christ's sake, like Lear compared to Simpson. I just couldn't be a party to that prick ending up with Reed's beautiful dead goddamn world. It was stupid of me."

"We were talking about you this morning."

"What about me?" His reflection in the mirror was gradually clouded by steam, like a figure receding in dense fog, then—poof!—it was gone.

"You're wasting yourself."

"Who said that?"

"Both of us." She stepped out of the shower, a gleaming pinkish woman with a rosy scrubbed face, a substantial woman with ample breasts and a glistening bush—a beautiful woman. "You're wasting your life."

Singer

Hastings. Anne Hastings. She was Astrid's best friend in London when they were both young mothers, that's how far back they go. Twice each year they pay each other visits. Every summer the best friend and her daughter would show up to spend a week of nonstop chatter. I missed her this year. But Anne Hastings right here in the world of the Boomfells, teaching, Val, at your old fancy-pants college—how's that for a coincidence? There are no men, Charles, that's her biggest complaint. All the men are married, or *impossibly* dull, *impossibly* young, *impossibly* threatened. It's hard for Anne. Astrid's best friend didn't want to see Eliot at all, let's face it, but by the time she'd finished her second glass of wine, it became difficult for me to get away. That's why I was late. She knows Ruth by the way—or her daughter does. They play in the orchestra together. Anne's girl plays the flute. I asked her to come along with us tonight. Eliot, I'm positively shit-faced, I couldn't possibly meet your Boomfells like this. She believes I was *beastly* to Astrid, who is one of the best humans ever born, in Anne's book. Try using the word "beastly" with conviction, and tell me how you feel. These English are so engaging, Charles Boomfell, they speak so crisply and engagingly and brightly, you want to gag them, don't you? Talking to Anne, I felt like I was on *Masterpiece Theater*—the Jew on *Masterpiece Theater*. I used to call her Hasty Pudding, she went through so many men—every six months another doctor or dean or African chief. In British Columbia one summer, she actually showed

157

up with an Oxford African, an economist. She can't find a man in New England—only pale married members of committees. She has her eye on a graduate student who comes to school in a cape that would fit Yeats. You'll like her. Her fingernails were dirty because she'd spent the morning making Christmas pudding—poisonous plum pudding made with suet. She sends them to her friends all over the world. Astrid and I used to put it in the freezer until May, then pitch it. She's tall like Astrid, like a tall ship, a tall pale English lady with large breasts and wide hips and short feet. I wanted to give her my version of Eliot and Astrid's demise to go along with Astrid's version. By the time she was shit-faced it was difficult to pry her hands off of my wrists and get away. But enough of Hasty Pudding. She's going to call you—ring you up, that is. I made her promise to ring you up. Thank God, you waited for me to return. I wouldn't have enjoyed returning to an empty house.

Val and I had a cozy morning talking in the living room about life, didn't we, Val? But after you left, it was very bad. Suddenly, I was in your house, a strange empty house, and I began looking around. You have a lot of stuff, you Boomfells. All this old stuff like that highboy in the hallway, the Windsor chairs, your candlesticks and andirons, the Queen Anne table, the Canton in your old cupboard. Isn't that Queen Anne, with the little feet like that? It's all very nice, all right, but I hate it. I hate all that stuff, this infatuation with . . . what? Lucky and her husband, the anti-Semite, they would go to auctions every Friday night, the preview, and then they would go and sit all day Saturday—all day, Charles Boomfell—and watch dreary souls, overweight shopkeepers and dried-up old women and womanly men, pale and sweaty with greed, buy useless old stuff nobody needed. Mindless people biting their lips, focusing all their energy on this junk, working themselves into a state of covetous anxiety over a chest of drawers or a set of dishes or a dead old painting. Lucky and her husband would sit there for hours and hours until the little oak table or the ladder-back armchair or the set of dolls came up, and then they would jump into the fray, hearts pounding, and make their calculated bid, hoping to take home another item to crowd into their empty married life. *Christe eleison*, Charles Boomfell.

Once I had to go to his house and tell the anti-Semite to his face to stop making his hostile phone calls in the middle of the night, and I saw all the pathetic dreck they had accumulated in their painful years of hopeless marriage. Lucky hated it. It was what they did together under the pretense of creating a home—in fact, it was a symptom of profound homelessness. All the possessions intended to hold them together were all the while sinking them. Poor Lucky would have to stand at the side of the auction hall and pose as a decoy, bidding against her husband the fool, because he believed their competition would discourage other bidders. He was quite a bit older, you see—my age—and Lucky did what she was told. She didn't know any better. When they got home he wouldn't rest until he had found the right place for his new acquisition. Her head and her house were full of all these things she didn't want, all the debris washed up in the wake of other people's dead lives, all the signs and symbols of other people's misery, basically.

Have I offended you? Don't take it personally, Valerie. This morning, after you went out, I was poking around, thinking how pleasant and tasteful and nice everything was, and suddenly I was overwhelmed by Lucky—Lucky imprisoned for years by old junk, Lucky attending dusty auctions to raise her arm and bid for things she didn't want, under pressure from grasping Andrew, the collector. That was his ambition, to open a shop someday where other collectors could admire his junk and recount their own great finds. Thinking about Andrew, Valerie, I could have taken your candlestand and snapped it over my knee and burned it in the fireplace. It was that bad. Suddenly Lucky, whom I had kept at a distance all morning, was back—Lucky imprisoned in the scary psychiatric ward, floor eleven, surrounded by madwomen with cigarette burns on their arms, rows of blackened burns like tribal markings. And I couldn't go to her. I was unable to race to the hospital and storm the concrete walls and save the day because I was in New England—can you believe it?—in the Boomfells' charming old house, of all places, which was suffocating me with its charm and order and decency.

Fortunately, just as I was about to do something stupid, like call the hospital, who should appear but the girl next door. I heard yelling, I looked out, and there was the next-door neighbor out on her porch—a blond woman wearing a green vest over her pale blue bathrobe. Between her cupped hands she was calling, Ocean, Ocean, Ocean. I seized the opportunity to escape the storm gathering in my mind and went out to see what the trouble was. Talk about beastly? Here comes an enormous black dog with a red bandanna around its neck to eat Eliot. Stay, Ocean, stay. She invited me in for some lentil soup. Holly, the neighbor. I learned that her sister is retarded, her parents' marriage has become a cruel ritual of complaint, Jeff the husband is never home, the traffic shines right into her bedroom window at night. Everything. I told her I had troubles of my own. Then I'm afraid I made a fool of myself with the Boomfells' neighbor. I took her wrist, the neighbor's thin wrist, to examine the nasty-looking wound she'd given herself at the stove somehow. I sprayed it with some medication that she had on her spice shelf. What happened to my wrists, she wanted to know. I told her, very briefly, and her eyes acquired this heavy, dead-serious look. Just to take that houndish expression off her face, I think, I asked her if I could stay with her tonight. I don't like being alone at night. I regretted it the moment I'd said it. She took one of my casts in both her hands like an eggplant. You better go, she said. But I couldn't return to the empty house. It was impossible for me to be alone in the house just then, I explained, with all the furniture and so on. So she told me what courses she was taking, and we talked about childhood development—how people fail to develop, how they remain children all their lives. We hung her wreath on the front door. Did you notice? You didn't notice Holly's wreath? She said she never sees the Boomfells except when they get in and out of their cars. You should get better acquainted. You can always use a neighbor.

All these Christmas decorations, Charles Boomfell, every tree on the street covered with little white lights, the glitter, the festivity, the merriment, I hate it. Everything nice I hate. All these affluent people in Cyrano's decked out in their holiday happiness, are they happy? No one's happy. I keep hearing people say that. Mention the word "happiness" and the automatic response is, *No* one's happy, despite the determination and energy and expense—the money—that goes into the appearance of happiness. The time and money and effort that has gone into the way these women look tonight, for example. Will they go home with their husbands and get out of their getups and fuck and be happy? They have too much on their minds for that. They have put aside childish things, don't you think? If you asked them if they would like to go home and fuck and be happy, they would laugh.

David, the brother, has everything. Money to burn, smart children, a loyal spouse, houses and cars and trips all over the world, works of art on the wall and works of charity in his heart. Everything, even his health, which he monitors very carefully at an expensive clinic in New York. And he can't bear his little brother, Eliot—unbearable was how I looked to him on floor eleven—because Eliot gets to fuck Lucky and try to kill himself. I took one look at his face and I told him to get a pair of pajamas and commit himself—give floor eleven a try. Trying to die, I am still happier than he is, that's what David thinks. Although he will tell Phyllis, the wife, how pitiful and tragic I seemed to him in the hospital. Although he will tell me I must be out of my mind to be so messed up over nothing but a girl named Lucky. He scorns me because I don't want everything, and all the misery that goes along with it. I only want to go home and fuck and be happy. That's all. Of course, David is mistaken. It's difficult for him to understand, but the truth is that the attempt I made on my life does not mean I am happier than he is. You're laughing, Valerie, because it's funny, isn't it? No one is happy, not even Eliot.

Of man's first disobedience, and the fruit of that forbidden tree, whose mortal taste brought death into the world, and all our woe, with loss of Eden, et cetera, sing, Heavenly Muse. Was Milton happy? By his mid-thirties he'd read everything that had ever been written in Latin, Greek, Hebrew, Italian, English, you name it. Everything known, Milton knew. What does the smartest man in the world do? He marries a girl half his age, who flies back to her family within a month. Thirty days, Valerie. A seventeen-year-old girl drives John Milton to focus his awesome resources on the issue of divorce for almost two years—wild ideas that would wreak havoc. The notion that you can split up just because you don't get along—chaos. Then she comes back. Is he happy? By the time he's forty-four he's blind. You'd go blind, Charles, if you read every book in the world by candlelight. The same year, his young wife dies, and a month later his baby son, John, dies too. He's a blind man with three daughters. A few years later his second wife kicks the bucket in childbirth, and a month after that, her baby dies. Is he happy now? Everything he's been working for, these past twenty years—pamphlet after pamphlet, treatise after treatise—goes to pieces. Back comes your namesake, Charles the Second, and Milton the radical is suddenly a dangerous man, who must be destroyed. They are going to take this extraordinary head, containing all the knowledge in the world, and put it in a hangman's noose. Milton dead—before he'd written *Paradise Lost*, Valerie. They want to take this head, containing *Paradise Lost*, and destroy it before he is able to put the poem into words. Instead, they just lock him up for a while, burn his books, confiscate his property. Poor, blind, haunted by death, his lifelong dream of the Commonwealth shot to hell, what does he do? He sits down to justify the ways of God to men—that's the spirit!—to compose the greatest epic poem in the language, a poem encompassing all heaven and earth—everything. And he succeeds. Milton does it. Meanwhile, he gets married again. Lucky Elizabeth Minshull. Meanwhile, the plague pulls into town, the indiscriminate death-dealing plague, and blind old Milton must run for his life, but he makes it, and subsequently produces his *History of Britain*, his *Paradise Regained*, his *Samson Agonistes*. A little onward lend thy guiding hand, Charles Boomfell, to these dark steps, a little further on . . . and a few years later he gets to die, apparently with gout, which is very painful. Gout hurts. Is he happy now? *Kyrie eleison. Christe eleison.*

I mope and pine in my ridiculous state, running to the Boomfells, running to the Boomfells' neighbor, running to Anne Hastings, crying in bed at night with my limp little dick in my hand, then I stop and think for two minutes about Milton sitting down in the midst of his overwhelming wretchedness and dictating *Paradise Lost* to his amanuensis word for word. Sing, Heavenly Muse! Sing it, Milton! He would go to bed, he tells us, with all the poetry of the Bible and classical literature in his head, then during sleep and the wee hours before dawn his Muse would confide to him his unpremeditated harmonious verse. Is that how it happens with you, Charles Boomfell?

Seventeen years old! Maybe that wasn't too unusual in the seventeenth century, but seventeen is still seventeen. Skin like a baby's, cute little breasts and toes, clear vacant eyes. It wasn't the Heavenly Muse that dictated the lines Milton poured into her seventeen-year-old ear as he guided her dimpled hand to his monstrous prick. And the Heavenly Muse didn't come to the rescue when little Mary Powell decided she couldn't deal with this living font of knowledge and wisdom for another five minutes. Poor John Milton. What did he do to the kid? This loftiest mind couldn't escape the tyranny of his mortal flesh any more than we can, Charles Boomfell. Of course not. It never ends.

My parents and their fifty years, my brother and his dead-end status quo, Anne Hastings and her impossible, impossible, impossible, your neighbor and her traveling salesman. Imagine what's going on in the minds of just about everyone who must return at the end of the day, after another miserable day of slugging it out in the world, and face the person they have promised to live with for the rest of their lives. Milton's wives died after a few years. Hardly a happy alternative, but decidedly a way out of a hopeless situation. Marriage *is* impossible. I've tried it. And Astrid wasn't a difficult person. She was easy. She was tolerant, generous, dutiful, hardworking, she knew how to make perfect eggs, she knew how to make the bed, she didn't yell at her children, she didn't fart all day long, she never complained. I was the difficult one. I'm the one who farted and complained. Despite Astrid's goodness, it was impossible. The living spouse soon becomes another boring possession—like a sailboat. We even had a twenty-one-foot sailboat, Eliot's family. Imagine! Everyone climbed into it on Sunday afternoons for a little ride on the big windy lake. You're like a sailboat, and only one person can take you out on the water. No one else can sail Eliot, and no one else can sail Astrid. And if that one person gets tired of sailing you, you no longer get out on the lake, right? Your sail no longer fills, your bow no longer presses through the mysterious water, and so on and so forth. Nicole would man the tiller, Astrid would hoist the jib, while little Alex sat bravely strapped into his jerry-rigged car seat, and Eliot basked in sunshine, pointing the way. For a while I dreamed that we would one day buy a big boat, a forty- or fifty-foot boat, and sail all over the world, Valerie. Have you heard that one before?

I think you're right, marriage with Lucky would become impossible even sooner than marriage with Astrid did. Lucky is not nearly as selfless and forgiving and good as Astrid. I agree with you, Valerie, it would be a disaster. That's the way life is now—we can't help it. Phyllis and David, they run their marriage like a business. They're so busy with their work, their trips, the children's comings and goings, so busy acquiring and accumulating, so busy keeping all their affairs straight, they don't have time to see each other. That's the secret, that's how it is with rich successful people. How can your marriage be a problem if you never see each other? On the other hand, with people like my parents, there's a convenient failure of nerve and imagination, call it. But that's not the case with the Boomfells, is it? How has the impossible turned out to be possible for the Boomfells? How has this tiny marriage withstood the pressure of an entire society—a promiscuous, tempting and teeming, wasteful and destructive society—to tear it apart? The Catholic Church has even broken under the pressure. Myths and truths of marriage and family collapse all around us, and there in the rubble stand Charles and Valerie Boomfell like a monument to the past.

Don't laugh, Valerie. Tell me! If you stay in the saddle for dusty mile after dusty mile, riding out every storm that comes along, stay in that same weather-beaten saddle come what may, do you finally pass between towering peaks and enter a kind of sunstruck Yosemite of knowable enduring love? Is that the prize for hanging in there, despite the boredom and frustration and doubt and anguish? Look at them laughing. I want to know. What have I missed? Or, on the other hand, is there nothing to report? What do my parents know, right? What does Blanchard know? What is Holly, the neighbor, going to know if she makes the horrendous mistake of standing by an asshole for the next twenty years—or the next hundred years? On the other hand, what have *you* missed, right, what discoveries and transformations? And fun—let's not forget fun. Remember our friend Strether, Charles: Live, live! Once you get to be on the dark side of forty you realize it's not just a literary discussion. Anything is possible. That's another thing I've learned. Everything happens. Unless nothing happens. Of course, if you came unstuck and went your separate ways at this point, the look of those almost twenty years would change, wouldn't it? A lifelong marriage could be reduced overnight to one more merely longish episode. That's what life with Astrid looks like from here—an episode. Whereas a lousy year with Lucky feels like a lifetime, which will never end. Everything is possible, and nothing is possible. That's why we're all so happy here.

Ah, we're going to have some celestial chimings. Angel music! There can't be much call for the harp these days, can there? You can't hear it with the noise in here. The poor girl must feel like she's pissing into the wind. Who does she remind you of, Charles—the harpist? Maybe it's just her straight back and blond hair. Our friend Wanda Gwertz, the cellist. I saw her in Toronto last summer. I've seen her a few times in the last however long it's been. Years ago we ran into each other at the Prado in Madrid. She'd dyed her hair black, but I recognized her. That was strange. Last summer I noticed her trio was playing in Toronto. The New World Trio, they call themselves. How's that for optimism? Three women. I think they're plugged into a couple of touring circuits here and abroad. Wanda teaches part-time in two or three places. I think they've made a record. Lucky wouldn't go to the concert. I wanted her to see Wanda Gwertz play her cello, but Lucky refused. After the performance Wanda and I had a drink. We only had an hour because she was catching a midnight flight out of there. To Israel, I think. She'd been through some tough times, our friend Wanda, but she was looking well. Back on her feet. Do you ever hear from her, Charles? Remind me to get you her address. I'm sure I have it. Wanda's a good egg.

One question, Charles Boomfell, do you think you're making a mistake? Real estate? When Lucky bought the house, here was this fellow in a trench coat with a slimy smile tucked under his tidy mustache. He opened the door with a key. Here was the kitchen. Did we want to go down to the basement? He told Lucky there was a wonderful crab apple tree in the backyard if she was interested in making jelly. Lucky making crab apple jelly! Is that what Charles Boomfell does? Everyone says they have to make a living, when what they need to do is live a living, and everyone knows it. Maybe I want Alex to go to Yale, and maybe I don't, but I'm not going to sacrifice my life to pay the tuition. For Lucky's cunt, yes. For tuition I draw the line. We know what happens to children who go to college to the tune of thousands and thousands a year. Nothing much. I know, I went to college myself. I went and went and went. My big brother, David, went to Harvard Business School so that when he sashayed out into the world he would have everything. He hates his little brother because he believes Eliot is less miserable than he is. Children grow up, at least they get older, and move out of the house into their own lives, and if you have failed to live your life because of them, they won't care. It's not their problem. My parents gave me everything, and I never want to see them again. Ruth and Benjamin will be fine, or at least, if you decide not to sacrifice everything to their mythical happiness, they won't be any worse for it.

I spent two months traveling in India, sweating my ass off. The heat and stench and throngs of humans, the starving eyes. Everyone should go to India. Not all at once. Eliot Singer, the American, had more worldly goods on his back than the average starving family of five, who lived, squatting, in the road. The enormous eyes of starved faces would follow my knapsack, the outrageous bounty of my knapsack in the midst of all this crippled suffering and overcrowded death. Go to India, Charles Boomfell, then come back and tell me if you can find the means to live your life as you please, or if you must spend your allotted time on earth selling houses for empty people to fill up with all their imprisoning junk. In Calcutta I tried to look up Mother Teresa. I wanted to catch a glimpse of her in her element. Hell. Calcutta is hell. You can't breathe for the pollution, an opaque smog. You can't move for the masses of paralyzed humans. What a hot shit she is, this shrunken old lady not much taller than a crutch. She cradles deformity and death in her bent-up tired old arms, and loves it. She says prayers of love for the loveless. Mother Teresa prays! If I lived in Calcutta, the first thing I'd give up is prayer. God doesn't seem to be within hearing distance. She was in the USA addressing students at a football stadium. I spent the day at the mission with two charming Missionaries of Charity, plain hardworking young women all covered up in their habits, with hands and faces sticking out. One was from Ireland and the other was from Italy, a nurse and a student of piano. Like Eliot. We talked piano for an hour. Guess what, Charles Boomfell? They seemed happy. These young people dying from the heat in their absurd garments, stuck in a place of moaning pain and clutching starvation and stinking death, they seemed happy. If they get to spend the day bathing the twisted bones of a little child who will die tomorrow, or emptying the diaper of a twenty-year-old man so severely brain-damaged he doesn't even know he's alive, they're happy. All day long they're cheerful and positive. Mother Teresa's nuns, they don't even get to play with themselves. When you join the order do your genitals atrophy and fall off and Mother Teresa comes along and sweeps everything into her dustpan and that's that? I don't think so. I'm sure that charity begins at home even for the Missionaries of Charity. Are these people selfless, I asked myself, in contrast to the nightmare of selfishness that the rest of us inhabit? Are they different? I don't think so, do you? Self-interest was what motivated them to join the mission in the first place. They didn't like the lives they were living. They came to Mother Teresa in search of personal happiness. They have liberated themselves to lead lives of worth. Whereas our narcissism destroys us day in and day out. We have insatiable egos here in the land of wants, but our inside selves have been shattered. We don't know the difference anymore between living and dying.

It does sound pretty good, doesn't it, Val? We should all become Missionaries of Charity and live to be a hundred and happy all the time. I couldn't stay and be a nun, so I went to Nepal. I could have stayed and lived out my life in Nepal, but at the time I didn't have the balls. I had to go home and live with Astrid and Nicole and Alex. Listen to Eliot Singer telling Charles Boomfell how to live! Everyone is out there selling one thing or another, hustling to afford all their headaches. Everything's for sale, which makes everything cheap. It doesn't matter what you do. It doesn't matter if you sell houses or starve to death, if you build bombs or write poetry, if you clothe the rich or feed the poor. Not a bit. It doesn't matter if you live or die. How could it?

But tonight we happen to be alive, Val. You're absolutely right. We're here. I can't get over it, really. Ten o'clock on a Friday night. Astrid has undoubtedly gone to bed with her latest book on single parents, or Hitler, or suicides. She would get along well with your neighbor, Holly what's-her-name. She has a tremendous appetite for all that psychoanalytic mumbo jumbo. She knows all there is to know about the causes and effects of Eliot. I wish you could hear her explain me to myself. Nicole probably has her friend Katie over to listen to records by candlelight, while Alex is alone under the covers, drawing drawing drawing. Oh God. Everything in Alex's world becomes a drawing. Here, see this truck on the top of my cast, that's the work of Alex Singer. Wonderful. And over here, this is a picture of his house, formerly our house. He drew a picture of me sitting in my hospital bed at the loony bin. He has me smiling with my pipe in my mouth, reading a book. That's his image of his father. I'm the greatest. You know all about that sort of thing. What am I doing, Charles Boomfell, cutting myself to ribbons when Alex is expecting me to come over and read to him, or kick the ball in the backyard? He only exists at all because I had to crawl under the covers of Astrid's bed in Italy and curl up against her goodness and kindness.

I was present at his birth. Were you in the delivery room, Charles? Astrid was as happy and excited as a child. She's having contractions in the car, big painful contractions, but she's laughing and smiling. Oh, Eliot, it really hurts now, she says with a smile. In the labor room I would put both hands under her back and pull up when the contractions came. At that moment I was happy. Then you have to get into your green tunic with the matching paper hat and face mask. There we are, a gang of masked figures gathered around this big marvelous woman with her innermost self nakedly thrust out to the world. A mound of woman with her long legs spread and a smile on her face, which was as white as a sheet. We're counting, and breathing together, and pushing—all the stuff we learned like two straight A students at childbirth school. I was having the time of my life, Valerie. You're doing fine, says acne-scarred Michael Frieman, the O.B., you're doing beautifully, Astrid. I didn't love her. The way the mind goes on in its secret life, you know, no matter what's happening. One of the nurses looked at me with smiling eyes, seeing us, I know, as a joyfully married couple giving birth here and now to a living symbol of our love. And I thought, No, I'm not in love with Astrid. This is not love. But I admired her tremendously. The way she was taking charge of the thing happening—her authority as a woman giving birth, if you know what I mean. I'm sure you were also fantastic, Valerie. Oh, Eliot, Astrid says, grimacing and grinning like an actress in a make-believe movie of childbirth, and here comes Alex. His big skull, you know, the messy top of it, appeared between Astrid's legs. We were both looking in the mirror that was suspended over the event. I couldn't imagine how this head was going to get through the smallish opening. You're doing real well, Frieman says. Then Astrid's flesh tore a bit around the head. Everyone was breathing, pushing down, grimacing and grinning. To make a

long story short, here comes Alex, his head, then—whoosh!—
his slippery blood-bathed mucus-clotted infant's body flops
out of Astrid's wide-open self into Frieman's plastic-gloved
hands. Tiny hands and feet, tiny balls and prick, face all
squooshed up, the whole thing. Astrid is half laughing with her
big happy smile, Eliot Eliot Eliot. A miracle, absolutely, Valerie, the ongoing everyday miracle of life on earth.

And also revelation. To me it was like revelation of what I
hadn't quite grasped before. We are born! There's no Alex,
then he is born. I may not be conveying what I felt at the time.
It was as though I were seeing my father being born, and my
mother being born, Eliot being born and Astrid being born,
Michael Frieman being born, and the black nurse with the
smiling eyes. We are born. We are this helpless scrunched-up
bloody creature born into the world. Suddenly I was overwhelmed. I fell on Astrid's neck, much disturbed, mumbling
love love love. I meant that at that moment I loved everyone.
I loved all the helpless strange infants born into the world. I
loved brand-new Alex and Astrid and Eliot, all our parents and
grandparents and—you name it—everyone. And along with
the emotions of love, love for the extraordinary creature who
comes tumbling willy-nilly out of brave innocent women of all
kinds, I was overwhelmed by the impossible unhappiness connected with the whole mess. Alex was crying. He was already
Alex as far as we were concerned. He was crying, while everyone else was smiling and laughing. I love you too, Astrid was
saying. I'm so happy, Eliot, so happy. We didn't mean the same
things at all. He hadn't existed—I hadn't wanted him to
exist—and the next minute the black nurse was placing
bundled-up Alex in my arms. A bundle of fear, basically. I
already knew that I was bound to make a major contribution—
I already had—to his inevitable misery and pain. Otherwise, it
was a wonderful night, a very wonderful three o'clock in the
morning. You've been there yourself, Charles. You know.

Here we sit in swanky Cyrano's surrounded by attractive

people in the prime of their lives, and meanwhile . . . what? Meanwhile Lucky is on floor eleven surrounded by insane women. We had everything. Sunday newspapers, coffee mugs, cross-country skis, our running statue. Lucky also began running. A mile, two miles, finally three miles at high noon. She even had a nifty sweat suit of some miracle fabric for the cold weather. She'd put a bright little band around her head like Pocahontas to keep her hair out of her face. Wonderful. We bought a bronze statue of a man and woman running, and put it on the window shelf. Unbelievably tacky and tasteless, Valerie. And yet I want that statue. I'm sure it's still there on Lucky's windowsill. Laugh, it's funny. It's very funny, Charles, isn't it? As far as we were concerned, the bronze figures on the statue looked exactly like us. I hate it, but I want it.

If I'm sitting in a fancy restaurant in another country, hundreds of miles away, thinking about her, what must she be thinking about, lying there all by herself in the loony bin on Friday night. She must be thinking Eliot Eliot Eliot. She must be! And yet she agrees with the make-believe Freud not to see me, not to speak to me. Thirty days! She must masturbate, right? Isn't that fair, Valerie? Lying there in her bed hour after hour, day after day, bored to tears? It would be impossible for Lucky not to masturbate. And when she does masturbate, what does she think about? Her psychiatrist? The anti-Semitic junk collector? The guy next door? Who must come to mind when Lucky touches the secret places that we have spent hours and hours discussing and exploring and discovering together as if we had a million-dollar research grant? Eliot Eliot Eliot. She must. And yet Eliot is here visiting the Boomfells, pretending to be sane, while she's lying in her bed on floor eleven pretending to be insane. I'm sorry, I don't want to ruin the evening. It's not all right, Valerie. It's not all right. I'm not myself.

On the one hand, there's Alex, the beautiful event of Alex, which I had been prepared to nip in the bud. I spent hours and days and weeks trying to persuade Astrid to skip the birth of

Alex. And on the other hand, there's Lucky's unforgivable act of abortion. The ecstatic scene of Astrid in childbirth surrounded by caring Frieman and smiling nurses and her happy husband in contrast to Lucky alone in a nasty bleak room waiting for a man without a face to enter and divest her as coldly and quickly as possible of the fetus she's carrying. My child, Charles Boomfell. There is Astrid giving birth—Alex's skull, the top of his miraculous bloody head forcefully emerging from Astrid's body—and Lucky lying on her back in the same way, with her feet in those stirrups. . . . I can't get these images out of my mind. Maybe that's why I want to bore you with them, in order to expel them.

It might have been easier to bear if I had been with her. She refused to tell me when or where she was going to have it done. She wasn't at home. It was a Tuesday. She hadn't been home the night before, and she wasn't home all day Tuesday. She had booked into a hotel, as I learned later, in order to go through the whole ordeal without allowing me to interfere. I was going out of my mind, of course. I knew she was going to have an abortion, but I didn't know where or when. Try to get information out of these people. I called several abortion clinics, they treated me like a criminal. Finally, Tuesday afternoon, I started making the rounds of abortion clinics. Outside one of these places there was a man and woman staging their own little pro-life protest. Utter imbeciles. They mistook me for a satanic doctor on his way to perform his evil deeds. I could have killed them. Inside, no one would speak to me. I described her, I gave her name, I said she must not be allowed to go through with it, I was the father, and so on and so forth. I pleaded. Singer was against abortion that day, Charles Boomfell. Nothing. To them I was a raving madman. There were people sitting in the vacant tawdry waiting room as if they knew what they were doing, leafing through magazines like maybe this was a dentist's office. I couldn't find her.

Unfortunately, I had only recently seen a show on television about abortion—a documentary portraying actual young women going through the sorrow and ordeal of abortion—so I had plenty of pictures in my mind of exactly what was happening to Lucky. You get past the mindless harassment of the moron outside, and you climb the cold steps of the ugly brick building. Inside, you must submit to an interview with a counselor, who asks you if you've thought about what you're doing. Do you know what you're doing, Lucky? Then they take you and put you in a bare room with a table to lie on and a strange-looking frightening machine in the corner, and you're left alone to think some more about what you're doing there. I can't get the picture of Lucky lying in such a room out of my mind. Lying there, staring at the blank ceiling, thinking. What's she thinking, for God's sake? Then the man in the mask, a complete stranger, enters the room in a big hurry and recites in simpleton terms the sounds and sensations you can expect to experience during the procedure. Just like a good dentist. The woman must lift her legs and put her feet in the stirrups, open herself to this anonymous joker with his gloved hands and brutal utensils. Did you see the documentary? He starts the machine, which sounds like a vacuum cleaner, and then he enters the woman with a plastic nozzle-type device, which sucks the embryo into the machine. The woman lies there and listens to her would-be infant being sucked out of her. I'm racing through town, with images of Lucky lying there allowing Eliot's son or daughter to be vacuumed out of her. When it's over, the counseling woman smiles and asks you if you're all right. Then you get to lie there alone, completely alone in this grotesque cell without one thing on the walls—as though no one is going to pretend, even by putting a decorative poster on the wall, that this process is anything but ugly and painful—to lie there and think about the horrible thing that has just happened to you, which you wanted to happen, and which is now done and can't be undone. *Christe eleison*, Charles. Really, *Christe eleison*.

I was able to imagine Lucky lying there too clearly. Smiling sympathetically at the counseling lady, telling the masked doctor to hurry up about it. She needed me, she needed Eliot to help and comfort and protect her, but I didn't know where she was. Tuesday night, there's Eliot camped outside her door in my car. She never appeared. Later she told me she was at a hotel because she simply wanted to be alone through the whole thing, from beginning to end, and be done with it. That was the only possible way for her to get through it. She was trying to make it easier for herself. Easier for *her*, Valerie.

The next day, Wednesday, I kept returning to her house every hour or so until, at noon, she finally returned with her daughter. She looked terrible—her hair, her skin, her eyes. It was abundantly clear that the last person she wanted to see waiting on her doorstep was Eliot. In order to get rid of me, in order to make her feelings as clear and final as possible, she merely stated what I already knew. I had the abortion. Those were her exact words. That's all she said. Then she continued into the house. I was unable to speak. If I began talking . . . if I'd attempted to respond, God knows what would have happened. We are born, everyone is born, but Eliot's child was not born. In the documentary they showed us what was inside the machine that had sucked the embryo out of the woman's body. We get to see the aborted fetus, which they put in a little plastic bag. Lucky and Eliot's would-be infant in a little plastic bag—garbage. Nothing but garbage. In contrast to gorgeous and colossal Alex, who screams, who begins to cry in his beautiful new voice, to open his eyes and move his arms and legs and . . . You know what I'm saying.

But where was Alex, or Nicole, who I loved, or Astrid, this marvelous woman, or my parents, who had been born, just helpless babies, and grew up and fucked and gave birth to Eliot? Where was Eliot, the innocent bright-eyed beautiful infant born into the world? They were all lost, as far as I was concerned. They had all been lost to me. I had lost Alex and

Nicole and Astrid because I couldn't get Lucky out of my mind. There was Lucky's body in my mind, and there was a big sign on it: No more for Eliot. I have lost everything, that's what I thought as I turned away from Lucky and her little girl and walked back to my car, afraid to respond to what she had told me. Unbelievably, I had the good sense not to express all the rage and anxiety that had been accumulating in my skull for days because I knew I wasn't in control of where that might lead. She looked so broken, so dreary, pale, nauseated—Lucky, this vital juicy young woman with her whole life ahead of her. I have lost her, I thought, and I've lost everything else as well. I've lost everyone in my life who was ever born, including Eliot. I was this beautiful baby, I became a handsome young man who played the piano, who brought home straight A's, who loved his life, who loved his parents and his home. That person had been buried alive. But then I met Astrid, a tall strong angel, who gave birth to Alex. Astrid, Alex, Nicole, these were my sources of worth and meaning, and I had lost them, along with everything else—my work, my ability to work, my love of literature and music, tennis, food, everything. And now, beyond a shadow of a doubt, I had also lost Lucky. I'd destroyed Lucky, a young woman who had done nothing but grow up, get married, have a kid, and try to live her life, until Eliot came along. It was very clear that I had lost Lucky. Otherwise it would have been impossible for her to lie down for some stranger and have our child sucked out of her womb into a plastic bag. Impossible.

Alex and Nicole and Astrid, Lucky, my parents, my brother, Eliot, and Eliot's unborn infant. They were lost and I couldn't get them back. For some reason I had the sense not to follow Lucky and her daughter into the house—our house—and all that might have ensued. I couldn't bear to look at her. I didn't say a word. I returned to the car without saying a word and drove directly to Astrid's. Where was I going to go? Incredibly, there was Alex. He was right there in front of the house on his bicycle. Actually, Nicole's bicycle. It was much too big for him. He couldn't sit on the seat and reach the pedals, but he was able to ride the bike standing up. There he was, six years old, having taught himself to get on his sister's bike and ride it. I was overwhelmed, of course. I hadn't expected to see him. I was horrified—that's not too strong a word, Valerie—horrified that he would see me. I was afraid to face him. Thank God, I hadn't followed Lucky into the house. Thank goodness, Charles, I hadn't gone into Astrid's house. I had all this in my mind too clearly—people being born and people being destroyed. Lives aborted every time you turned around. I spread towels on the bed, on the floor, towels everywhere. A big mess, that's not Eliot. I spread towels all over the hovel. Then blood, my blood, like I'd never seen blood before. My mind was full—above the brim, Charles Boomfell, like our friend Robert Frost—but I wasn't thinking anything. If I was thinking, I didn't know it. And then I was one of the boys on floor eleven. I wasn't surprised, I wasn't reborn. Nothing had changed. It happened like everything happens and continues to happen, and you go on from there. Later, when I was able to think about it, one hundred and sixteen stitches later, it became impossible. . . .

In answer to your question, Charles, of course your presence would have prevented it. If you had flown to Toronto immediately, right, and I'd picked you up at the airport, and we'd gone out to dinner and so forth and so on? Of course. I was alone, going from abortion clinic to abortion clinic, my mind crowded with menacing phantoms. No, I couldn't possibly have killed myself that day with Charles Boomfell sitting there in my hovel having a beer. How's your duck? Is it all right? Valerie, eat, the salmon is out of this world. Incidentally, I'm going to insist on getting the bill tonight. That's the least I can do.

The phone was ringing as they entered the house, shortly after midnight. It was Holly next door. Was Eliot there? The south facade of the Lawson house, clearly visible from the casement window over the sink, was illuminated, a light in every window.

Singer appealed to his hosts with open arms. "She wants me to come over. How can I possibly go over there at this hour? I'm exhausted."

"How ridiculous," Val said irritably. "Don't go if you don't want to. Period."

"This is our neighbor, Holly Dean Lawson?" Boomfell asked. "This is the person I never see from one week to the next?"

"I told her I could come over for a minute. She sounded excited, you know. I might as well get it over with."

"Shit," said Val.

"Turn out the lights and lock the door when you get back," Boomfell told him.

"Don't wait up for me." Wrapping his black wool scarf around his neck, Singer went out.

"Is he going over there to sleep with her tonight? Can you believe that?"

Boomfell couldn't.

He was worn-out, having trudged through the disappointing day half hung over, short of sleep, and having stupidly drunk another bellyful of wine tonight, listening to Singer. Yet he couldn't rest until he'd found the most recent issue of the

Valley Weekly, a local newspaper that contained a list of all current and upcoming concerts in Boomfell's corner of the world. He'd been alert to announcements on the radio lately, but until tonight he hadn't known what he was listening for. The New World Trio. Three women. She's had some tough times, Charles Boomfell, but she looked well. In the next half hour he must have dug out every issue of the newspaper for the past two months, but he couldn't find the most recent one. He resisted the impulse to wake Val and demand to know what she'd done with it.

He was visited in his sleep by the, for him, rare pleasure of an erotic dream—his dreamed self groping under layers of an anonymous woman's clothing while seated in a crowded auditorium, it looked like, fingers tracing the edges of dampened underthings, a violin playing, the lady snaking fingers into trousers. . . . He awakened with a start. An intuition of danger jolted him upright, waking Val too.

Singer, taller than the simple tapering pencil posts of their antique four-poster, stood fully dressed at the foot of the bed.

"This is marriage? This is marriage, order, sanity?"

"Jesus, you scared the hell out of me. How long have you been standing there, Eliot?"

"I don't believe this," Val muttered.

"Good night," he told them.

Boomfell found his watch on the night table and pressed the tiny button to light up its face.

"What time is it, Charlie?"

"Three o'clock in the morning."

Before he had quite fallen asleep again, Singer was back at their doorway.

"Charles?"

"For Christ's sake, Eliot. Go to bed!" That was Val.

"It's snowing out," he informed them.

"Is it?"

"It's very beautiful. Very disturbing."

. . . .

Snow outlined the branches of bare trees, topped each picket of the picket fence, metamorphosed the squat hemlocks into friendly gnomes, and covering rooftops and windowsills, it endowed the houses on Boomfell's street with a fanciful gingerbread charm. The snow leveled the boundaries of yards and driveways, unifying the neighborhood, burying all odds and ends of disharmony and everyday debris, so that the familiar outdoors had become—overnight!—another world.

Indoors nothing had changed. In the bathroom mirror the bleary face of Boomfell wasn't handsome. A single hair sprouted offensively from the top of his ear. He pulled it out. His winterish gut, pale and full, repelled him. His penis dangled discouragingly. With sudden resolve he collected his cross-country gear from dresser and closet—thermal underwear, wool knickers, red wool knee socks—and went downstairs prepared to make the most of the day.

Val sat at the kitchen table, rather diminished in Boomfell's baggy yellow bathrobe. Singer sat behind her administering a back rub with fingers and thumbs. They both looked up when he entered the room.

"Don't stop," Val said. "It's working." Her hands cupped one of the large white coffee mugs they'd received for donating to listener-supported public radio. "Right there, and down a little farther."

After Singer had excused himself to get ready—"Sven and Hans, ve ski now, ya?"—Boomfell said, "You said it was working. What's working?"

"Eliot was trying to cure my headache. His back rub was working. It's back already."

"How long have you been up?"

"For hours. I couldn't sleep after he woke us. I finally came down and made coffee. There's fruit in the refrigerator. We had waffles. There's some batter left, if you want one."

"Has he been up long?"

"He was lying on the couch in his clothes when I came downstairs. I guess he slept for a few hours."

"What's the story, did he fuck the next-door neighbor or not?"

"He hasn't said anything about it, and I haven't asked. She must be mortified this morning."

"You're gorgeous this morning, by the way. What happened to your hair?"

"I'm never going back to Richard's. He hates women. That's why he's a hairdresser, so he can make women ugly and steal their money." She raised her cup to her lips. "God, I can't drink any more of that. My head is spinning."

"Are you coming skiing with us?"

"I promised Ruth I'd meet her in town. She wants to do some Christmas shopping." Val pushed back from the table, picking up two mugs, and crossed to the sink. She was in her bare feet. Longish feet with crooked square-ended toes and pink unpainted toenails.

"Are you in the mood for Plum's party tonight?"

"Not right now I'm not. I wish I could go back to bed."

"Why don't you?"

"I'm too awake. I'd just lie there and feel worse."

"Aren't your feet cold?"

"Of course they're cold. This floor is like ice, goddamnit."

Val's fruit cup consisted of grapefruit, oranges, green apples, banana slices, and slices of kiwi that sparkled like jeweled fruit. How nice of her.

"Charlie."

He turned to face her. "What?"

She stood before the sink, holding the bathrobe open so that it looked as if there were large wings attached to her naked body. In the daylight of the kitchen, the bright robe, yellow as sunflowers, infused her pale winterish flesh with a pinkish luminosity.

He smiled. "What?"

Val's face, sallow this morning compared to the rosiness of her body, was fairly expressionless, as if she were regarding herself in a mirror.

"What?" he asked.

Singer

What's the story? I didn't know there was a story. The next-door neighbor is a fledgling psychologist. She loves to discuss relationships, motives, meanings. Everything has a reason, everything is a question. She says she's worried about me, then she asks herself, What do I mean by that? Why am I worried about you? It can be tiresome. She went to get all dressed up in her diaphragm. I was sitting in the rocking chair, his rocking chair, with his ornate initials on it. Everything in the house is monogrammed. Did you ever notice that? I was exhausted. She has framed posters decorating the walls. Giverny, van Gogh's wheat field with black crows, Klimt's unbearable kiss. There are pictures of her family everywhere. Her retarded sister, her brother, their weddings and gatherings, the grandmother as a little girl. The salesman has his collection of decoys on the windowsills. I loathe decoys. Then there's the log cabin quilt hanging in the doorway to conserve heat. The stereo on its fake teakwood entertainment stand was emitting transcendental synthesizer music to meditate by. And sitting in the middle of all this was Eliot Singer—smack in the middle of all this stuff that meant so much to her and nothing to me. To make a long story short, I put on my shoes and when she returned in her monogrammed nightgown, wide-eyed and half-smiling, I told her I had to leave. I left. I'm certain that the moment I closed the door behind me she was as relieved as I was. She wanted to help, to live up to the situation she had bungled into with this character from Canada.

The minute I got back here, the minute I stretched out on your couch, I had second thoughts. Third and fourth thoughts. Lying in the dark with all your dark furniture around me, thinking about Lucky lying in the dark of floor eleven with dark moaning madwomen around her. You lie there in the half-dark with light from the nurses' station coming through the glass doors. I was thinking about Lucky and all the parts of Lucky—everything that adds up to Lucky. Light from the neighbor's house was shining right through the twelve-over-twelve window sash, casting a grid against the wall. I got up and went to the window. She's got every light in the house turned on, as usual, but guess what, Charles? Holly is standing by the living room window in her blue-and-white flannel nightgown, looking directly toward the Boomfells' darkened house, directly at the window where I'm standing, it looks like, although I don't think she can see me. It had begun to snow, beautiful snow falling on the bushes and trees, falling down between the two houses. I was exhausted, and wide-awake. Across the way in her warm house, in her warm mono-grammed nightgown, Holly the neighbor was wide-awake, looking at the gorgeous snow. Holly and the parts of Holly. We're both looking at the beautiful snow falling between us, except I can see her, and she can't see me. She raised her arms above her head, stretching.

Well, the weather outside is frightful, and the fire is so delightful. . . . That's what popped into mind as I stood there, looking out the window. A song my mother used to sing. Little Eliot comes home in his loden coat with the hood up, stomping my boots in the entryway, shaking the snow from the hood and shoulders of my coat, and the warm wave of Toll House cookies baking in the oven, that smell engulfs me along with the general cheerful warmth of my wonderful house, and my beautiful mother is singing, Let it snow, let it snow, let it snow. Was there a happier child in the world at that moment? The answer is no. No child could have been happier than Eliot Singer at that moment. That's what we can do, the wide-awake neighbor and I, we can bake Toll House cookies. What an idea! We can have the time of our lives making them, and eating them. We'll save some for the salesman when he gets home, a surprise, and I will give some to the Boomfells, who were sound asleep upstairs in their sane marriage bed. I was excited. I pulled on my sweater and shoes, humming with anticipation, but the next time I looked, Holly had moved from the window. I was sure she wouldn't have chocolate chips or walnuts or baking powder. I'd go over to bake cookies with the neighbor in her nightgown at three in the morning, and some ingredient would be missing. The Toll House cookies would never happen, yet all the ingredients for some fly-by-night fucking around would then be present. I repressed my impulse to run next door to bake cookies. Are you proud of me, Charles? I've had my fill of reckless encounters. That was my thinking. You can't go tampering with an impressionable neighbor during your weekend reunion with the Boomfells. Honestly, it was like a tiny turning point. I didn't have to go bother the newlywed in her monogrammed nightgown just because she happened to be awake, watching the snowfall. Her husband, the salesman, tomorrow he'll enter his living room and everything will look just the way he left it, just as he expects it to look. Eliot Singer won't be sitting in the middle of it, changing the appearance of everything.

Let it snow, let it snow, let it snow. Rosy-cheeked and bright-eyed, I'd step into the cookie-scented kitchen of our town house on Sixty-seventh Street and my aproned mother would surround me with a hug. Isn't the snow beautiful? Look what I have for you. Do you want milk or hot chocolate? Milk, Charles Boomfell. I wanted milk. She didn't want to destroy me, she loved me. Toll House is also Alex's favorite cookie. Did he have a choice? My son, he'll never be as happy as I was as a kid. I laid back on the couch. Sleep, sleep, sleep, I chanted to myself, but the more consciously I made the effort to sleep, the less likely sleep became.

I was exhausted and wide-awake. Empty and full. Holly under her nightgown, Alex snug in his bed, Lucky flat on her back in the abortion clinic, Eliot curled up like a fetus on the Boomfell couch unable to sleep while the Boomfells slept like babies right over my head. The idea of everything made the idea of sleep impossible. It must have been four A.M. My prick felt like a pathetic appendage, dispensable as my appendix. I heard footsteps on the stairs and closed my eyes. It was Val, of course, not you. She stopped when she saw me on the couch, and proceeded to tiptoe across the room toward the kitchen. Val? I said, lifting my head. To make a long story short, Charles, she allowed me to rest my head in her lap, the terry cloth pillow of her nice lap. Like magic, I fell asleep, fast and deep asleep. Then daylight, the aroma of coffee like a whiff of forgiveness, the world out the window like brand-new. Val was cutting up fruit in the kitchen, whipping up waffles in your yellow bathrobe. Golden waffles with Grade A maple syrup. Pale amber. At that moment I loved your wife, Charles Boomfell, this marvelous woman cracking eggs in a bowl, giving orders, telling Eliot to get out two plates, plug in the waffle iron, hardly aware that I was present, really. A dependable woman engaged in the serious business of breakfast. Valencia, that was my name for her in the other life. Not Val—Valencia. Here she was in her kitchen, ten years later. I hadn't thought that name—Valencia—until just then. Our old life, Charles, it's like light-years ago, isn't it? What a marvelous person, I'm thinking, sitting at your kitchen table, watching your wife whip up waffles in her clear efficient way, and it hits me. Valencia! The name had started out as a joke between us, which grew more and more serious, until it finally lost all its original humor. It was her early-morning demeanor, I suppose, her disheveled unguardedness and efficiency as she broke the eggs and ordered me around that made me think of it. The same person she ever was, you know. Val is so solid, Charles, so thoroughly herself and no one but herself. That's what I love about her. That's what I love about Astrid—her sanity. Somebody has to be sane. Astrid is as solid and sane as stone. You need that. I don't know if you can live without it. I know that I couldn't live with it, though. Astrid's solid sanity and goodness was impossible. Jesus, Charles, it's a beautiful day. First a wonderful breakfast prepared by your excellent wife. And now, here we are driving out into the middle of snow-covered nowhere. Perfect. Just what the doctor ordered. I was damned lucky they had my size at the Ski Haus, wasn't I? You and Val, you've both been far more generous than I had any reason to expect. The way you've come through this weekend, the concern and patience you've lavished on me . . . Most people wouldn't put up with Eliot for five minutes, let's face it. I won't make a speech, but believe me, I'm moved. You have no idea. Are we here? Yes, Charles, let's open the lungs, disturb the blood. Sven and Hans, ve ski now, ya?

Silence. The narrow unused logging road, canopied over by snow-laden hemlocks, was a welcome white tunnel of silence, except for the hushed thrust of his skis in the undisturbed snow, and the wind that intermittently gusted overhead, above the tall trees of the woods. He named them as he went: pine, hemlock, oak, maple, birch, beech. Valencia! Every other tree was Valencia. At the top of the first climb he stopped to wait, and the muted thudding of his heart, too loud and rapid, filled his ears. Slow down. A chickadee in the upper branches of a dying ash—chickadeedeedee—heightened the surrounding stillness. Into this peace and quiet, like the dogged approach of a disturbed ghost, came the slapstick clatter of Singer's struggle as he fought his way up the slight grade, a relative newcomer, as it turned out, to cross-country skiing. When he came into view—black running suit, the dark blue tam that belonged to Val, the red mittens Ruth had knit for her father the winter before—Boomfell pushed on.

At the bottom of the first exhilarating downhill run, he waited again. Singer waved to him from the top, sweeping a ski pole in a wide arc. When he shoved off, you had to smile. He gave out an unexpected hoot as he gathered speed in the track Boomfell had made. Where the hill took an added dip, giving a boost of acceleration before leveling out, Singer lost it, tumbling ass over tea kettle in an explosive burst of snow. At that moment Boomfell was fond of him. The brittle fluttering leaves of a young beech, caught in a sudden breeze, sounded like a smattering of applause.

"Are you all right?"

Tangled up in skis and poles, a tall man caught in a trap, Singer didn't answer.

He took a beating the whole way, falling a half dozen times before they reached Graves' Hill, their turnaround point. Twice the skis slipped out from under him on the uphill, maddeningly. Two of the downhill falls hurt, Singer wildly out of control, a result of dangerous recklessness in his case, rather than overcaution, which typically tripped up newcomers to the sport.

"Snowplow," Boomfell urged. "For Christ's sake, Eliot, you want to go home in pieces?"

Singer slowly hoisted himself to his feet and slapped snow from his clothing. "My big brother would have been dead an hour ago. David dead in the snow with a stopped heart. It's a tribute to my way of life that I can do this at all. Do you think so?"

The casts visibly bulged like the arms of Popeye under the snug sleeves of his running jacket. What sort of a tribute did they represent to his way of life? In the heat of the moment that irony had evidently escaped him. "How do your arms feel?" Boomfell asked pointedly, although Singer had already assured him that his wrists had healed enough to stand the stress of the activity. The casts were scheduled to come off on Monday.

"I'm healing, Charles Boomfell. This is why I came."

The view from Graves' Hill made the long trek to the top worthwhile: a panorama of distant New England hills with a town in the foreground—water tower, steeple, a cluster of buildings—like a tenuous outpost in an inhospitable wilderness. Behind him Singer was a solitary black figure on a white field. Valencia! A joke that had become serious. When he finally reached Boomfell, he was breathing hard. He'd shed the tam and mittens. His brow was beaded with sweat, the back of his jacket was wet through, and Singer's long gloomy face, though bright pink, looked tired.

"Mankind," he said, gesturing with his pole to the scene before them. "Look at mankind, the big deal." A moment later he said, "I just want it to end."

The long haul back became work. Singer fell twice more and stayed down longer. At various points Boomfell continued to wait for him to catch up, then they pushed on without speaking. At last, just before dusk, they came to the top of the first long hill they had climbed almost two and a half hours earlier. Boomfell reviewed the precipitous descent, the way the road dropped sharply to the left, then swung to the right before the fast straight drop to the town road where they'd left the car.

"Bend your knees, will you? And maintain control. Snowplow!"

"Go, Sven," said Singer wearily. "Hans vill come behind you, don't vurry."

Soon after Boomfell reached the bottom, Singer's attacking howl, more like a man going over a cliff, startled him. Singer came hurtling down the final shoot of the narrow tree-lined trail like an upright piano strapped to a sled. No snowplowing, no attempt to control his speed. He wavered fatefully, the poles jutting awkwardly askew at his sides. Disaster, that's all. But—why?—he didn't fall. As he coasted toward Boomfell, he displayed an exaggerated grin, the lower teeth enlisted for effect. The very grin, Boomfell recalled, that had formerly punctuated a Singer goal in a pickup game of soccer, or an overhead smash deep to Boomfell's backhand. It was the very grin the scholar once had sported as he crossed home plate on the strength of his own home run. Maniacal.

Myth of the Golden Age!

"Glorious," he shouted as he glided toward Boomfell, his arms flung wide. "Glorious."

Unprepared for a hug from Singer, Boomfell was caught short, his arms pinned to his sides.

"It's over. Good-bye, that's what I was thinking as I hauled my ass up that last frozen hill, the heart churning. Good-bye good-bye good-bye. Coming down, I knew. I didn't fall, I stayed up, Charles Boomfell, and it was very clear. It's over."

On North Cummington Road, as they entered an alley of sugar maples, a buck leapt before Boomfell's lights, clearing the stone wall, the tail on it a white plume.

Singer groaned as if he'd been struck in the gut. "It's over. But O the heavy change, now thou art gone, now thou art gone, and never must return!"

Which struck Boomfell funny. "What's that from?"

"Where were ye nymphs, Charles, when the remorseless deep closed o'er the head of your loved—"

" 'Lycidas.' "

"Thanks for today. Thanks for busting my ass, Charles Boomfell. Today we were nursed upon the self-same hill, fed the same flock, by fountain, shade, and rill."

Boomfell pointed his finger at him. "You're nuts."

"That's what they say."

At five he tuned to National Public Radio for the evening news. As they drove through the December dark, comfortably bushed from the afternoon outdoors, they discussed issues of the day, exchanging opinions on the present disastrous state of the nation and the globe like men without a care in the world.

In his black turtleneck, and wearing an expression of doom— something like doom—Singer followed the Boomfells into the Plums' brightly lit holiday party like a bear on a chain. He had tagged along because he couldn't face the night alone in the Boomfell house. As Val and Boomfell circulated amongst the guests, Eliot posted himself next to an eight-foot tropical plant in the cathedral-ceilinged living room. For the first hour, each time Boomfell looked, he appeared to be frowning glumly at one person or another who, surely in the partying spirit, had approached him. For a time a small group seemed to have gathered around him, although Eliot didn't seem to be the one talking. Later Boomfell spotted him at the far end of the room, settled in an alcove window seat presumably intended for viewing sunsets, in earnest-looking dialogue, legs crossed and arms folded, with a broad-shouldered blond woman in a black evening dress.

"That's Miriam Gunther," Val said. "Daniel's wife, the emergency room doctor. You know, they're clients, the ones that don't cook, but had to have the six-thousand-dollar restaurant-type six-burner stove."

"Right, your new boyfriend." Val had spent half the evening talking with pale Daniel Gunther, plainly enjoying herself.

"He's a great guy," she said, "he has all these wonderful gory emergency room stories, annals of medicine, he's a riot."

"Is your friend dangerous?" Irene Plum asked them, slightly slurring the second syllable of the last word. "I don't want an incident."

By eleven Eliot turned up at Boomfell's side, ready to leave. The determinedly cheerful people present had gotten to him. "There are so many doctors here somebody should be sick."

On their way out they met Plum, splendid tonight in red cummerbund, his cheeks inflamed from tending the fire, all the excitement, and drink. Boomfell went through the flimflam of introducing the youthful graying urologist to the Milton scholar. Singer excused himself from the ritual of the handshake, and Plum asked him what had happened to his wrists.

"I cut them to ribbons," Singer volunteered, deadpan.

As if his remark had been a wry piece of wit, the urologist laughed.

"That woman," he told them in the car, "the blond shrink

192

with three diamond rings and lipstick on her teeth, she told me that destructive relationships don't end until someone gets destroyed."

"How thoughtful of her," Val said. "She looked as though she was recklessly flirting to me. A psychiatrist out of control."

"I agreed with her," Singer said from the backseat. "But she didn't seem to understand that she was describing all relationships—everyone."

He was patient, his encased arms flat on the kitchen table. Ruth drew one of her exotic flowers on the underside of his left cast, while Ben, biting his lips in concentration, drew a picture of an airplane on the right one. Under the plane he wrote, "Good luck Ben." Val, a fair caricaturist, contributed a tiny version of herself and Charlie, two surprised-looking nudes shyly concealing private parts with hands. Singer studied his decorated arms as if examining indecipherable hieroglyphs, evidently moved. Then, in a space along his left wrist, he wrote, "A fool and his blood are soon parted."

"Look at mankind in a hurry on his jet planes." Outside the entrance to the airline terminal he was reluctant to leave the car. "How can I endure this? I can't breathe on the plane."

"You'll be fine. Call me when you get in. You'd better hurry if you're going to make your flight."

"I feel like a wild animal being led back to captivity. And who is leading me back? Eliot Singer, a civilized fiction, that's who. I shouldn't return, Charles, should I? I should go any-where else in the world."

"No. You live there. You'll be in New York in a few days, right?"

"A week. Seven days. Yes, the wild animal visits New York. That should be a howl. But now I must return to my cage."

"You'd better get going."

"We'll talk soon. I'm not going to thank you again. I've thanked you enough."

"Go. Run."

He didn't hurry. With the overnight bag slung over his shoulder he was a tall lumbering hunchback. He nodded to a black porter, who paused with his trolley of baggage to permit Singer to precede him through the automatic doors. The wild animal returns to captivity! The grandiose hyperbole of the man. Yet as the glass doors of the terminal slid shut, and as Boomfell put his car into gear, that came close to what he felt: an unmanageable burden safely delivered out of his hands. Settled back into the northbound flow of traffic on the interstate, he felt the sudden lightness, the unanticipated exhilaration, of relief.

April

Sunday afternoon I took a break, walked around by the pond, amazed by yesterday's snowfall, the tropical silent greenhouse made me miss Pauline, made me horny even, I had a cup of coffee at the Bookstore Café, I spotted Don on the street in his Icelandic sweater and blue wool hat before he saw me, I cut across the quad and ducked into the museum where I hadn't set foot all year. He'd probably been to the house looking for me. I didn't recognize her from behind, the long forest green coat, her new shorter hair, she stood before that Eakins portrait of the sad handsome older woman, her hands in her coat pockets. Your haircut, I said, I love it, Val. Her eyes were bigger and bluer, she looked younger. Her favorite here was Sargent's small oil of his dining room, the absolutely convincing dinner plates on the table were single deft brushstrokes up close, she'd give anything to be able to do that, she'd taken a painting course in college thinking that would be fun and found out it wasn't, she had no talent. I was afraid Don would suddenly appear in his furry sweater with his hungry face. I accepted a ride back to the house, we talked about the way snowfall made you feel, I invited her in, Sue and Ellen were in Boston, I said, and Mac had taken a pack of kids skiing. She wasn't in a hurry to get home, she was treating herself to a whole afternoon of doing as she pleased. She liked the tall ceilings, for example, Mac's kitchen cabinets, the Victorian detailing around doors and windows. We went to my room on the third floor. You can do this stuff? she asked, reading the titles of textbooks. I was still getting required courses out of the way, physics, chemistry, biochemistry, my microbial genetics, but what I was looking forward to, I volunteered, was virology and immunology. I can do it, I said. I'd brought along two wineglasses and a large bottle three-quarters full of the house red, Sebastiani zinfandel. Maybe my hand shook pouring it. She sat in my new stuffed chair, Barbie pink, stained and faded, but really comfortable. I assumed a cross-legged position on my bed, facing her. I couldn't believe Val was in my room. It was cozy up here in the treetops, she said, looking out the dormer window. The weird original art, I informed her, was by Pauline, who was going to be the real thing someday, the large unrecognizable earth mother nude was me, could she tell? She asked about the framed photographs near her on my desk. The black-and-white picture was my mother age twenty in her beautiful bare shoulders, the brand-new baby she was nursing was me, naturally, we were living in Boston at the time, I loved that picture. It's wonderful, Val said. The other photograph was one I took of my mother on the windy beach in San Francisco two years ago, October, just one week after she'd learned she had breast cancer, I liked it because she looked so determined and brave, it captured her. Val said something offhandedly stupid like, So now she's all right? She'd known so many women who had had . . . I realized she didn't know anything about it. I was here at school my junior year, I said, living in a dorm, all excited about my liberal arts courses, dance, for example, Mom said she'd discovered a lump in her breast, she was going to have an aspiration done, no big deal, ninety percent turned out to be cysts. When the aspiration wasn't conclusive, I remember joking with Pauline that my mother was becoming a hypochondriac over this lump. She called the night before her needle biopsy, she was nervous, which made me nervous. Mother, you don't have breast cancer, I said, forget it, and she said, I know I don't. She was very calm when she called me with the results a couple of days later. I didn't know squat about cancer, I read the section in *Our Bodies, Ourselves*, which showed me the scary tip of the iceberg, everything was suddenly different, going to sleep and waking up was frightening, impossible things could happen, cancer happened. I was afraid to think the word *death* as though thinking it could bring it about. I thought, Okay, we'll do what we have to do, you'll be all right. Am I boring you? I asked Val. She shook her head no, holding her wineglass in her lap with both hands. At the airport she looked the same as ever, of course, we chattered away and carried on, we drove through the park with all its healthy beautiful people, we walked on the beach, people were surfing, I took that picture. If it had just been an ordinary day, I never would have taken her picture, we knew this was a special moment, a point of no return. That night I went into her room and got in bed with her for the first time since I was seven probably and went to pieces. She'd already been through that, the shock, she comforted me, she guided my fingers to the lump in her breast and said, It doesn't seem like a big deal, does it? Val had taken the more recent picture of my mother from the desk, she was looking at it closely. What's your mother's name? she asked. We entered the overcrowded underworld of cancer, which no one quite knows about until forced into it. You're not alone is one emotion when you see so many people suffering too, then you go back outside and you are alone, you get home and shut the door and you're completely alone. I could only guess what it was like for my mother, although we talked a lot. The surgeon was a joker, upbeat, aggressive, everything was a piece of cake for him, he wore impeccable clothes and tasseled loafers. My mother didn't want him to do it, but the oncologist insisted that he was the best, finally you have to believe in somebody even though it still might not feel right. If the disease was systemic, the total mastectomy was pointless. What do you do when the best people tell you it has to be a total mastectomy and it has to be right away? They know everything, you don't know anything. Where did the cancer come from? Why do I have it? No one would entertain those questions, nothing was more irrelevant than those questions. They know everything compared to what you know, but they don't know enough to speculate on the most important questions. We had to trust them. She felt fine, that was part of the weirdness, she had to believe in her illness, and part of her couldn't believe it—cancer—I don't think she ever believed it at some level, I know she still wonders maybe she didn't have to lose her breast. At seven in the morning we were herded down the corridor to the surgery prep area like sheep going to slaughter, that's how I felt. She was brave, but when I had to leave her she didn't want to let go of my hand, her eyes were frightened. The surgery waiting room was packed with anxious people, the surgeon, Hinkle, came out in his alien green surgeon's outfit and took me aside, he thought everything went well, the lymph nodes looked good to him, he smiled, he looked pale and tired rather than pink and successful. I asked him if she was going to be all right now, I knew it was a stupid question. The cancer in her breast was gone, he said, which almost seemed like a joke, but it was an honest answer. I wanted to be hugged, that's what I really wanted from him. She looked childlike to me in her hospital bed. It hurts, she said, and she kept repeating that in her drugged voice, she needed me as much as I needed her. Val had put the framed photograph back on the desk, and now took the black-and-white snapshot to look at it more closely. It isn't fair, she said. There was no evidence the cancer had metastasized, we decided she didn't want her body subjected to toxic chemicals, that was her decision, we didn't know if it was the right decision, no one knew, it had only been two years, but it was over as far as we were concerned. My mother began exercising regularly, she became intense about her diet, she worked hard, she meditated, she made up her mind to be as happy as possible, life had become so important and serious and scary it became necessary to be as happy as possible. I didn't want to return to school, I took a job in a restaurant. At the beginning of the spring semester I signed up for courses in calculus and general chemistry at a local college, I'd never taken calculus or chemistry in high school, and guess what, I discovered I had an aptitude for that sort of thing, I was quick, so when I returned here—we both wanted me to take my degree here—I decided on microbiology, my mother's doctors were okay, but I can do better, that's the plan. Val smiled, but in a good way. Most of the bottle of wine was gone, it was dark outside, Charlie would be wondering where she was. Back from skiing, Mac was in the kitchen in his knickers making lentil soup, So this is the extraordinary Val, he said, grinning, I could have killed him. At the door, Val said she'd had a wonderful afternoon, she'd love to have me over before I went home for the long holiday, although things got pretty wild just before Christmas, then maybe because of what I'd said about Hinkle, and because she was half-drunk like me, she leaned forward and hugged me. I called my mother in San Francisco. I told her we'd had a wonderful snowfall, Val had come over, we'd spent the afternoon talking, I'd told her the whole story of the cancer, I thought Val really listened, but I also felt funny about it, talking about you, I said, I just wanted to call. My mother laughed good-naturedly, Talk about me as much as you want, she said. Are you getting involved with Val? she asked. Mother, come on, I answered, she's a happily married woman with children. I called Don, his wife answered, I asked to speak to Mr. Candy, I'm drunk and horny, I said, come on over and make love to me, make it snappy. Before he arrived, I called Pauline, afraid she wouldn't be home. She was. Love me? I said. She said, To death.

IV.

As the holidays approached, the real estate business—that is, Boomfell's part in it—slowed down. He spent Monday afternoon walking through a hundred-acre woods with the landowner, Bryce, who dreamed of turning it into an exclusive development of high-priced homes where all residents would have maximum privacy in a beautiful woodland setting. The project was complicated by unknowns, but the possibilities were too great for Boomfell, as possible listing agent, to ignore. The price of land was out of sight. He left Bryce with his thoughts on the most creative planners in the area, the name of a reliable forester, a copy of the state law pertaining to wetlands, and the assurance that if the project went forward come spring, Boomfell would like to be involved. He welcomed the opportunity, he said, to be part of something that would demonstrate the power of imagination more than the everyday power of greed. The landowner, a chiropractor from New Jersey who had inherited the land ten years ago, nodded as though Boomfell had stated the case perfectly. While the afternoon with Bryce would probably come to nothing, it gave Boomfell the feeling that he'd done a day's work.

Eileen Salter called to say they were taking their house off the market. We both love the place so much, she explained. It's packed to the rafters with memories, especially at this time of year. Her voice had the definite ring, the intense cheerfulness, of a woman who was kidding herself. Boomfell wished her the best.

Tuesday afternoon he learned that an agent from Perkins, Odyssey's main competitor, had a buyer for Eichenberg's glassy contemporary house. Boomfell stood to make his modest piece of the action. Otherwise, he was happy to be done with those two.

By Tuesday night he was surprised they hadn't heard from Singer. On the one hand, you couldn't wait to get rid of him. It had been like having Raskolnikov around after he'd axed the old lady. On the other hand, you'd think he'd be considerate enough—courteous enough, Val—to let them know what was happening after they'd put up with his crap for over seventy-two hours.

"Why would you expect Eliot to be considerate, Charlie? That's hardly his style."

"He said he might drop by after New York—sometime after New Year's."

"Spare me."

"You seemed to enjoy having him around. You were downright gracious."

"How did you expect me to behave? You invited him."

"Maybe he didn't have to sleep with his head in your lap. That may have been beyond the call of duty. What was it, four in the morning?"

"He told you that? That he slept with his head in my lap?"

"Just a detail. In passing."

"I'm surprised you'd even bring it up, Charlie. He asked me to sit with him so he could get some sleep. You know exactly how that happened. He gave me a back rub too, remember?"

"I'm just surprised at your attitude. Here he's sleeping with the head in the lap, and on the other hand, spare me, you never want to see him again."

"I'm sure we won't see him again."

"Why not?"

"We just won't. Will you get the phone please?"

"You're standing right next to it."

"I'm not getting it. Let it ring if you want to."

"What's wrong with the phone? You have a problem with the phone all of a sudden?" he shouted.

She'd already left the room.

"Charles Boomfell, are you sick of Singer? You must be. I wanted to give you an update. The moment I set foot on Canadian soil—guess! I got off the plane, hailed a cab, and for a punitive price I went directly to Lucky's with my prick in my hand. I knew she was in the hospital, but I also knew the hospital would be an impossible struggle, so I went to her house. Our house. I wanted to see it, I guess. Maybe I'd look through a window. There were lights on inside. Who opens the door? Who? The door of fate opens, Charles, and Lucky is standing behind it. That's what I thought at the time. Pale, lonely Lucky, whose brain will turn to dog food if she sets eyes on me before thirty days have passed. We don't even talk. Her little girl wasn't there because Lucky had just gotten out of the hospital and was still supposed to be resting. The little girl was with Andrew learning to be a whining little fascist junk collector. We don't talk, Charles, we just fuck like two demented deaf-mutes whose only language is the language of fucking. I spent the night with her. Can you imagine?"

"No," Boomfell interjected.

"The next morning—yesterday—I went to have my casts removed, and everything became clear, clearer than ever before. The removal of the casts was more disturbing than I'd foreseen. Profoundly disturbing. I saw what I'd done to myself, Charles Boomfell. The ugly hurtful wounds I'd inflicted. My arms! I wasn't prepared for the sight of them—pale weak arms lacerated with tender scar tissue all sewn together with black thread. It repelled me. I returned to my hovel depressed and agitated. There was nothing I could do but look out the window or lie on my bed. I was drifting to the bottom like the *Titanic*, Charles, I was afraid I wouldn't be able to get off the bed—ever. Do you know what that's like? Quick, I called Lucky. She came promptly, zipping through the dark streets of the city in her little car with her pale face and her messy hair. I told her it couldn't go on. It's over, those were my exact words. I'd visited my friend Charles Boomfell, I'd gone skiing, I'd had the casts removed, and at last it was over. The end."

"And?" Boomfell asked.

"She left. In her black boots from France and her Italian leather jacket and her long snug skirt. Charles, the relief. The sickness has passed. It's quite unbelievable. Today I straightened out the hovel—Eliot the housekeeper—I threw out garbage and did dishes, I made the bed and swept the floor. Everything. I went to the post office, I went and sat in my office with all my sad books, I wrote copiously in my notebook. This afternoon I took a long walk, all the way to the river and back. I have been alone all day, and I'm alone now, completely alone, and I feel fine. Do you know what I'm doing right now?"

"What?"

"Reading a book! How long has it been since I've read a book? The joy of reading, Charles Boomfell, I'd forgotten. Just you and this compact object of paper and glue—a private complete world. Ruffle the beautiful pages! Smell! The excitement of page one, Charles. I ask myself, where have I been? Eliot had stopped reading. I look at my arms and say, Who did this? Alex and Nicole and Astrid, especially Astrid, what I've put them through, it's frightening. What I've put myself through, Charles."

"But now it's over, right?" said Boomfell by way of encouragement. "That's good news, Eliot."

"Completely over, Charles. Lucky—it's so clear to me—she's a little girl. I simply overwhelmed her, everything overwhelmed her. But how did I in turn become overwhelmed?

The whole thing baffles me. But now, tonight, the relief is visceral. I can feel it when I breathe. I haven't breathed for months. Ask me what I'm doing this evening, Charles."

"You're going to a movie," he guessed, seizing upon that as an expression of normality.

"I'm about to take two lamb chops out of the broiler. We have carrots, a baked potato, a small loaf of sourdough from my favorite bakery, a '78 bottle of merlot from Bulgaria. We have a square meal. No movies. I haven't been to a movie in years. I hate actors, for one thing. I will read, and then to bed. Like Pepys, a calm complacent citizen."

"I'll drink to that."

"It's a wonderful feeling, Charles Boomfell. You played your part. And now the lamb chops, I don't want to overdo them. Hello to everyone. We'll talk soon."

"Take care, Eliot."

Astrid's number was written in purple ink under Singer's name. He listened to the mysterious connections snap into place that would cast his voice to Canada, and bring the voice of Astrid Singer to Boomfell. When he heard the somewhat muffled foreign ring of her distant phone, his body tensed. He swallowed, an anticipatory gulp, as his excitement took him by surprise. It was a little past ten.

"I'm sorry, please repeat your name." When he gave his name a second time, she said, "Yes, hello." The tone of her reception was disappointing. She had not been waiting this past month to hear from Charles Boomfell.

"I saw Eliot this weekend. Did you know about that?"
She didn't.

He succinctly sketched a general picture of the visit, the improvement he thought he'd seen in Eliot between the time he'd arrived and his departure on Sunday, then promptly came to the point of his phone call, the encouraging news Eliot had shared with him earlier that evening: the end of Lucky. "He sounded very convincing about it. He can breathe again, he said. He sounded tremendously relieved."

Boomfell's glad tidings elicited long seconds of silence from his listener on the other end—someone he'd never laid eyes on, speaking to him from a place he'd never been. He saw his mistake.

"I realize you must be tired as hell of all this. It simply seemed like very encouraging news. I wanted to let you know."

"Mr. Boomfell—"

"Charles," he reminded her.

"I'm sorry, but this thinking is naive. I'm sure it is not the end of Lucky. Anyway you're right, I'm very tired of the whole story of Eliot. He was here last night. He wanted to see the children. Alex. Of course Alex had to go to bed in order to get up for school. Eliot should have come earlier to see Alex, but he doesn't think of that. Never mind. He said nothing about endings. The casts were gone. He looked tired and sad. We argued stupidly about when he should see Alex. That was last night."

"He didn't mention that to me."

"It wasn't important to mention to you."

"I won't keep you up. I just wanted to touch bases."

"I'm sorry, touch . . . ?"

"I guess we'll just have to wait and see."

"You wanted to be helpful. I understand. Thank you for calling."

They said good night. The excitement he'd felt as he dialed her number had become a numbing fatigue. He was certain that his meddlesome phone call marked a turning point—the end of Astrid. They'd spoken together for the last time.

Tonight Singer was reading! He wished he had thought to ask him what the book was.

. . . . . .

The *Valley Weekly* came out on Wednesdays. Lo and behold, the New World Trio appeared in bold caps halfway down the lengthy list of musical events. Notable women's trio . . . toured internationally . . . program of baroque . . . Blakely Recital Hall, Saturday, December 20, 8:00 P.M. Blakely, that was Boomfell's own backyard! Wanda Gwertz and Eliot Singer descending on him simultaneously from almost ten years ago. Boomfell revisited! The fact that he'd stumbled upon the event at all—that he'd heard her name mentioned on the radio, that Singer had flown from Canada with the phrase "New World Trio" on his lips only the week before—the force of the coincidence urged him not to ignore it. He should attend the concert. But when he tried to imagine himself stalking backstage, presenting himself before the unsuspecting woman like an assassin, he balked. Wanda Gwertz didn't know Boomfell existed here. Leave it at that.

Ruth's Christmas concert, in which his dazzling daughter accompanied dark short Jane Yasuho in a quite convincing performance of the Corelli Christmas Concerto, took place Thursday night. Afterward, in the festive perfume-scented lobby of the church, hung with pine boughs and echoing with the hubbub of holiday good wishes, a tall woman, unknown to Boomfell, lunged toward Ruth just as he was helping her into her red wool coat.

"I must congratulate you on a most impressive performance indeed." The woman was English. "Anne Hastings," she informed them, and shot her hand out first to Ruth, then to Boomfell. Her brisk grip, thin but firm, caught only his fingers rather than his whole eager hand. "I'm sick to death of all these damned holiday things, to be frank, but this one has been a pleasant surprise. I've promised our mutual friend Eliot Singer that I would ring up the Boomfells, and I positively intend to do it the minute I return from a very needed R and R with my very ancient aunt and uncle in London. Isn't Eliot full of surprises? Those mummified arms of his. Good heavens." She grinned. Above her cape-like outer garment her narrow face was pallid, the day's makeup worn off. She had small imperfect teeth and an imposingly large nose. Her dark put-up hair had here and there come undone. She spoke as though speaking were a race. "I'd love to just flop somewhere and chat, but I have a late supper for my poor neglected urchin to prepare—this is my Gillian—and shitloads of dreary papers to read. It's been lovely meeting you. I'm starved for company in this vast friendly country of yours. I do hope we'll see you soon. Have a merry."

Before he or Val could do more than nod and smile in response, she was off, the arm holding her handbag partly upraised as she made her way through the boisterous music crowd. Her daughter, a stout girl in a navy blue coat and a red tam, was close behind her.

Hasty Pudding. Astrid Singer's best friend.

Acidly Val said, "Wasn't that nice of Eliot?"

Outside, a light dusting of snow.

Late Friday afternoon Louis Weisman informed him that Simpson had made an offer on the Reed place through Jane Kahn, Odyssey's star earner. Not only the house and ten acres, but the land, too, over two hundred acres that had been listed separately. Simpson the art thief, vile in his fur coat, he was going to become a gentleman farmer. He'd decided he wanted to see glossy black Angus embellishing the pastures outside his windows.

Fool! You fool, Boomfell! He didn't deserve to go on living, that was the feeling as he drove home to his patient hopeful family. Tonight they were planning to set up the tree. The sale of the entire Reed spread, what a surprise present that might have been.

Wanda Gwertz in the town where he lived—the difficult idea dogged his steps most of the day as he and Val, searching for last-minute gifts for their children, plowed through throngs of shoppers engaged in the same craziness. The rehabilitated downtown, five stories tall, if viewed from a casual visitor's perspective, hardly looked like the ideal place to live that Boomfell, for years now, had taken it to be. This "rural city" whose unique blend of colleges, agricultural countryside, and reborn mill town had attracted a lively mix of young entrepreneurs, healers, artists, and academics, all seeking an alternative to urban stress, homogeneous suburban sprawl, as well as the impoverishment and punishing isolation of more distant boondocks—today it looked to Boomfell like small potatoes.

Twice he was sure he spotted her—a woman sipping coffee, a woman at a cosmetic counter—but in each case the blond possibility turned out to be at least ten years too young. Did Singer say she had dyed her hair black?

New World Trio. Blakely Recital Hall. 8:00 P.M.

Impossible! Suppose she spotted him suddenly sticking out of her audience like a bad dream. What a drag! Or afterward, say, long-gone Boomfell stepping up to blunt her postperformance high with his half-forgotten face. It was the sheerest chance that the event had come to his attention at all. Yet how could he fail to go?

At the end of the day, the shopping done, they awarded themselves Chinese food at Panda West, and didn't get home until after seven. Ben reminded them that tonight's TV special, starring Scrooge, was starting at eight. They'd anticipated Dickens's classic for more than a week now—the whole family, plus Ruth's friend Lisa, bundled up on the couch with bowls of popcorn, the fire going, everything.

What in fact would be the point of running over to Blakely Recital Hall to sit in the back row like a voyeur? Wanda Gwertz, whoever she had become in the last ten years, wasn't in town to see Boomfell. The truth was, he told himself, trading shoes for slippers in the mud room, he didn't want to go. He didn't need to go. He would not be missed.

As he entered the room where his family had already arranged themselves for the show, he felt like a man dodging into a doorway to avoid a familiar face coming down the street.

Sunday he avoided the *Times*, which Val had gone out and bought before breakfast. The front page, Business, Arts & Leisure, the Book Review, Travel: guilty of avoidance on all counts. He prepared a breakfast of bacon and eggs. Bacon: guilty of four slices. Ruth wanted him to look over a rough draft of her psychology paper. He'd been looking over his daughter's shoulder since grammar school, overly anxious that she do well, eager to make a positive contribution to her development as a thinking person. Sunday he couldn't face her essay, that's all there was to it. Ruth became assertive: Fine, she thought he wanted to read it, she wouldn't bother to ask him again. Child abuse, guilty on numerous counts, probably, although it might be decades before the verdict came in. He began a game of computer chess, one of Ben's unused Christmas presents last year, and quit when he foresaw the inevitable defeat level four had in store for him. He attempted to finish the long article he'd been reading in *The New Yorker*, but found himself rereading passages, unable to follow the thread. Val, meanwhile, had made three loaves of Grandma Welsh's fruitcake, an offering her assembled family expected her to deliver each Christmas. She made two large jars of cranberry relish. She and Ben arranged a red-ribboned spray of pine boughs, complete with pinecones, and tacked it to the back door. By afternoon she, Ben, and Ruth, too, were ready to drive to the Long Barn Christmas Shop to choose this year's special ornament for their tree. Boomfell refused to go along. "Let the old shit stay home," Val said. "Yeah, Dad, let the old shit stay home," Ben added merrily.

Boomfell roused himself and went off for a run, his familiar five-mile figure eight through the neighborhood. That had become increasingly difficult to fit into his schedule this year, ever since they'd turned the clocks back. The exercise gave a lift—not a thought in his head, basically, for five miles. Minutes after he returned he was startled by a forceful rapping at the front door—relax, for crying out loud, the most everyday occurrences had the power to startle him these days—which turned out to be the April he'd been hearing about lately from Val, a face you kept looking at, Val said, plus brains, balls, and determination, just really something, but he'd figured college girl, they were all beautiful now, nothing Val told him had prepared him for the young woman's appeal. She was dressed for out West today, a weathered cowboy hat, boots that made her damn near his height, jeans as faded as that folk song, a chocolate waist-length suede jacket. Her handshake was serious, her look was through-you, she was all business delivering her package, she didn't smile. She hoped it was something they could use, she said, and jumped backward off the front step, turning on her heel, and leaving Boomfell, endorphins already aroused by his run, stirred up, disturbed.

"I told you," Val said later, "she's like new blood. I want her around, I want to be around her, she picks me up."

"So let's get to know her," Boomfell agreed. "Get her over here."

Ruth took charge of April's unexpected package, she placed it under the tree and forbade anyone to touch it, that included her mother, who kept wondering out loud what the present for everyone could be.

April

Marjorie and Eleanor were still dressed up at noon, they looked beautiful, I told them and meant it, Marjorie in a green wool suit with a matching little velvet hat, and Eleanor in a navy blue dress with a white collar and pearls, they'd been taken to the Episcopal church by one of the pillars of the community, Marjorie said, the choir was thrilling, but she couldn't figure out what the minister was trying to say, what in the world did she care about Palestine. I'd dropped in to say merry Christmas and to let them know that Val had arranged to have someone else clean the house for the next three weeks while I was in California. Marjorie said, I hope we're alive when you get back. Eleanor said she'd always wanted to see California, the redwoods. I brought them Don's poinsettia and a small tin box of Scottish shortbread, which they made a fuss about. I couldn't stay for tea. Eleanor said, Now wait a minute, dear, she shuffled to her bedroom with her cane, she shuffled back. With knotty disfigured hands, she pressed an ivory cameo brooch into my palm, a woman's head in profile, a bird in her hair, my heart beat faster, I couldn't take it, I said, I just couldn't. I couldn't tell if the gift was spontaneous on Eleanor's part, or planned. It was meant for a young woman, she said, her mother had given it to her when she turned twenty-one, the pin had been sitting in her drawer so long it made her nervous. I wouldn't feel right, I said, you'll miss it. Eleanor said, It's only an old brooch, dear, but we wanted our favorite person to have it. I told them I'd treasure it, I'd wear it all the

212

time, I kissed them both, I wished I'd refused, I couldn't refuse, I was afraid for them. I'd decided to give Val a full body massage by Haleya Priest for Christmas, Bliss Come True, I wrote in the O'Keeffe card that I'd chosen to contain the gift certificate, laying it on thick. I had rewarded myself with a full body massage following my last exam Friday, the brilliant New Age hands of Haleya Priest felt like revelation, they knowingly undid the concentrated tension my body had accumulated through the week, I felt open, peaceful, whole, my body hummed from head to toe by the time she was done with me, Yes, I thought, that's what I want to give her. But I'd missed her on Friday, I wanted to see her before I left for the Coast, I just wanted to see her, I drove to her house with a wrapped present for the whole family. Val wasn't home, her husband, Charlie, opened the door ready to jump down my throat, he was layered in green-and-purple rugby shirt over turtleneck, blue-and-white-striped shorts over red long underwear, an orange hat pulled over his ears, his cheeks were bright red patches, he'd been running, Christ, he thought I was that pair of Jehovah's Witnesses, he said, he'd seen them making their way down the street. I identified myself, I thrust my package at him. April, he said, yes, of course, he said, the premed student from California, he said, come in, Val would be home soon, come in, she'd love to see me, come in. He was overanimated, too eager, I had to go, I immediately regretted the package, which contained a half dozen anatomically correct gingerbread men and women, Ellen and I had made them Saturday night, stoned, listening to old music, primitive male figures savagely hung, opulent female fertility goddesses. Suddenly they seemed like a bad idea, not funny. The premed student from California! What else had she told him about me? She had her husband, her children, her house and garden, she didn't have a life of her own. I regretted the Haleya Priest gift certificate, which I'd already mailed that morning. She had her husband, her children, her house. . . . When I returned to our house,

Mac said, Too bad, I'd just missed the extraordinary Val, she'd come by with her son and her willowy daughter, she'd left this little something for me and my mother, not to be opened until I got to California. The small package was beautifully wrapped with some exquisite flamestitch paper—For April and Delight from Val—I tore it open: a tree ornament, an upright pink pig in a white gown with transparent wings and a gold halo, a pig angel. I forgave her, I forgave her husband, I forgave her children, I forgave her house and garden.

Singer

I'm in a coffee shop on Madison Avenue. Grown men and women in ankle-length fur coats, Charles Boomfell, like all the bears from the Bronx Zoo are on a field trip. Rich people strolling around with loathsome expressions on their spoiled faces as though they were not exactly as invisible and inconsequential as the bag lady curled up on the church steps across the street. The sidewalk is lined with good-looking black men selling shiny watches on cardboard boxes. I keep bumping into young families—like yours or mine—on their holiday weekend, skipping, Charles, skipping with happiness because they are looking at the window displays and eating in the restaurants and sleeping in the hotels of hell on earth. The blind man sticks out like a sore thumb with his cup of pencils and his depressed dog, but it's very funny, Charles Boomfell, because everyone here is blind. That's not why I called. Everyone has been to New York.

I feel about fourteen years old. This is my hometown. All these people and buildings, this is my old neighborhood. I hate it. I don't know why there aren't bombs going off all day long on every block. In front of Cartier, Charles, a car went out of control and plowed into hundreds of people on the sidewalk. Moaning bodies littered the sidewalk with red-and-white-striped bags and gift-wrapped packages scattered around them. My thought was, Why isn't someone swerving onto the sidewalk every five minutes? There are many insane people here, that goes without saying—but most of them act as

215

though they were sane. It's frightening. I squatted by a very old man and held his hand until help arrived. The air was screaming with the approach of many ambulances. They couldn't get through. He was all dressed up in shiny black shoes, his face was white as a sheet. Maybe he broke his hip. He said, Now they're running me over with cars. Imagine! All of New York City was running him over.

Yesterday I got into a cab at the airport and gave the driver my brother's address. He said something about the weather, and I said I didn't want to talk. That upset him. I didn't get out of the cab for two hours. Ulysses Freeman locked me in from the driver's seat. Eliot the hostage. He took me to Harlem, up and down the cold deserted streets of Harlem where groups of men hung out in blank doorways. Whole blocks looked deserted except for the piles of garbage blowing down the street. The ride down FDR Drive was cops and robbers. Ulysses Freeman was reckless, but talented. We went to Brooklyn— flew to Brooklyn. He was in a rage. It amazed me that he could maintain his rage for so long—shouting and threatening and carrying on. It was frightening, of course, but I was also amazingly calm. I think that's why his anger wouldn't subside. The truth was, I didn't really mind. I was in no hurry to get to my brother's. I didn't want to get there at all. And when I finally did get there, Charles—Ulysses Freeman finally took me right to the door, raging the whole time, running red lights, shouting out the window, missing pedestrians by inches—it was much worse than captivity in the cab. Now the real hostage crisis began. My parents were present. They asked about Astrid and the children. I won't bore you with all the sordid details. One of David's neighbors was there—a woman. David had invited her for me, if you can grasp that. She asked me if I wanted to go to her apartment for a nightcap. Eliot's cure. David's children immediately began to drive me crazy. Uncle Eliot, Uncle Eliot, as if I had come to New York to play with them, to play all their games and sing songs in front of the

Christmas tree. Each year Phyllis and David celebrate both Hanukkah and Christmas. I have to stop talking about them. I'm not interested in these people, but when I'm around them I can't stop thinking about them. Their toothbrushes and slippers and newspapers disturb me. Their pills and boxes of cereal and milk cartons. Phyllis is so nice to her children you want to scream. I didn't go home with the neighbor for a nightcap. I spent much of the night looking out the window at the sad sparkling city.

Today I left the house before anyone was up. I walked from Eighty-third Street to the Village, devoured a big omelet with bagel and coffee on the way, then walked back. I won't tell you everything I saw on the way, Charles, but that would make quite an epic poem. If I happened to be a poet, I'd write a mind-blowing epic poem entitled "The Walk," describing everything I saw. It was windy, there were intermittent snowflakes. I was feeling better. I felt nonexistent in a good way. I felt nothing mattered. I decided to go to the van Gogh show after all. My brother had gotten me a surprise ticket to the van Gogh show for today at four o'clock. All mankind wants to see fifteen months' work by our poor friend van Gogh. People are admitted in groups a half hour at a time. I had no intention of going until I'd taken my walk, then I decided it was better to go there than to return to David's townhouse. What was I thinking, Charles? How could David do that to me? How could I go? Saint-Rémy and Auvers. The poor son of a bitch. Here's mankind the art lover—hundreds and hundreds standing ten deep as if spellbound before these paintings. What a cruel joke. All the art lovers smiling blissfully or staring slack-jawed or frowning as if they knew what was going on here. Explaining the paintings to one another, choosing their favorites. He really puts a twist into it, doesn't he, someone said. Everyone loves van Gogh. They wouldn't want him living next door maybe, but hanging on the wall they love him. I wanted to take my headache and my sore back and flee the crowded rooms, but I couldn't tear myself away from the paintings. Looking at the self-portraits, I felt ashamed. Painting after ecstatic painting, as we smile and frown and mutter opinions—our opinions and appreciations—we approach the fact that he shot himself dead at thirty-seven. Look at everyone who gets to live to be seventy, eighty, ninety years old. He didn't die right away, you know. It took three days for him to die. Death was one of his major interests. But only because he loved life, I said to myself, staring at paint. There was the crows-over-wheatfield painting that your neighbor, Holly, has on her living room wall for decoration. That was a bad moment. Everyone leaving the exhibit enters an enormous room filled with books and posters and notepaper and garbage featuring van Gogh this and van Gogh that. The profitable van Gogh religion. He sold a single painting—Theo sold it for practically nothing—during his anguished joyful life. Now mankind shuffles past oohing and aahing, ready to put up millions upon millions for one painting, which he probably did before lunch. Meanwhile, living artists go on starving and dying. Why hasn't some ardent artist-lover walked into the van Gogh show with a bomb strapped to his behind?

Of course, now what I want for Christmas is paints. Twenty-five tubes of white, lots of yellow, ocher, green, blue, red. I want to commit myself to an asylum for a year and paint every one of the paintings van Gogh painted during his long lucid ecstatic periods between breakdowns, then shoot myself in the chest and spend three days dying with friends dropping in, then have my canvases nailed up around my coffin by my brokenhearted brother. The poor son of a bitch, the poor fucking genius, we say, and yet his brief life is also appealing. Of course, no one's going to give Eliot paints for Christmas. I must return to David's and endure the holiday. I must return to Canada and endure the rest of my life. I left the exhibit and walked over here for a cup of coffee and needed to talk to someone—someone, Charles, before returning to my brother's house where there is no one to talk to about anything. Who could I call?

A whole family of Bronx Zoo bears has just walked out of the Ralph Lauren store. Four of them. They shouldn't be allowed on the street. The bag lady has come to her feet. She's talking, Charles, she has something to say. She raises her fist to high heaven, she has something to say, but no one will look at her. Ulysses Freeman, I wish you could have heard him. You don't feel like talking today, man, what the fuck? He hated the rich, the limos passing us, he hated everyone on the highway, all the fuckers, man, who didn't know fucking shit. He hated the buildings and streets of Harlem. Why didn't they drop their fucking bomb on fucking Harlem. His rage became general, all-encompassing. This country is a cunt trying to fuck you over, and you don't feel like talking today, man. You pick the wrong cab, motherfuck. Ulysses Freeman's cab. He was inspired. Of course, I agreed with him. I hear you, I kept repeating, and that only refueled his tirade. I was sure he would run over some poor family from Ohio. He was brilliant behind the wheel. We ended up right in front of David's building. Get your ass out before you get fucking killed, man. And what happens today? Someone actually plows into the crowds on the sidewalk. Now they're running me over, says the old fellow. He never let go of my hand. He was English, neat as a pin with the white mustache, crisp white shirt collar. There's always a bit of good with the bad, he says when they laid him on the stretcher. Now they can't make me go to my daughter's for their bloody Christmas dinner.

The bag lady has returned to her catatonic state on the stone steps. She's homeless, Charles. That's got to be one of the loneliest words in the world. *Homeless.* The old fellow would rather be in the hospital than go to his daughter's, while this homeless lady has no one to talk to but the thin air. I love it. I hate to bother you, Charles. The van Gogh blockbuster was too much excitement on top of everything else. Now I must return to David's town house and be Eliot the wacko brother, Uncle Eliot the unbelievably funny uncle. I must pretend to be Phyllis's brother-in-law and my parents' son. No, it's not easy. It's hard. Hello to Val. No, don't put her on. I can't talk anymore. I must save my energy. David, he's having friends in tonight. He doesn't want to be alone with me. If you have friends over, you don't have to talk to your brother. Snowflakes are falling again. Flurries. Why are snowflakes so beautiful in New York? Is it because they are a reminder of nature, the sudden occurrence of nature in this world of total artificiality? The effect is magical. Alex would love the excitement of snow-flakes in New York. I can't think about him. Alex, Astrid, Nicole, I can't think about them. No, I haven't mentioned Lucky, Charles. You noticed. I haven't mentioned her once, have I? I don't know what that means. I have no idea. I'm not thinking about meaning. Merry Christmas? Oh my God, Charles Boomfell. Christmas morning in my brother's house! Uncle Eliot! Imagine.

The first week of the new year Boomfell saw no point in biding his time at Odyssey. Except for the day he was obligated to take calls and be on duty for the odd walk-in customer, he stayed away from the office. He and Ben went cross-country skiing twice. That felt worthwhile. His son in his sky blue wool hat, the beautiful navy blue knickers, the boy's smile at the end of a good run. At night he read, randomly browsing through centuries of poetry in an old anthology, unless there was something to watch on the tube. At the end of the week a wonderful blizzard struck. The world was canceled. Val suggested they tackle the upstairs bathroom, a project they had been postponing for ages. The rolls of wallpaper were piled on the top shelf of the linen closet. Boomfell accepted the challenge, as good a way as any to seize the obliterated day.

Neither of them had done wallpaper before, not in all the years of their shared domesticity. It soon became clear that it wasn't going to be easy. Handling the wet paper, hanging it straight, cutting and trimming, contending with air bubbles, wrinkles, rips—no, it was a tedious damned business, trickier, more time-consuming than they'd bargained for. By day two they were down each other's throats. He tore one stubborn strip off the wall, crushed it into a sticky ball, and—Valencia!—bounced it off the top of his wife's kerchiefed head. Pushed to her limit by the infuriating corner above the sink, Val threw her scissors into the bathtub rather than, as she laughed later, driving them into her helpmate's heart. There was a predictable sense of satisfaction in the end—the upstairs bathroom had been renewed—but Boomfell was unable to muster his wife's unqualified enthusiasm.

Now it seemed obvious, as he stood before the mirror, framed by the new wallpaper, that too much value, too much of Boomfell, had been wrapped up in this place. It was only a place to live. There had been years and years of projects and chores. At the end of almost three days of wallpapering a bathroom, one week into the new year, he saw more clearly than ever that his labors had been misspent. It was only a *place* to live. Under the guilty pressure of bills to be paid—the extravagance of Christmas, plus another heating bill, plus the monstrous equity loan, plus insurance, the car, damned town taxes, plus plus plus—the discontent signaled by the stint of wallpapering flared into anxiety. All he had failed to live, paying these bills! That was what the striped wallpaper reminded him of: a prison uniform from an old slapstick comedy.

Val went off to her massage by Haleya Priest skeptically, Boomfell observed, the way she'd gone to that homeopath one year for canker sores, or to the crackpot chiropractor that time for the shooting pain in her hip. She'd never had a so-called professional massage, she protested, she was shy about submitting her body to all that hands-on scrutiny. What kind of a name was Haleya Priest anyway? she asked. Her reluctance to offend April, she told him, was the main reason she'd decided to go through with it. But she returned in a daze, her underpants in her purse, her hyperenergy subdued, her smile blissed-out, like a New Age flake, he accused, fresh from a close encounter with a herd of unicorns. She didn't yell when Ben marched salty slush into the kitchen, she asked Boomfell to turn down *All Things Considered*. Her exotic mood largely wore off by the time she had dinner on the table, but the massage, she insisted, had been magic, Haleya Priest was for real. They weren't living right, she told him, there were other ways to live.

April

I was nervous going up to her office, over three weeks felt like a long time, but she told whoever was on the phone that someone had just come in, she'd get back to them. She said, I missed you. We went to Angelica's, which was quiet because most people weren't back yet. She asked about my mother. It looked like Mom and her boyfriend were together again, I said, I was happy for her, she'd followed a lot of false leads where men were concerned, drawn to the political activist type who usually came laid-back without money and turned out to be into himself. I told her about Sue, who had been attacked by some psycho husband at the women's shelter, she had bruises on her neck, the wife in question went back home with the guy New Year's Eve, Ellen wanted to run him over with her car when he came out of his house. I didn't intend all this to be funny, but Val and I laughed, really laughed. Speaking of men, Don was seated at the kitchen table Sunday morning when I came downstairs, talking to Mac about government funding for AIDS research, Eastern Europe's future, etc., I told him I didn't want to be his lover anymore, I'd figured it out on the plane, although I wasn't sure until I saw him again, now I hoped he'd leave me alone. The bad news was that Pauline had decided to go to Jamaica for the winter, escape the dear dirty Boston scene, her brother knew someone with a little grass shack, she'd be back when she got sick of it. I've entered my celibate phase, I said, just as well, it was time I checked in with myself again. Snow flurries arrived outside at dusk to contribute to our mood. I said, Tell me about you, I'm always talking about me, how about Val? What about Val? she said. Okay, how about Val's love life? She was married, she said, remember? Yeah, but . . . She'd been involved with one other man since, years ago, when Charlie was teaching, probably because she knew he was screwing around, number one, everyone was apparently, it was a safe, convenient setup, number two, the man seemed pretty exciting at the time, it went on for more than a year, until it couldn't go on, etc. One lover in over sixteen years, I said, I was smiling, I guess, because she asked, Have I said something funny? She said, What's this lover business, she never would have used the word "lover." She explained how sixteen years passed, from one minor crisis to another, always something more important than anything else, holiday following holiday, children's needs, sixteen years later you didn't know where the time had gone, one trip to Washington, D.C., one trip to Europe, one week in the Caribbean, one trip out West in sixteen years, one so-called affair, but so busy the whole time you couldn't catch your breath, hardly knew how you'd pulled it off, etc. So you're lucky, I said, you were lucky, you married lucky. There was no one at their wedding, she said, except Charlie's repressed homosexual teacher-friend, who tried to talk him out of it, that's where they were coming from. They'd been banished by their families to go off and get the disappointing misfortune over with, no one gave them a snowball's chance, they'd done pretty damn well for themselves, damnit, they were the only ones who knew the whole story—their story—which was one of the things they needed each other for, it wasn't easy, they had each other, that's all there was to it, she wasn't going anywhere, although she'd had a half-assed offer recently, no kidding, not worth discussing, a desperate friend from somewhere, the whole time shredding her napkin into thin strips, pinched bits, with her clean fingers. I couldn't wipe the smile off my face. Is it that funny? she asked. No, I said, no, laughing, I think it's great, I grabbed her hand, I love the whole thing, I was laughing, I'm sorry, I said, you're so serious, I'm not laughing at you, I said, you're great. A bearded man alone with his book was clearly tuned in to us, grinning behind his dumb-ass pipe. Let's get outta here. We agreed to start swimming once a week.

"New York was despair. I tried but failed to get anything out of relatives, parties, buildings, concerts, bookstores, new clothes, restaurants, women, millions and millions of people of all kinds. I tried—you would have been proud of me—but I failed. Eliot received an F in New York. I had a towel stiff with sperm from fantasizing lost love. I threw it away at Kennedy. I won't bore you, Charles, you get the idea. Back in Canada I ran with all my might directly to Lucky the minute I hit town. Someone should have been timing me, at least for the last half mile. To make a short story shorter, we're together again. I'm happy, Charles Boomfell. Can you believe it? We're going to sell her house—our house—and together we're going to buy another house. That's necessary. Are you there? Say something."

"I'm surprised. Flabbergasted. But . . . wonderful, Eliot. Happiness no less."

Quietly, as though sharing a secret, he explained, "You have to know what you want."

"Where are you now?"

"In bed. It's a perfect Sunday afternoon, Charles—dark with flurries outside, and light with blessings inside. Here, would you like to talk to her?"

Before Boomfell could answer—no, God no!—a woman's voice came over the phone. "Hello, Charles Boomfell."

"The real Lucky?"

"The real Lucky."

Say something. "This has been quite an adventure." Groping, he added, "I'm glad things have finally worked out."

"Charles, everything works out." When he didn't reply, she said, "Thanks for your help."

"Keep an eye on him. We're fond of Eliot."

"So am I. Here he is."

"We were lying here in the warm bed of our renewed happiness, Charles, counting blessings, and we wanted to give you a call. Thanks for everything. You and Val, you're an inspiration."

"Don't be silly," Boomfell protested.

"Take this number. Got a pencil? Under Eliot and Lucky—ready?"

He took down the number Singer gave him, quite certain it was not a number he would have reason to call.

"Maybe in February we could come down to see you," Singer suggested. "You should meet—you and Val and Lucky. We could return to Cyrano's. How does that sound?"

"We'd enjoy that. Give us a call."

"Incidentally, I thought of you the other day. I've had a card from Wanda Gwertz. Sent to me at the school. She always sends me a Christmas card, although neither one of us are Christians. She enclosed a copy of her schedule for the next few months."

"No kidding."

"No kidding. She's going to be in Boston—let's see, I've got it right here—yes, the first Sunday in February actually, at the Isabella Stewart Gardner Museum. Her trio. Wanda Gwertz has quite a schedule, Charles. Busy, busy. She's going to be all over the place. I thought I'd let you know, it's so close to you. I went there once when I was in college. I was visiting a girl in Cambridge. Kim Bells! The name just broke in on me. A very wonderful girl in a pleated wool skirt who had read everything ever written by Henry James. She insisted we go to this little museum. It has a courtyard, doesn't it? We used to sleep with each other with our clothes on. Those were the days. Charles, I've got to go. There's a beautiful madwoman pestering me. I wanted you to be the first to hear the news from Canada. Singer is happy. That's tomorrow's headline. Singer is happy."

"I'm glad, Eliot."

"It's very simple, you have to know what you want."

"Is that all?"

In the background he heard the woman call, "Good-bye, Charles Boomfell."

In every word out of her mouth he'd heard the voice, the overwhelming influence, of Eliot Singer. How profoundly disappointing. Everything works out! How disturbing. The news from Canada—Singer is happy—how depressing.

April

She'd never learned to breathe, she sliced through the water with rigid arms as though not to disturb the surface, she could thank her mother for that, she said, trying to swim without splashing. By the end of the hour I had her doing several laps without stopping, with a fairly relaxed efficient motion, a quick learner, delighted with herself, red-eyed, panting, she'd always wanted to be able to swim, really swim. She was less shy in the locker room after the pool than she had been before. We stood side by side in the horizontal mirror over the sinks. Val started laughing, Let's see, shouldn't this be up here, lifting her larger and lower breast to match the other one. Everyone's equal, she said, you call this equality? You have a beautiful body, I told her. Late Sunday afternoon we had the place pretty much to ourselves. Is this good for you? she asked, entering the sauna, she'd never been in one before, it felt a little like a torture chamber, didn't it? She wanted to know the story behind my tattoo, she'd never understood tattoos. Just something I did for fun with a friend once, I said, I didn't want to say Pauline. She talked about her son's recent obsession, carting home library books about dogs, desperate for a dog all of a sudden, she'd love a dog too, but no one was home all day. Ruth had embarked on a quasi-vegetarian phase, no beef, pork, lamb, and now not even chicken, which was getting on Val's nerves, what if she decided to stop eating altogether all of a sudden? What phase are you entering? I asked. She said, Spontaneous combustion, feels like. I described my dream in which my mother and I were climbing a snow-covered mountain, connected by a rope, the rope came undone, she fell sliding down the snowfield out of sight, I couldn't find her, I had to continue to the top against my will. When I reached the summit I went into a small dark hut full of people I recognized, friends of hers, bending over a table, bending over her body. She opened her eyes and smiled when I looked down at her, I'm all right, she said, and when she took her hands off her chest she had both breasts, then I woke up. Val said she used to write her dreams down, years ago during her quest-for-self-knowledge period, now it seemed she couldn't remember them anymore, she was aware of having dreamed but couldn't remember what it was about the next day. Does your mother have a lot of friends? she asked. A gang. I asked her who her friends were, she never talked about them. There were women in her building she had lunch with now and then, she and Charlie saw certain couples every so often, but friendships had become superficial, merely social, rather than vital, she hadn't had what you'd call a close friend, the best friend, for years now. Divorce had definitely taken its toll, people had moved away, everyone got older and more resigned to their differences, work and family didn't leave much time for much else, but she definitely missed that, a real friend, life was weird. I had stretched out on my back on the top bench of the sauna, my folded towel under my head, Val sat against the adjacent wall, I closed my eyes. The heavy close heat was always almost too much until you started to sweat. Copious sweating was one of the things I liked about myself in the sauna, spreading small pools of it upward over breasts, neck, face, and down over pelvis, thighs, Hmm, I hummed, doesn't this feel great, a kind of cleansing release, pure sweating, kindness to nipples, kindness to vagina, as Ginsberg says, as though all the heat here had become concentrated between my legs, cunts are so great, Pauline liked to say, with all their complicated textbook parts, bulbs of vestibule, clitoris, hood of, labia this, labia that, full warm wet. How about this little game you can play with yourself, maybe come without touching, just concentrate, focusing heat plus pressure, kindness to clitoris, kindness to vulva, but not with Val present. She sat with her knees together and her hands flat on the bench on either side of her, head back, like the resigned victim of a sacrificial rite. Let's masturbate, do you mind? Instead I said, I love it when the sweat pours out of me like this. Val stood up, Whew, I think I've had enough. In the shower she said she almost felt guilty, being so nice to herself for a change, wasn't that wacko? She dropped me at the house, she couldn't come in, everyone was waiting for her, Yes, let's do it again.

Val woke him up before it was light outside to describe the girl in the sauna, sweating, rubbing herself down with both hands, into it.

"While you sat there petrified and not sweating, I suppose, Jesus, what time—"

"I became totally aroused, my heart started beating, I was practically dizzy, I'm serious, Charlie, I still feel strange, thinking about it."

"Is that what you had to tell me?"

"Yes."

"So, you think you're a lesbian all of a sudden?"

"No. I'm just telling you what happened."

"Was she getting turned on, the lovely April?"

"She was enjoying the sauna, she's completely uninhibited, I don't know. It wasn't funny, it was erotic."

"When are we having her over?" he asked. "I thought she was coming to dinner."

"Yeah, you'd like that." She was out of bed. It was six-thirty, it was Monday morning, they had to get moving. "She has a tattoo right here," Val said, pointing to a spot on her behind.

"A tattoo of what?"

"I'm not telling you."

When he entered the bathroom moments later, she was standing before the mirror covering her left breast with her left hand. "I think she's infatuated with me," she said, "can you believe that?"

The coat of arms above the main entrance depicted a phoenix rising from ashes, and bore the motto C'EST MON PLAISIR. Who did Isabella Stewart Gardner think she was? He entered at a less forbidding door into a dark anteroom. In the last ten years he had visited the small museum maybe twice—the last time five or six years ago—yet it remained eerily familiar. Whenever he stepped from the dim entrance room to the tile-floored Spanish cloisters, with its medieval sculpture, its plants, Sargent's *El Jaleo* there under the Moorish Arch, he was brought back to his discovery of this place when he was not yet twenty years old, a copy of his hero, William Butler Yeats, in the large pocket of his hooded parka. Nothing here had changed since then. It was Isabella Stewart Gardner's pleasure that her personal museum remain in perpetuity just as she had left it.

He had introduced Valerie Welsh, the girl destined, as it seemed, to become his wife, to his exotic find. The opulent galleries and darkened stairhalls of the interior had inspired many horny Sunday afternoons. From the cool serenity of the cloisters, with its vaulted ceilings and marble columns, you looked into the central courtyard, a glass-roofed quad four stories tall. The marbleized facades of the courtyard were composed of arched Venetian window frames, balustrades, medallions, and stone reliefs. A Venetian fountain at one end provided the peaceful sound of falling water. Palm trees grew in massive terra-cotta pots. A winter afternoon in this light-filled space was a tropical holiday in an ancient higher world.

Valerie Welsh, viewed from below as she stood on one of the balconies in her plaid skirt and white blouse might have been a nymph in transparent gossamer for the satyriasis she aroused in her gawking boyfriend.

That hazy memory, along with memories of another young woman—pasts within pasts—aroused Boomfell now, as he paused in the dimly lighted cloisters again, disturbed by the play of winter sunlight on the old-world walls. Just now he had the Gardner Museum largely to himself, at least the first floor of it. Evidently other visitors had already gathered in the music hall. He scanned the balconies, listening. Evidently the concert had not yet begun, despite the fact that he had arrived intentionally late. Slowly climbing the wide stone staircase to the second floor, he felt like a thief. This was nuts.

A woman without a coat was the only other person in the Dutch Room. She stood near the vivid pair of Holbein portraits. They flanked the doorway that led, he seemed to remember, to the Tapestry Room, where concerts were held. Boomfell crossed the floor to the early Rembrandt of a man and woman in black. The burgher marriage depicted in the painting looked like a pain in the ass. The gentleman's complacent face, looking directly at the viewer, seemed to ask, What the hell do you think you're doing here?

The Vermeer, which stood on a small table behind glass, stopped him. Whenever they'd visited the Gardner, he and Val Welsh had not failed to pay homage to it. He stooped and peered into the exquisitely lighted world of the painting. It was entitled *The Concert*. The central figure, a long-haired man, had his broad back to the viewer. He was playing a mandolin, looked like. To the man's left, on clavichord, was a girl with her back to the light, a bright pearl on her ear. To his right another young woman stood singing. An idle cello lay on the black-and-white floor in the foreground. The private seventeenth-century world of Jan Vermeer. What was the story between these people. No one knew. On the other hand, he considered, they were just like us.

Hurrying heels clattered on the tile floor behind him. From the opposite side of the room the woman by the doorway said, "Thank God. Jesus Christ, Wanda."

He didn't turn around to look.

"I lost track of the fucking time." The distinct reply, a little breathless, carried the length of the room. A voice he knew.

"Ssh! It's packed." They were gone.

He fled into the maze of galleries, staircases, corridors, walking fast, like a man who had lost his way. One long gallery dead-ended at the museum's small chapel, a dark enclosure with a single stained-glass window. Relax! Movement to his left, in an alcove roped off to visitors, startled him, and he spied an outlaw couple furtively making out, heedless of Boomfell. His double take revealed that they were grown-ups, not kids. The woman's hand was out of sight beneath the man's waist. Arrest them!

The Gothic Room was oppressive with dark carved furniture and darker paneling. He stood at one of the tall windows, which looked into the daylighted courtyard, and listened. The soulful sound of the solo cello came from somewhere below him, trailing resonant memories from another life. He looked at his large useless hands resting on the marble railing. You have to know what you want.

When the applause began, he hurried down stone steps. At the rear door of the concert hall a girl Ruth's age handed him a program. "Three Great B's in Concert," performed by the New World Trio. The first piece had been Bach, although Boomfell hadn't recognized it. The next piece was a cello and piano sonata in C major by Benjamin Britten.

The teenage girl touched his arm. "Excuse me, sir, but I won't be able to let you in once they start playing again."

He took a seat on the aisle a half dozen rows from the back.

The vast room was dark as a cellar, the walls draped with acres of Flemish tapestries from—he knew—the fifteenth century. The seating, filled almost to capacity, was all on one level. It was not likely that he could be spotted from the performers' platform at the faraway front of the room, yet Boomfell didn't look up from his program, reading and rereading the names of the three musicians, until the first decisive note of the Britten sonata was struck.

From where he was sitting Wanda Gwertz looked unchanged. As if Boomfell had been sped backward time-machine fashion to the one and only other Wanda Gwertz recital he'd ever attended. Same face, same hair, same upright posture as she sat passionately manhandling her instrument, all that, but also the same sort of black dress with thin straps over pale shoulders. It couldn't be the same dress, could it, ten years later? Here, as unchanged as Isabella Stewart Gardner's personal museum, was the spit-and-image Gwertz of Boomfell's memory. Seemingly as unaltered, say, as Rembrandt's self-portrait, a Grecian torso, the famous Vermeer, or the courtyard's square of Roman mosaic pavement from the second century. All his imagining hadn't prepared him for this twist. Wanda Gwertz was in her mid-thirties by now. Apparently she had eluded all manner of everyday wear and tear, busy with her three great B's, mastering the possible. Bach, Britten, Brahms had served her enviably well. Music making was an elixir.

What was he doing here? Leave her alone.

By the final movement of the Britten sonata he'd adapted to Wanda's onstage presence. During the Brahms Piano Trio in B Major, he was able to sit back, safely distanced from his self-involvement, and listen. The New World Trio was first-rate as far as Boomfell could tell. Judging from the applause, the audience felt the same way. Their energetic performance conveyed a sense of creative excitement—of worlds to come. Wanda Gwertz had come through! Boomfell's merely personal interest in the afternoon's performance, how extraneous. When the concert ended, he got up from his seat, and casually shuffling along with the crowd, smiling to fellow music-lovers as one whose Sunday afternoon was now complete, he left the hall.

Descending the staircase to the cloisters and the now shadowed courtyard, the Isabella Stewart Gardner Museum suddenly repelled him. The place was dark, decrepit, even creepy. A marble torso of Dionysus, the head and penis missing, turned him off. The fragments of ancient sculpture, chunks of marble columns and railings, fugitive bits and pieces of once splendid busted-up buildings—it was a random hodgepodge of uprooted rubble. She had pillaged Europe to satisfy her pleasure. The ultimate decorator. All this stuff piled up like so much pilfered loot, it was a rich American's makeshift attempt at instant aristocracy. The place reeked of a reckless philistinism. Maybe James and Sargent and Berenson had been taken in. Charles Boomfell, for one, wouldn't be back here in a hurry—maybe never. He hurried to retrieve his wool overcoat from the cloakroom. All around him staid members of the middle class raved about the inspired performance by the New World Trio.

He took deep breaths in the welcome winter air. It was dusk, the darkening fens encircled by lighted buildings and the bright lights of passing traffic. He had once lived in this city. He no longer did. He would be home by seven, seven-thirty at the latest.

He had already crossed the street and was halfway to the parking lot when he realized, buttoning the top of his coat, that his scarf was missing. It was the purple scarf Ben had given him last year for his birthday—purple with a gray-and-black stripe. The boy had picked it out himself, without his mother's help, and had paid for it with his own money. It's a hundred percent wool, Dad, he explained when he presented the gift. They said you can exchange it if you don't like the color.

Boomfell wouldn't have exchanged it for his life, in a manner of speaking. He would have left any other scarf there and counted the loss of it one of the costs of the afternoon. He had to go back for this one.

The concert crowd had thinned considerably by the time he talked his way past the young woman at the side entry and returned to the cloakroom. The scarf was still on its hanger, a bit of luck at the end of a weird day. Someone touched his arm from behind, and he turned.

"Charles Boomfell?" Wanda Gwertz pulled a heavy wool sweater over her bare shoulders and pushed her hair back from her face with both hands. A boldly patterned sweater of many colors. "This has been happening lately. Last week I ran into a woman from Juilliard who I hadn't seen for fifteen years. She was teaching at the school where we played. Hey, weren't you going to say hello?"

He hadn't been there in ages, he said. He was still surprised. "The day I stumble into the place, guess who's giving a concert? You sounded great—inspired."

At closer range, her face was thinner than he remembered, the nose maybe more pronounced. Lines he didn't recall framed her mouth, which looked larger, the lips larger, although that may only have been the new style of makeup, her features more dramatically outlined. Her smile was, as ever, childishly wholehearted.

The pianist intruded, a tall stocky woman who wore her hair in a braid twisted up on top of her head. "Let's split, Gwertz. I'm famished." She handed the cellist her coat.

Wanda Gwertz stuck her hand out to him, smiling big. "I wish we had time to shoot the shit, but my friends here are hungry." She pulled on her coat—a double-layered affair, wool beneath a weather-repellent outer sheath, taupe-colored, with broad shoulders. A new coat. "Are you teaching around here?"

Instead of answering her question, he said, "Do you have time for a drink?"

"Giovina!" The pianist, getting into her own coat, turned. "Do I have time for a drink?"

"Our flight is at ten, I want to leave for the airport before eight, Susan is making dinner for us, remember?" Giovina had not looked at Boomfell yet.

The third member of the trio, all buttoned up in a man's secondhand oversize tweed coat, approached them, carrying her violin case. She was younger than her colleagues, still in her twenties. "Let's roll," she said.

"I'd better not," Wanda told him. "We've been staying with friends who planned this dinner and everything."

Boomfell checked his watch. "It's only five-thirty. I'll drop you at your friends' in an hour," not at all sure why he was pushing it.

The violinist asked, "Who is this guy?"

Wanda Gwertz smiled. "I'll grab something to eat now," she told Giovina. "I'll be back by seven."

They had little to say in the car, as if waiting until they had drinks in their hands to broach the subject of the last ten years. Yet once they were settled side by side at a bar on Newbury, she seemed content to sit there observing her surroundings as if no significant time had passed since she and Charles Boomfell had gotten together for a drink. She was in no hurry to catch up on what had become of him, or to fill him in on the last decade of her life.

Her meal arrived promptly, arranged before her on the bar. Fish chowder, a Greek salad, French bread. Boomfell wasn't eating. He ordered a second scotch.

"Where are you headed tonight?" he asked. "Home?"

"New York is home for the time being. Tonight we're flying to London, then Yugoslavia. That's why they're so uptight, especially Giovina. She needs hours to get ready to go any-where. I drive her up the wall because I'm not like that. I travel light." She slurped a spoonful of soup, bending over the bowl.

239

"So tell me about it. What's the story—the New World Trio?"

"The story is we starve, but we get to play. When Giovina isn't collapsing with anxiety we have fun. It's almost impossible, being women, but that also has its weirdo appeal. We all teach, which makes the future feasible, at least for a while."

He learned, when he asked, that she and Giovina had met at the National Symphony in D.C., let's see, maybe five years ago now. They'd picked up Karen in New York.

"We had a couple of breaks, then lucked out with an agent. Albany loved us. Columbus loved us. Israel loved us. This is our first trip to London. We're gypsies. After two weeks in the same place I want to kill. Wandalust, that's what Giovina calls it, she's the wit."

Her life as a musician—the places and people—raised too many questions to be pursued just now. He observed her hands. Nothing ended, he thought. Ten years later you're sitting in a bar with this person, same teeth in her smile, crow's-feet a little more pronounced. Lives went on, turned up. Only weeks before, that had been something he had yet to learn.

"It was a shock, how much you looked like your old self up there playing."

With her mouth full she said, "So tell me about Charles Boomfell." She swallowed. "In twenty-five words or less, what's up with you?"

"Lately, I feel like I've been living in the past. Wanda Gwertz—live at the Gardner Museum. In December Eliot Singer spent a long weekend with us."

"Eliot? Really?"

"Not the Eliot we knew, believe me."

When he mentioned the attempted suicide—Singer shattered, one hundred and sixteen stitches, the casts—she jerked toward him as if she'd been pushed, taking his arm with both hands. "Sorry, that just scared the shit out of me. I saw him for a minute last summer in Toronto. I'm in love, Wanda Gwertz, I'm very happy. That sounds farfetched, doesn't it—Eliot happy."

He hadn't intended to bring up Singer. It made a good story—his Lucky, his Astrid and Nicole and Alex, his tribulations, the insanity of his recent good news. The story of Singer allowed Boomfell to postpone the subject of himself. He soon had her laughing. Eliot on skis, Eliot at the foot of the bed, Eliot and the smitten neighbor, Eliot in New York.

"Who is us?" she asked. "You said us, like Eliot visited us."

"He stayed at the house with us."

"You mean Valerie? You and Valerie are still together? Really?"

"Is that surprising?"

"A little, yeah." She smiled. "It amazes me that people stay married, that's all. I couldn't work married. It would mess me up. I tried being married. What time is it?"

"You tried?"

"That's over. Look at your watch." She pushed up the sleeve of his jacket. It wasn't seven yet.

"Who turned out to be the lucky man? Or the unlucky man."

"His name was Joseph. Not Joe. Joseph. Whenever someone called him Joe, he corrected them. Not Joe. Joseph. He was only twenty-four. I met him in Seattle."

"I thought you were in Halifax," said Boomfell. "What happened to Halifax?"

"I left after the first year."

When she didn't continue he asked, "How long did you live in Seattle?"

"Not long. He was working as a fisherman to earn money to go to Africa. That was his plan. The adventurer. Everything had to be an adventure. Michael was the same way. His brother, Michael, not Mike, he was two years younger, he was part of the deal. They'd lost their parents when they were little boys like ten and twelve and they were raised by their uncle, who already had his own family, so basically they'd been on their own since high school. Anyway they were inseparable. Christ, don't get me started on this, Charlie. What are you drinking?" She hailed the bartender and ordered a beer.

"So you married two guys instead of one?"

"They were wonderful together. The whole thing was all wonderful. We rented sailboats, you know, and sailed in Puget Sound. When we had enough money I quit the symphony and we went to Africa, the three of us, to poor Tanzania. Everybody got sick, everybody got better. I played the guitar, Joseph played recorder, and Michael played harmonica. We were vagabonds, basically. Michael did most of the cooking. I felt good with them. Oh"—she touched his arm again—"we climbed Kilimanjaro with our porters, our Chagga guide, assorted tourists from Germany and Japan. Michael came down with altitude sickness and had to stay behind at the twelve-thousand-foot hut. Joseph and I made it to the top, that was probably the highlight of the last ten years, that was major."

He wanted to know what happened after the African adventure.

"We went to Greece. That was my idea. I wanted to see all the famous things you have to see. Anyway, it was all downhill after Greece. I should really get going, Charlie, what do I owe you for this?"

He insisted on getting the bill, but it wasn't necessary to go yet. "Don't leave us in Greece," he said.

"Are you really interested? It's a sad story, Charlie, it's a drag, he died on me. The original plan was to go to New Zealand after Africa, but Wanda had to go to Greece, right, I needed to see the Parthenon, which turned out to be awful. At that point we didn't have enough money to go to New Zealand, so we went to Spain. We went to Pamplona. That was a zoo. From the minute we arrived I knew it was a mistake. We went for the fiesta, right, but once we got there it was too crazy, I hated it, we decided to keep moving. By then we had Kati with us, an Austrian who'd been living in Rome, a very pretty anti-Semite with red hair. Michael was all over her. He'd had Joseph and Wanda stuffed down his throat all year. There were two army dumbbells from Alabama, stationed in Germany, who wouldn't leave her alone either. They were going to participate in the *encierro*, running the bulls, you had to be an idiot to go near the bulls. The second day Michael announced that he'd decided to run too. Perfect! Joseph couldn't let him do it alone. I should have insisted we leave, but I was so sick of the whole scene I said screw it, I refused to watch. You can guess the rest, can't you?"

"No."

"He was helping a boy get up, some little Spanish boy who shouldn't have been in the street in the first place. Lots of people get hospitalized during the so-called Fiesta de San Fermín, people get killed. It's like channeled hysteria when the bulls are released, charging through narrow streets with everyone running for their lives ahead of them. Evidently Joseph got the kid back on his feet, according to Michael, but then he was knocked into the wall of a building by one of the berserk bulls, he never saw it coming. I wasn't even worried about Joseph, Joseph could handle anything, I was worried about Michael. It never should have happened, a stupid freak accident."

"He died?" Boomfell said, unwilling to take the obvious for granted.

"Two days later. He never regained consciousness. Michael blamed himself, he was inconsolable. I felt like it was my fault. My father sent us money, he didn't come to the funeral—Joseph had destroyed my career as far as he was concerned, my almighty career—but he sent money. I managed to get a teaching job in New York, and I started working very hard on my music. I'd been away from it for over a year. For one year I got to be somebody else, one lousy year out of a lifetime. How about that? Michael went to British Columbia, I haven't heard from him since."

What could he say? "I don't know what to say. I'm sorry."

"You don't have to say anything." She took his wrist, shoved up the sleeve of his jacket, and read the time. "Let's go, Charlie." She had gotten off the bar stool and was struggling with her coat. "Giovina is going to kill me. How stupid, getting into all this, aren't you glad you asked?" She smiled, but her smile had lost its spark. She looked lost in the largeness of her new coat. "I used to talk about it constantly, about Joseph, I mean, like the Ancient Mariner. I was a mess. Now it's like the past in capital letters. It happened, I got through it, and it's the past, my past. Anything after that has to be up."

They were in a hurry then. She directed him through the narrow streets, although she might have simply said Marlborough Street. Boomfell knew Marlborough. He slowed down, trying to read the numbers on the doors of the dark red brick buildings.

"How are you doing?" she asked. "I still don't know a thing about Charles Boomfell."

Peering through the windshield, Boomfell told her he was doing all right.

"Oh God, they're all waiting for me. Do you see them? Straight ahead."

He pulled up behind the blue Volvo station wagon. The car was double-parked and running, a man behind the wheel. The other two members of the New World Trio stepped from the sidewalk toward Boomfell's car.

"Your stuff is packed," the violinist shouted.

Giovina stormed the passenger side, opening the door before Wanda could find the handle. She thrust her broad face into the front seat, reaching for Wanda's arm. "I'm going to kill you," she yelled.

Wanda Gwertz resisted, leaning toward Boomfell. She was smiling again, beaming, wholehearted, the stress that had come into her face as they sat at the bar was gone. "Wouldn't you love to live with this?" she said. She kissed the side of his face as she was pulled the other way. "Good-bye, Charlie, thanks for coming."

On the street Giovina tugged on her sleeve while Wanda waved, antic, the coat half off, grinning back toward Boomfell. The two women disappeared into the backseat of the station wagon. The cello, he saw now, filled the rear window. They were accelerating as they approached the intersection some fifty yards away, they didn't brake at the stop sign.

Charles Boomfell, that name had been long obliterated by her subsequent experience. Her past involving Boomfell had been superseded by *the past*, in which he didn't figure and from which point her life had had to begin again. And now, following the encounter she counted a matter of chance, she certainly knew none of the panic, as she took flight for distant lands, that closed around Boomfell's skull, the base of his skull, and began to exert its nauseating pressure as he sped out of the city—it felt like an abandoned city this Sunday night—like a man fleeing a crime, strapped behind the wheel of his car.

"Joseph," he said aloud, and his voice broke on the second syllable of the unfamiliar name. The poor kid!

Wanda Gwertz, the cellist, she had quit the symphony to go to Africa! Singer, the scholar, he had slit his wrists! To the bone! With self-disgust Boomfell thought, It was a shock, how much you looked like your old self. . . . On Route 2, once the four-lane highway became a road of two-way traffic, each trailer truck that thundered by in the oncoming lane—and they passed with regularity—made him consider, as he squinted against the glare of headlights, how little it would take, a jerk of the wrist, to swerve into its momentous path.

Flurries. The remarkable designs of large individual snow-flakes, like the paper ones children cut out and tacked to the

245

walls at Ben's school, were fleetingly visible on the windshield before they dissolved and were intermittently swept away by the windshield wipers. Not Joe. Joseph. Within minutes a dense white whirlwind, a squall, canceled the night around him, and the road leading through it. He braked, slowing to third gear, and switched on his emergency blinkers. The amber lights visibly flashed before him. He wiped the inside of the windshield, as if that might help him get his bearings again, and in that instant a glare of tall powerful lights emerged from the clotted density of the storm, bearing down hard. He swung to the right, fishtailing this time as he hit the brakes, and stopped just short of the guardrail. A pickup, streaming out of nowhere, blared past him from behind, the chassis jacked up three feet above its outsize tires, the cab a carnival of yellow lights. Boomfell looked in time to see a young face, a bareheaded teenage girl, cigarette raised to her lips, calmly looking down at him with an expression of bemused condescension. Like a phantom truck, it disappeared, engulfed by snow. He let go of the wheel. He had overreacted. Relax. Minutes later, the wild dose of blizzard abated. By the time he resumed his former speed, the snow had stopped completely, leaving the night clearer than it had been before.

He turned onto the long wide street, bordered by old houses, half of them already in darkness. The Boomfell house, toward the end of the common, was well lighted. He had been gone since eight o'clock in the morning, saying only that he wanted the day to himself. It was almost eleven. By ten Val would have begun to be concerned. He hadn't intended to tell her about his visit to the Isabella Stewart Gardner Museum, their old hangout. Now he would. Not Joe. Joseph. His visit to the Gardner Museum, whatever he had expected from it, had turned out to be an adventure. Like an adventurer home from distant exploits, exhausted and anxious, yet unexpectedly uplifted at the sight of his sturdy house, its welcoming windows, the familiar life that awaited him inside, he steered into his familiar driveway. Adventurer! He remained in the car for several minutes. Several minutes passed before he was prepared to reenter his warm bright kitchen, his house, containing everything.

April

I met her at the Bookstore Café when I got through at Marjorie and Eleanor's, they'd been in a dither about last night's basketball game, their knight in shining armor, Gary Bird or Jerry Bird, the nicest boy in the world. Val was wearing a houndstooth-check wool dress with a black scarf, The entrepreneur, I said. We hadn't really talked for two weeks, except briefly about work, I was getting new courses straight, she'd been tied down with the usual, last weekend she visited her parents, which turned out to be unexpectedly pleasant, her father's condition under control after months of carrying on. I gave her an update on the Don front, he kept coming around saying he loved me, one night he cried, which was awful, he's forty-something, I warned him that I would call his wife if he didn't lay off and now haven't heard from him all week. I'd received a postcard from Pauline, I reported, which said, Get your butt down here. Val was subdued, Oh nothing, she said, Charlie seemed down lately, maybe it was getting her down. You didn't have to worry about Charlie at all, she said, but he was going through a rough patch, hated the job he was trying to fit himself into, he'd painted himself into a corner, he didn't talk about it, but she could tell, so-called reality sinking in. I said it sounded pretty familiar, which was the wrong thing to say. Does it? she asked, her tone said, What do you know? For years he'd put everything into his so-called work and it hadn't panned out, he was in mourning for his old self, as far as she was concerned, he didn't expect anyone else to give a hoot. She wanted to talk about him, which was a new twist. Soon after they'd moved here, she said, his father came down with that devastating Lou Gehrig's disease, ALS, whatever that stood for. Amyotrophic lateral sclerosis, I told her. Charlie commuted hours a day two and three days a week, whenever he wasn't working, to be with his father in the last year of his life. He fed him, dressed him, all that sad depressing stuff, he did what he had to do, she said, and got little in return. That's too bad, I said, I didn't know what her story was about. You know what he said to Charlie before he lost the ability to speak, one of the last things he said? I shook my head no, I couldn't help smiling, like of course I didn't know the last thing Charlie's father . . . When are you going to do something with yourself, Val said, why do you want to waste your time with that nonsense? Charlie couldn't get back to his work for months after his father died, he abandoned the project he'd been working on, he couldn't take it seriously. Charlie couldn't say no, she said, he lacked some sort of important self-centeredness— worried about doing what was right, he got it wrong. Instead of nursing his terminally ill father, he should have spent that year getting his act together. I asked, But what about his father's question, why waste your time? She looked across the table, speechless for a second, as though I'd slapped her. That's what he wanted to be, she said, he thought he was Yeats or somebody. So I asked, Did you? Frankly she'd never read the stuff, long convoluted narrative poems, she didn't know any more about that than she knew about . . . microbiology. She looked unhappy. Why real estate, I asked then, if he couldn't stand it? My mother became a nurse, I said, because she decided to do something worthwhile. He wasn't looking for a career, Val explained, he was after something quick and simple with a chance at money so he could eventually get back . . . but the truth was sinking in, he was drifting farther and farther from where he wanted to be. Charlie was Charlie, as far as she was concerned, as long as he was doing his thing in his room at the back of the house, he was always positive, Val said, he was fun, as long as he was busy back there, hey, who knew what might happen. Lately it was as though his fire had gone out. She missed him pacing around the backyard, bursting into the kitchen inspired and full of shit, I guess that's what I'm saying, she said, I miss him. I said, Want to know what I think, don't hate me, I wouldn't worry about Charlie, I don't think it's that important, what he wanted to be, I think you've both been robbed, you're tied up in knots with one another, but don't sound that good for each other, you should go your separate ways, that's what I think, Charlie gets to be Charlie, Val could be Val. She said, You sound like Singer. Who's that? I asked. The last word on happiness. I couldn't tell if she was pissed. Happy Valentine's Day, I said, which was the next day or two, that made her smile. Snow had turned to rain the night before, followed by freezing rain until morning, so all the trees and shrubs, rooftops, fences were glazed with ice, the world a shining crystal palace, winter fantasy. The sun had come out, the day had warmed up by the time we stepped outside, and as we walked down the narrow tree-lined street toward the center of town, the ice began to let go the length of it, tinkling down at first like chimes, then crashing from the tall trees so we ran excitedly to get out from under them, not knowing whether to be happy or frightened.

Tuesday morning I turned up as usual at the Gunthers', Daniel was just getting out of the shower in his burgundy robe and bare feet, like royalty, he'd just done his sixteen-hour stint at the emergency room, he looked ashen pale, his hair sticking out, Miriam had been gone since Thursday to one of her prestigious high-power conferences, wonderful little Norman was at his grandmother's, who lived right in town as it turned out, the place was a disaster, like a gang of fraternity jerk-offs had been camping out there. I said, Holy shit, Daniel, I started picking up newspapers, pitching cans and Styrofoam containers into the garbage, kicking toys and clothes out of the way. He was making his cup of espresso at the sink, he drank mugs of muddy espresso all day. Screw that, he said, have a cup of coffee with me. I had to be out of there by noon, there was no way I was going to get through this mess if I sat down and had a cup of coffee. April, sit down, suddenly very assertive in a calm way, he pulled out a chair, poured me a cup of scary liquid from his fancy little espresso thingy, I killed somebody last night, he said, I feel like shit. An eighty-nine-year-old lady, I immediately thought of Marjorie and Eleanor, scared, holding my breath, came in with her late-middle-aged sons and their wives, he said, so I knew it wasn't them, she looked terrible, complaining of nausea, dizziness, head pain, couldn't focus, couldn't walk, her blood pressure was off the charts. He took my hand and rubbed it between his hands, she felt cool and clammy, he said, like dead meat, and let go of my hand. He gave her a drug to bring down her blood pressure, that was routine, that's what any competent physician anywhere would have done, he said, her blood pressure started going down immediately, as intended, but kept going down after it should have stabilized, Come on, lady, for Christ's sake, the blood pressure dropped more, wouldn't come back up, he could have wrung her neck, she died. What did he tell the woman's family? You don't go out and tell them you just killed their wonderful old mother, he said, he told them that she'd been on the threshold of a massive inevitable stroke, he'd tried to interfere, but the outcome couldn't be prevented, fortunately she hadn't suffered, etc. They shook hands with him, they were grateful to him, thankful she had passed away so mercifully, Daniel slumped back in the chair in his burgundy robe, his smooth pale chest vulnerable, his ankles thin and hairless,

Annals of medicine, he said miserably. That wasn't your fault, I told him. He said, I caused it to happen, that's one of the first things you'll learn, mistakes happen, we live in an imperfect world, you have to accept that or you can't practice medicine, etc. I stood up, intending to get back to work, I leaned over and hugged him the way you'd hug anyone who had had a really rough day, I started filling the sink with water. He asked me if I'd like to get something to eat with him that night, Miriam wasn't getting back until tomorrow, but I couldn't, I had a class I was afraid to miss. He said, Okay, let's skip dinner, we'd been doing this little flirtatious number with one another for months, I decided okay, let's skip dinner. I hadn't made love to anyone since Don, since before the holidays, for crying out loud, we went into the guest bedroom rather than their bedroom, we weren't very successful, I didn't think, he was nervous and tired, came too soon for either of us, but his kiss was sweet, he was sweet, Daniel Gunther was a sweet man, mistakes happen, we agreed, we live in an imperfect world, we decided to leave it at that. Val, who had seemed preoccupied when I turned up at the office and had warned me that she only had twenty minutes for a cup of tea, now became fidgety, she started up from her seat and sat down again. That's just great, April, the last time that happened the man's wife went bananas, she'd fired the pathetic little dope, she was trying to run a legitimate business, not a sex ring, the Gunthers were good clients, she'd designed their kitchen, damnit, she knew them well, this put her in an awkward position, etc., trying to keep her voice down. I was blown away, I didn't know where she was coming from, Daniel Gunther and I had nothing to do with her or her business, maybe I shouldn't have mentioned it. I don't understand you, she said, I can't deal with this, stop looking at me as if I had a problem, she said, she stood up. What's the matter with you, I asked, where are you going? I don't understand you, she said. She had her coat on, I took her arm. What's bugging you? I asked, Talk to me, don't leave. How about Sunday, I asked, were we going to the pool? She didn't know, she'd call me. When she didn't call Sunday, I phoned her house, Ruth answered, and it was Ruth who returned to the phone a moment later, her mother was in the middle of something, she couldn't make it to the pool this afternoon, she said she'd be in touch. Fine, I decided to give Val a rest, I went through the weekly routine, the Gunthers' on Tuesday, Daniel was working, Marjorie and Eleanor on Wednesday, James Gill's desolate bachelor pad on Friday, up to my eyeballs with course work, everybody in our house was bitching about the weather, work, meals, the three of us had begun getting our periods simultaneously like clockwork. Friday afternoon Val had two suburban ladies in the office talking about colors and fabrics, she was friendly in her chipper competent entrepreneurial way, she smiled as she handed me my paycheck, the connection between us, the special something, clearly wasn't on. The following week I called to let her know that I was going to Jamaica from the fifteenth to the twenty-fifth, spring break, Pauline had to see me, I could stay there for practically nothing, I'd just purchased a nonrefundable fourteen-day-advance-purchase airline ticket in the nick of time, I hoped it wouldn't be much trouble to have someone temporarily take over for me, etc. Val said it had been tricky to cover for me during the long Christmas holiday, she couldn't do it now, the difficulty with hiring students was they were always taking off for distant . . . The trip was important to me, what was she saying? I asked her. If you have to go to Jamaica in March to see Pauline, I'll have to let you go, I'm sorry, April. I went to her office directly from my microbiology-of-cloning lab, storming up the stairs with my barrage of questions and accusations. I'm sorry, April? What are you doing? What's going on, Val? What's this about? etc. She was wearing a black turtleneck, her gold chain, her khaki skirt, she was brisk, controlled, official, she wasn't in the mood to be interrogated, she said, she had explained her position over the phone, she believed she was being reasonable, she had nothing to say. I hated her, I hated her life, I could have attacked her with my clenched fists, I was ashamed, I was a fool, I said good-bye and meant it.

The second week of February, despite his ambivalence about it, he had called Singer, ostensibly to set up their tentatively planned weekend.

"What can I do for you, Charles?" That was Singer's abrupt and off-putting greeting. When Boomfell said he'd been thinking about him, wondering how he was making out these days, Singer replied, "I can't talk now, Charles." That was the end of the conversation. Singer couldn't talk!

Yet two minutes later, almost immediately, he called back. "Charles Boomfell, are you all right?"

"Am I all right?" Boomfell repeated, as if hard-of-hearing.

"The question occurred to me."

"It's February, the darkest month. Otherwise we're fine. Everyone's fine."

"Not we, Charles Boomfell. Not everyone. You."

"I was just calling to—"

Singer cut him off. "You understand what I'm saying. We understand each other. Let's not belabor it."

He and his Lucky didn't come down in February as tentatively planned. They didn't return to Cyrano's, the four of them, to celebrate the way everything works out. By March that seemed never to have been a real possibility. Just as well, you figured. The real Lucky, Boomfell didn't need to make her acquaintance.

Then, the night of St. Patrick's Day, when they returned home from the O'Beirnes', there was a message on the kitchen

255

counter. Eliot Singer called. And several nights later, a Saturday, the first day of spring in fact, they got back from the movies to find another note awaiting them. Dad, Ruth had scrawled on a paper bag, Eliot Singer wants you to call him in the morning. Call him underlined. But that tone—what can I do for you, Charles?—he couldn't get past it. No, in March he didn't feel like returning Singer's unforeseen phone calls. In March it was Boomfell who couldn't talk. Evidently Singer grasped the point of his silence; they didn't hear from him again.

V.

Fueled by still favorable interest rates, real estate began to move again with the arrival of spring. New housing starts hit an all-time high in April. High-priced condo development seemed rampant. Toward the end of the month Boomfell managed to pay down a portion of the punishing equity loan. Soon he would be in a position to buy a better car, which was vital to his line of work. He was making a living. If he wasn't crazy about the job, at least he was getting paid for it. Then, right around Easter, he got lucky. Bryce decided to sell. One hundred plus or minus acres of deciduous woods containing two streams, bordered to the south by a large pasture, and with over nine hundred feet of frontage on Field Hill Road. Owing in part, Boomfell believed, to a long agreeable talk they'd had one day, touching on everything from global warming and nuclear arms to AIDS, track housing, children, and alternative medicine, Bryce, the healer, had latched on to Boomfell as his consultant in the development of his land, offering him, Boomfell, an exclusive listing, looking to Boomfell to bring in the right sort of buyers. Land prices were out of sight as people scrambled to possess the precious little that was still available in desirable locations. It was as though Boomfell, for the first time in his life, had found himself in the right place at the right time.

One rainy weeknight, after everyone had gone to bed, he had the temerity to unearth his untitled work in progress from the

257

bottom drawer of his oak desk. He experienced the thrill of possibility. The work was better, far better, than it had seemed to him when he'd abandoned it more than a year before. If his luck held through the summer and fall, if the Bryce project panned out, he'd be able to take some time in the winter, take most of the winter, and complete the manuscript. Then what? That wasn't a question he had to address at the moment. If his plan was fraught with uncertainties and had the overripe smell of wishful thinking, it was nonetheless a move in the direction of Boomfell, which might make his present dislocation more bearable. He might pull it off yet—his life. On good days that seemed distinctly possible. His year in real estate, it was an episode in a much bigger story.

Sad, but funny too, the Salters put their house on the market again, the new season opening old wounds or freshening dormant wants. You hardly went down a street anymore without spotting one or more FOR SALE signs posted on front lawns. Transience, lives in flux, greed, such were the givens of the day, he considered, and they were good for business. One day Swift Realty's green-and-blue sign turned up in front of Holly Dean Lawson's house, as they thought of the place next door. Circa 1830. The next evening, when he noticed her outside, he strolled over. She was squatting by the west side of the house, peering into the opalescent faces of tulips.

"You aren't moving, are you?"

"Yeah, it looks like it." She would have called him to list the house, she said, but she felt awkward about it, being neighbors.

"We're going to miss you."

"I bet." She cupped a tulip in the palm of her hand. "Isn't that beautiful?" Jeff was taking a job in Cleveland, she volunteered. Greeting cards. More money and less travel. "His family lives out there, which is another reason."

"In that case, maybe you should stay here."

"They love me, that's not a problem. I'm ready for a change. I fell in love with this house, but it never felt like home." She stood and slapped her hands on her blue jeans, smiling at him with closed lips.

He had never noticed her mouth before, for example. She didn't wear lipstick. Her fingernails were closely trimmed and unpainted. Her look was direct. Her skin was more like Ruth's, for example, than his wife's skin. Circa 1830. She was too young to be locked up in an old house.

"It seems like only yesterday that you moved in."

"Not to me." She sat on the front stoop with her legs out in front of her, and leaned back on her arms. She held her face up to the low westering sun, closed her eyes. "This winter lasted forever. I was fine until New Year's. By February Carlo Rossi and I were getting a little too friendly. That was my big discovery of the year." She opened her eyes. "Alcoholism! I couldn't wait to get home and sit down with Carlo. My phone bill for February was like the defense budget. My best friend lives in San Francisco and my mother lives in La Jolla."

"You're not an alcoholic. You're the picture of health."

"That's what I said. I was very heavily into denial. I went to an AA meeting and stood up and said, I am an alcoholic, then came home and said, See, I can admit it. That must mean I don't have a problem. Instead of going back the next week, I thought I'd just have one little glass of wine while I made myself a skirt and taped some records. I downed the whole jug. I don't remember how I got to bed that night, number one. Number two, I couldn't find the material for the skirt. I began to wonder if there ever was any material. Come on, Holly. Finally I found a piece of it in the fireplace so I knew I hadn't gone completely out of my mind. But I had no idea that I'd burned it up. That terrified me. I went back to AA. I haven't missed a meeting in five weeks. At first everyone looked gray and pasty. Everyone chain-smoked and drank gallons of coffee.

I couldn't be one of these heavy losers. Denial is a powerful thing. In fact, people of all shapes and sizes turn up there."

"If you're an alcoholic, I wonder what I am." Printed on her faded blue T-shirt, he noticed only now, was the legend HANDLE WITH CARE, and the pattern covering the shirt, at first glance abstract, was composed of large handprints. "Look at you," said Boomfell. "It's all ahead of you."

"Jeff doesn't think I'm an alcoholic either. He thinks I've created a manageable crisis for myself. If I'm an alcoholic and go to AA and quit drinking, I've licked all my problems. In other words, deciding to be an alcoholic turns out to be another form of denial. The real problems go unresolved. The truth is I feel a hundred percent better. I was hiding, dying inside, and now I'm doing something about it. Jeff just misses the blow jobs."

"Is that a metaphor?"

"I don't want it in my mouth. That's my real problem as far as he's concerned. I could only face it if I had a skinful of Carlo Rossi red. Maybe it's not the penis per se. Maybe it's Jeff's penis. I really don't know."

"I wish you had come over to see us this winter. There we were, right there hibernating, buried in our routines, while you're sitting over here with Carlo Rossi, burning skirts. How are you supposed to know what's going on with people?" The Boomfells hadn't seen their next-door neighbor all winter. Nothing more than a wave had passed between them. "This is the first time we've spoken to each other in months, isn't it?"

"Put up a For Sale sign, that does it every time. I'm feeling good now. That's not what was going on this winter. I would have come over and quaffed up all your wine on you, and you would have hated me for it. Nobody knows their neighbors," she said cheerfully. She came to her feet again and returned to the flower bed—jaunty, bouncy in her Top-Siders, up. "I thought you were coming over to compliment me on my tulips. I planted these tulips, isn't that amazing? Look at them! Big wonderful tulips. Oops, watch where you're stepping, there's dog shit all over the yard. Ocean!" she shouted, and twice more, loud. "I think he's found a girlfriend down the street. You know who I was thinking about the other day? Your friend from Canada."

"Eliot."

"Actually, I wasn't thinking about him the other day. I think about him all the time. I didn't forget his name either. Believe me, I'm not about to forget his name. How's he doing anyway?"

Fine as far as Boomfell knew. He hadn't spoken to him for a while. "I need to call him, in fact. He liked you," he told her then. "He appreciated what you did for him."

"I'm sure I didn't do anything for him."

"You had him over, you kept him company. He appreciated it. I know that."

"He was great," she said, smiling. "I think I was obsessed for about two months. Isn't that off the wall? We only spent a few hours together. He was like a mind-altering drug that wouldn't wear off. He was so . . ." She waited for the word. "Here. He was so here."

The first of May, a Friday, you had sun shining through newly leafed-out trees, money leafed out in your pocket for a change, plus bird song in the backyard, Ben there with his brand-new baseball mitt, the neighborly buzz of a lawn mower across the way, plus Val in her skirt, relaxed tonight, cheerful, plus a bottle of zinfandel with your London broil, beauteous evening-type feeling all around. Hail, bounteous May! Dogwood, lilac, viburnum, apple blossoms. All that going for us, see. What was wrong with it?

May 1 was also the night of Ruth's last school concert of the year, which is why she wasn't at home for their cookout. The event was dignified by being held at Blakely rather than the high school's cavernous auditorium. When the Boomfells arrived, the well-lighted recital hall was almost full, noisy with the chatter of cheerful, well-meaning parents who had almost reached the end of another school year. The flowery May, he thought, who from her green lap throws the cowslip . . . the yellow cowslip, and the . . . what? Singer, you figured, would know the poem by heart. One of his Milton's youthful verses. The happy young Milton.

At that moment, coincidentally, Val said, "There's Eliot's friend, the woman in gray and white just sitting down over there. What's her name?"

"Wait, it's on the tip of my tongue."

"Doesn't her daughter play the flute?" Val pointed out a name on her program under Flute/Piccolo. "Hastings."

"That's it. Anne." He grinned. "Hasty Pudding."

She had not gotten in touch with the Boomfells when she returned from England after the holidays, as she'd seemed so determined to do. Val had run into her at the grocery store months ago. She'd been suffering from a cold, nothing but frozen food dinners and ice cream in her basket. Boomfell hadn't laid eyes on her since the night of the Corelli concert. There was something different about her tonight. A haircut, yes, that piled-up business updated to a trendy short affair. Younger-looking from across the hall, the look of today, yet the soft old English something missing. She had entered with another woman, as tall as herself, dressed in a long khaki skirt and a baggy off-white cotton jacket. The safari look. Huntress. They immediately began talking to the couple seated in front of them, who came to their feet to be introduced to Anne Hastings's friend. I'm pleased to . . . just delighted . . . lovely day . . . positively bounteous.

"I wonder how he's doing these days."

"Who?" Val asked.

"Eliot. I should give him a ring, see what he's up to now that winter is over. Maybe they'd like to come down some time."

Val, facing forward, didn't respond.

He had thought of Singer earlier today, as he tossed the ball with Ben. Boomfell Special. He'd like to tell him about the Bryce break, for example, and the plan that the promise of money made possible. Boomfell's plan. Singer was an unwitting partner in that—the imagined reader to whose standard the work would measure up. Who apart from the likes of Singer was likely to give a damn about the fool's labor that Boomfell wished to undertake? Who but the likes of Singer understood what drove the likes of Boomfell? Myth's Poet Homers!

Are you all right, Charles Boomfell? That was the last time they'd spoken. It had only become clear recently, months later, that he hadn't been all right. For weeks, following his trip to the Gardner Museum, he'd been at loose ends. Whenever conditions permitted, instead of going to work, he'd spent whole days in the woods, wearing himself out on cross-country skis. At night he'd sit up late, randomly leafing through books, playing old records, and drinking recklessly. The day began with aspirin. And because nothing would relieve the ever-present lumps of tension that knotted his shoulders and sent painful spasms up the back of his skull, he ate aspirin all day long. He began to suffer episodes of insomnia. One bout, lasting three consecutive nights, made him feel he was losing his mind. Shitting became an anxious chore. The day he went shopping for a pair of pants on sale, he lost his wallet— license, credit cards, fifty bucks—for the first time in his life. The day he was to join Bryce and his attorney for lunch, he left his keys on the kitchen counter, locking himself out of house and car, and missed the meeting. Was he being squeezed out of a life that had never fit right in the first place? He didn't want to see people. He stopped playing squash with Weisman on Wednesdays, for example, and he refused to go to the Nelsons' Valentine's Day party. The routine and crucial sex he shared with Val dried up completely. Snap out of it, she shouted after him as he left the house in the morning. What's the matter with you? she wanted to know as he came through the door at the end of the day. Nothing is the matter with me. That was his reply. You're always scowling lately, Ruth told him. Their almost nightly discussions concerning everything under the sun had stopped. And Ben no longer asked his father for help with homework. No, he hadn't been all right the day he called Singer, or for weeks afterward. Unlike Singer, he hadn't realized it at the time.

"Wouldn't you like to meet the real Lucky?" he asked.

Ignoring his question, Val pointed out that this evening's performance was dedicated to Timothy Pratt, the ninth grader who had died of leukemia in March. "That poor family," she said.

The members of the orchestra, boys and girls in white tops and black bottoms, filed onto the stage. Taking up the rear, shorter than most of the boys, and only distinguished from them by his balding head, was Louis Weisman. Oh hot shit! Boomfell repressed an urge to stand and shout his friend's name. Louis took his place to the right behind the cellos and, all business, began tuning his instrument. His was the only double bass in the Wildwood High School orchestra.

"Louis!" said Boomfell. He sat up straighter in his seat.

Val shook her head as though she found the sight of Louis up there discouraging.

Mr. Baggs, a black man in a dark blue suit, bustled across the stage like a happy stout old woman hurrying to catch a bus—stepped onto the podium exactly like an old woman boarding a bus. The audience applauded, the members of the orchestra stomped their feet. Single-handedly, by dint of abundant energy and a monomaniac's will, and with an ever-present smile on his dark bulging face, Baggs kept music in the high school alive and well.

The first piece was "Procession of the Nobles" by Rimsky-Korsakov. He couldn't take his eyes off Louis. Better late than never, better this than nothing. At Odyssey in his serious suit and striped tie, Louis looked like Manhattan, a visitor from city life. He claimed he only missed the restaurants and, occasionally, the prevailing mood of carpe diem, midtown's shove of momentum. But Louis must have also missed the man-about-town sense of himself, a flattering self-portrait that had been taking shape just about the time his fortunes at Shearson Lehman nose-dived—a story Boomfell had never gotten straight—and sent him packing to New England quaintness and his uncle's business, Odyssey. In his present storefront setting he often seemed to feel uncomfortably visible. His chin-up posture came close to arrogance. Boomfell could imagine him hustling along Fifth or Broadway with not a moment to spare—one of the numberless young men faking it through throngs that took you at face value. Yet he had never known him to hurry along the Main Street of his new life. Past Jacob's, the law firm of Lynch, Pundt, and Urbanowski, past Foster's Hardware, Michael's Shoes, Normand's Bakery, Saint Mary's, Archangel's Bookshop, Pioneer Bank. Louis lolled and sauntered, flying his tie of a spring afternoon like a retired country gentleman who had whole days on his hands. Louis was not one of the aggressive members of the Odyssey team. His wife, Laura, complained that he was too laid-back when it came to getting ahead. With his fly-fishing gear and his skis, his tennis rackets and cameras and the double bass, Louis seemed to have adapted too readily to life under no pressure at the end of a dirt road. Boomfell suspected there was an inheritance coming up one day, which took the pinch out of preparing for the future. He and Laura didn't have children.

Yet for all his seeming composure as he strolled down Main Street in expensive clothes, appraising the simple life with a smile, Louis was pushing forty along with everyone else, coming to a boil, Boomfell knew, with worries, wants, doubts. They got along best when they stumbled into being honest with each other. It was useful to admit a little reality into the conversation at the end of the day: the hollowness of another Monday in the real estate business, the stale monotony of marriage, a sudden pain in the chest or running along that tube, vas deferens, into your right testicle. It was more useful to talk about receding gums, receding hair, how you got there, to this time and place, how you were going to afford the next ten years, than to discuss, say, the economy, the madness of SDI, the scandal of acid rain, the sickness of celebrity worship. No, Louis's swagger, his self-styled, good-natured aplomb, was bluster, the displaced New Yorker's version of grace under pressure.

His passion, as he called it, what made all the difference to Louis, was his bass. He spent several hours a day droning away in the guest bedroom. There were kids in junior high who could play circles around him. The Orientals on violins, Charlie, what drives them? He was thirty years too late, yet that was all he wanted to do. Tonight was a rare public performance.

Their friendship had lapsed since the New Year. Now, watching him onstage, a short balding man working up a sweat, wagging his head like suffering Christ, Boomfell missed their afternoons of squash and beer and bullshit. The close white-walled squash court, humid with body heat and resounding with the friendly violence of the game—for an hour nothing mattered but your next breath—had been a welcome midweek break. In his own way Louis was a character. There was a good deal to be said for the bargain he'd struck with himself. The man had accepted his lot, and pursued his passion however he could. His passion! How many people could claim such a thing? Louis's reward was evident in the way he carried on up there. His presence onstage with the Wildwood High School orchestra represented a kind of courage—an unworldly success. Boomfell scanned the audience for Laura but couldn't find her. Louis's passion was one of the things she held against him.

He glanced toward Anne Hastings and it came to him—of course!—that the woman with her tonight was her friend

Astrid Singer. Down for her visit on the glorious first of May, the daughter's last concert. That made sense. She looked right—the woman's composed demeanor, call it, her height, her shortish hair. Boomfell resettled himself in his seat, pleased with the possibility. Singer's tall strong angel!

Intermission. Fresh air. Anne Hastings had withdrawn to a corner of the building, the first white pillar, apart from the clusters of overbearingly cheerful people that had formed just outside the front doors. She sent a cigarette arching toward the sidewalk, snapped from thumb and finger as a smart-ass kid would do it.

"Lovely evening for the last concert, isn't it?" said Boomfell, approaching her.

"It's a lovely evening for anything but the last concert. It's hell in there."

"How was your first winter in New England?"

She looked at him for the second time. "Have we met?"

He told her his name. "Eliot Singer stayed with us when he was here before Christmas. We met you at the Corelli . . ."

She touched her face as though momentarily startled. "Of course." Small teeth in her smile. "Actually, I knew there was something familiar about you." She went about the distracting business of lighting another cigarette. "I've never smoked before in my life. Last week I noticed all these lovely packages of cigarettes while standing in the queue at the grocery store." She brought out the pack again—Camels—then dropped it back into her purse. "I bought this one because it's so exotic. Whoever thought of calling them Camels? I felt wicked lighting up the first one—a fiend—and promptly became quite dizzy. In answer to your question, winter was deadly. Interminable. Fortunately, I have a friend in New York and a cousin in Boston, that sort of thing. We survived."

"May is bound to be a lift."

"We're off the minute Gillian is finished at school. That will be a tremendous lift. I must visit my precious aunt in her impeccable garden, then Switzerland, and finally Italy. Friends are renting a villa together in Positano."

"How nice for you," said Boomfell.

"Have you been? It's amazingly reasonable. Not a bit more than one of your ordinary cottage rentals at the beach."

"Will you be back?" he asked.

"I wasn't prepared for the punishing isolation. Everyone holes up in their cozy little houses out here. There's hardly a vestige of community. The glorious individual withers and dies in his inglorious solitude. Students have been my only consolation, and they're all women. Men are married, or unhappily married, or gay, or dull as dishwater." She exhaled noisily.

"That bad?" Singer's name for her was perfect: Hasty Pudding.

"I did manage to finish the bleeding manuscript I've been carting around for years. That's something, I suppose."

"You're an anthropologist, aren't you? Where did I get that idea?"

"That's for ape lovers. I'm not that desperate yet. My little racket is Irish literature, oddly enough. The book is on keening." She dropped the cigarette, largely unsmoked, under her foot. "Anthropology of a sort. They're reading it at Cambridge at the moment. If I had it to do over again, I'd do anything else. Economics, law, medicine, something."

"Economics?"

"We literary academics with our elitist critical isms of the moment, it's a hollow killing fraud. All week long I've been mesmerized by the Lanzmann film on public television."

She referred to the film, he felt, as if testing him. "Yes," said Boomfell, "I felt obligated to watch it as well."

"If anyone doubts that mankind is entirely capable of destroying the world—his one and only precious world—watch

Shoah." With peculiarly British liveliness, the head wagging, the eyes dancing, the tongue going two forty, not missing a beat, she recalled highlights of the spellbinding testimony that Claude Lanzmann had elicited from death-camp survivors, Polish witnesses, and former Nazis during the eleven years he worked on his nine-and-a-half-hour documentary. The stubbornly smiling man who finally cried when he recounted taking the bodies of his wife and children from the gas chamber. The curtain of flames, all colors, that rose from the pyre of corpses. The peaceful quiet of Sibibor as the people there went quietly about the mass production of death. The sounds of men, Jews designated to work at the camp, hanging themselves in the barracks at night. Mothers opening the veins of their sleeping daughters in order to spare them the horror of the next day, before taking their own lives. The Polish peasants who went about working the land that abutted the camp as though what occurred there had nothing to do with them. The constant arrival of trains. The stench as bodies accumulated faster than they could be disposed of. The starved Jewish workers who welcomed the renewed arrival of death trains because the work meant they would eat again. The silence that followed the screams of the dying. The villagers gathered around the returned Jew—he had been the boy who once sang on the river—in front of the Catholic church, clammering for the attention of Lanzmann's camera.

She was as animated and articulate as a character on *Masterpiece Theater.* Boomfell suspected that her account of the program had been rehearsed with other people in similar conversations, a performance conditioned by her profession, by years of academic cocktail parties. Just now, outside Blakely Recital Hall on this May evening, they were far removed from Sobibor, Treblinka, Auschwitz, Belsec. Anne Hastings's impressive summation called more attention to herself, her gift of expression, than it did to the horrors others had suffered. The

Douglas Hobbie

silence that followed was awkward, as if there were nowhere to
go from here—no transition from the topic of annihilation to
something lighter.

"One of my dear friends in England is an astronomer," she
said. "Whenever I bore him with my strident fear that the
earth is bound to be blown to bits, he rather shrugs his thin
shoulders and says, It won't be missed. That's an especially
hideous point of view, isn't it?"

He'd been waiting for an opportunity to bring up Anne's
companion tonight, the tallish woman in the khaki skirt and
off-white mannish jacket. And then the woman joined them.

"There you are." Disappointingly, her accent was also English. "I was terrified that you'd left me to endure the conclu-
sion alone. Care for a sip?" She held out a can of Coca-Cola.
"There's a machine in the basement. Look, I spilled it on my
damned lapel."

"We've been talking about the Lanzmann film," Anne
told her.

"I skipped every minute of it without a twinge of guilt. My
holiday is doing nicely without the Holocaust, thank you."

Pamela was Anne's younger sister. She'd been in America
for three weeks; she'd been staying with Anne for the last three
days. She recited her itinerary: San Francisco, Los Angeles,
the Grand Canyon, Dallas, Atlanta, Disney World, Philadelphia, Boston, New York. Loved every exhausting minute of
it. "It's so vast, isn't it? Do you teach at the college with Anne?"

"We've only met once before," said Boomfell. "A mutual
friend."

"Eliot Singer," Anne told her sister. "You know."

"Oh yes." She smiled brightly at him. "See you back inside,
Anne. You won't abandon me, will you?" And to Boomfell she
said, "Bye-bye."

"I saw the two of you come in and take your seats," he said.
"I was convinced that your sister was Astrid Singer. I've only
spoken to her on the phone a few times, but I'd acquired an

270

image. I was intrigued. Here was Astrid Singer visiting her friend. I was sure of it."

"I intend to see her this summer. Between England and Italy. Astrid has been through so much. It's so sad, the whole stupid business, I can't bear to think about it. Astrid amazes me. She goes on."

"I can't imagine what his Lucky is all about. The last time I spoke to him he sounded like he'd arrived. I'd like to get them down here this spring." He tapped her elbow. "Listen, maybe we can all get together."

She was looking at him now as though Boomfell had undergone a disturbing and repellent transformation before her eyes. "I didn't realize that you didn't know. You don't realize, do you, that Eliot was killed? Isn't that ridiculous, the two of us standing here like this, chatting away—"

"Eliot just called me. In March sometime."

"It was only weeks ago. Isn't that ridiculous, it's the first thing that popped into my mind when I realized who you were. How tactful and clever of you, I thought, to spare us talking about it. I simply assumed . . . Were you close?" she asked. She had regained her composure. "The way Eliot went on to me about the Boomfells this winter, I gathered you were quite close. You hadn't seen each other in years or something, wasn't that it? I went up immediately. A Sunday. Astrid is completely alone in that country. She has no one. There was Nicole, of course. Nicole makes me feel prehistoric. An early crude version of the species. But Nicole was devastated. She wouldn't eat, she wouldn't speak to a soul. Evidently his wife, his Lucky as you put it, couldn't begin to cope with the situation. Astrid had the whole mess in her lap. It was a great relief when the brother arrived. He was quite helpful. Alex was in a complete fog. We spent hours drawing in his large pad. I didn't see him shed a tear. Are you all right?"

"You haven't told me what happened."

"Sorry?"

"You haven't told me what happened," he repeated clearly.

Most of the people outdoors had already moved back inside. Now the lights in the lobby of the building, large globes suspended from the high ceiling, went off and came on again.

"They're about to start," she said. "Evidently he went out to get the Sunday papers and never came back. He'd taken out his motorcycle, I believe. The first rumor of spring, you know."

"Eliot? A motorcycle?"

"Exactly. Astrid was petrified that he'd take Alex on the damn thing. Some British vintage model. I gather he was positively terrifying in his helmet and his leather and his boots. They were scared out of their wits the first time he drove up. You can imagine."

"This is impossible. What do you mean he went out and never came back? What occurred?"

"I didn't want to know every gruesome detail. The coffin was closed. Suicide was the first thought, of course. But Astrid is convinced that was not the case. He was returning, you see. He'd already purchased the newspaper. The insane details that stick in your skull. Such as what was awaiting him for breakfast. French toast, for pity's sake. Why do we know that?"

"Did you say they'd gotten married?"

"That's another thing. They'd only recently gotten married. As you say, he'd got what he wanted. I liked her very much—his Lucky. She was more . . . what? . . . substantial than I'd anticipated. Astrid, however, is extraordinary. I was also there the first time, with the first husband. I don't know what Astrid is made of. I urged her to return to Switzerland, but of course she has to stay in Canada until the children are through with the school term because that's what is best for them. She intends to visit her family in the summer. They don't have a clue. That's best for them, you see, because they're elderly. I love Astrid, but her virtue absolutely drains me."

The sound of muffled applause reached them through the

open doors that led from the lobby. Ebullient Baggs mounting the podium for the finale.

"Pamela will have my throat if I leave her in there alone. Are you all right?"

"No."

"It's not fair, springing this on you out of the blue, is it? Are you coming?"

"In a minute."

Momentarily, as he stepped inside the door of the dimmed recital hall, the place was unfamiliar to him, as if he'd never been there before. Val, he realized, wasn't in her seat in the back row. Relax! Then he spotted the back of her head, her padded shoulders square as a cadet's. She had moved to a seat on the center aisle, halfway down the auditorium. If the audience had been in silhouette, he could have picked her out, she was so unmistakable to Boomfell, like another sort of creature seated amongst the homogeneous gathering of humans. Their life of sharing! The sight of her disturbed him, and he looked away. He also avoided his daughter, dead-serious about playing her part to the best of her ability in the Wildwood High School orchestra. Heat came into his face at the sight of Louis vehemently engaged with his double bass. Play it safe, that was his strategy for getting by. Dilettante! His passion was a hoax. Everyone was poised to jump up and give their precious flesh and blood a brave standing ovation fit for the New York Philharmonic, make Baggs run back and forth across the stage three times with that shit-eating grin on his face. Clap hard enough, you figure, everything will be all right. Won't bring the Pratt boy back, but maybe everyone else will get to grow up, survive dangerous drugs and sex and cars, get married to something or other, cure cancer, war, poverty, pay all the fucking bills, live to be a hundred, get reincarnated. Everything works out. Lucky Lucky Lucky. He had to get out of there.

The next moment arrived. The entire audience came to its feet, the hands roaring already. Whistles! Cheers and bravos! The young people in the orchestra appeared fairly stunned, at first, by the excitement they had inspired. There was Ruth with a wink and a smile for her stand partner, a pint-size boy all tied up in his old man's necktie, a genius so far. Most of the boys were gawky kids, while half the girls looked like women already. Baggs signaled for them to rise, and the applause mounted. We love you; come through. Redeem us. The hot-shot on drums there, an earring catching the light, what's he up to? A squirt gun! Is it? Jesus, nailing his buddy with the trombone in the back of the neck, bang, nailed him again, water down the back of the neck, beautiful. Boomfell hadn't seen a squirt gun in years. There was Louis turning to his young colleagues with his old prep-school we-came-through grin on his face. Thumbs up. Baggs bustled from the wings for the second time, a hand raised to one and all. Heroic. Molly Maloney, stumbling to center stage, terrified, met him with a bouquet of roses, and the wave of applause crested. There was Val clapping her heart out, moved, not to be outdone. From here, from behind, he could tell she was happy just now. Relax. Look alive. Clap, for Christ's sake! The distinct sound of his added applause was spontaneously swallowed up in the general hurrah.

Val listened to what Anne Hastings had told him during inter-mission, then she left the room without saying a word. By the time he pursued her upstairs, she was seated naked on the toilet with her face in her flannel nightgown. She'd been cry-ing. When he placed a hand on her shoulder, she raised her head, pulled away. Her face, mottled red, distressed, could have been fifty years old, older. She offered Boomfell no com-fort, and she wouldn't be consoled by him. She wanted to be left alone. "Please, Charlie, I don't want you in here."

Within half an hour, though, she came down to the kitchen. She draped herself over his back as he sat at the table, and pressed her lips against the back of his neck. Her touch made him uncomfortable, but he didn't move out from under it. In a moment she sat in the chair across from him. They looked at each other like two strangers sharing a table in a diner at two o'clock in the morning.

"The last time he called us, in March, I didn't call back. Do you remember? Ruth talked to him."

"What's that supposed to mean?" she asked.

"He called twice, remember? I wish I'd called him, that's all."

She reached her hand across the table toward him. "I did call him, Charlie. I called him from work one day."

"Why?"

"I wanted to. I wondered what was going on. He said he was getting married, that's why he'd called. He wanted us to know."

"Why didn't you tell me that?"

"I would have eventually, I suppose. I guess I thought I'd let him tell you himself."

"I'm surprised you didn't tell me."

"I'm telling you now."

"What did he say? Did he mention a motorcycle? A motor-cycle, for God's sake!"

She shook her head no, looking at her veined hand flat on the maple table. "But Astrid is right. Whoever Astrid is. I believe her. I'm sure he was on his way home to have breakfast and read the newspaper with his wife, his Lucky." When he didn't respond, commiseratively or otherwise, she added, "So now the world can breathe easier."

"What?"

"That's what he said to me. I'm getting married, Valerie, so now the world can breathe easier. No one is invited. I'd love to invite you, Valerie, but no one is invited. Not even the Pope."

275

"Not even the Pope?" You had to smile.

"Say hello to my friend Charles Boomfell. Tell him Eliot is going to be on *The Newlywed Game*."

He felt his pulse race as the phone distantly rang. Why he was calling, just what he would say, he didn't know. After four long rings, just as he was having second thoughts, a voice came on the other end, an answering machine, not a person.

"Hi! This is Nicole. Astrid and Alex and I have gone away for the weekend. Leave your name and number so we can call you when we get back. Au revoir."

He called and listened to the tape again, without leaving his name and number, and then, after pouring himself a drink, a third time.

Au revoir.

He stretched out on the couch in the living room, listening to the dark through the open window, and finally slept for a few hours. In the morning he still wanted to be left alone, which was possible a while longer. It was not yet six. Quietly, he ventured outdoors.

Above the narrow border of evergreen and sumac, interlaced with vines, that divided Boomfell's property from his neighbor's, sunlight streamed into the yard. The wet lawn gleamed silvery, the foliage of shrubs and trees had a lustrous shimmer. The birds this morning! It was crazy. He left the yard. No neighbors were abroad. Holly Dean Lawson's back-porch light was on. Patches of mist hung over the broad green common that lay, two hundred and twenty rods wide, between the old homes the length of the street. The sun-spangled row of stately trees, the long silent green featuring wafting mists, the sweet air this morning . . . Glorious may not be the word.

Don't panic!

He returned to the woodshed at the rear of the ell. There he put on his leather work boots, stiff from lack of wear, and took the long-handled shovel, which stood behind the plank door. In the northeast corner of the backyard, between the bed of peonies and the cluster of three flowering crab apple trees, he paced off an area twenty-five feet square, marking the corners with sticks, and began turning over the sod. *Glorious may not be the word.* He settled into a rhythm, the steel of the spade came clean of rust, and soon he broke a sweat. It was a mistake to forgo a garden for so many years. He stepped the shovel sharply into the ground. *No one is invited.* He turned over the sod. *Not even the Pope.*

Gradually he became aware of the neighborhood awakening around him. Some damn fool up and at 'em with the lawn mower, fighting the good fight. Cars rounded North Lane, headed for the dump. Aggressively, the sound of chain saws started up across the way—the towering elm there that had not leafed out this spring. The sounds of the day merely accentuated the stillness in Boomfell's backyard. If Val had spotted him out there, digging up the yard beyond her peony bed, she'd decided to let him be.

My friend Charles Boomfell. Tell him Eliot is going to be on The Newlywed Game. You knew exactly how he sounded saying that. Famous last words. He buried the blade of the shovel. *So now the world can breathe easier.*

April

    It had rained for a week, which made the sunny day, puffy
storybook clouds in blue sky, seem like a major event. I was
edgy, waiting outside with second thoughts in a white T-shirt
and my white cotton skirt, Mac's old-fashioned lilacs in full
bloom, my favorite spring smell, I decided, period. I was more
excited than I'd anticipated when Val's car turned onto Crescent, out of the blue she'd called after two and a half months.
Would I like to go on a little outing Sunday, someone's garden
in one of the hill towns. I was scheduled to work brunch at
Cyrano's, which promised to be packed, Mother's Day, but
Tony said he'd take it for me. I thought, Shit, when I saw
someone in the backseat, why couldn't she come alone, but it
wasn't her children she'd brought with her. I can change my
mind right now, I thought, I can say no. Like members of
another species, as far as I was concerned, Marjorie and Eleanor beamed at me as I climbed in beside Val, Good morning,
April. Good morning, April. They were dressed for a day trip,
Marjorie in a pale blue cardigan and a straw hat, Eleanor in off-
white linen with a sailor cap pulled down on her head like a
bowl, her makeup out of vaudeville, her little lifelong teeth
see-through in contrast to Marjorie's unreal snow white set. I
had promised to drop in on them when I returned from Jamaica, I never did. I decided to go with the day, I twisted
around in the Toyota, each leaned forward to be kissed, I
blushed, Oh God, you guys, while Val, the mastermind of this

unlikely scheme, put the car into gear. I'm glad you could come, she said. She was attractive in her blue-and-white-striped skirt, an open-necked lavender jersey top, her hair was fuller, the thrill was gone. So where are we off to, everybody? I asked. Eleanor, reaching forward to touch my shoulder, said, We're exploring, dear. An hour into the hills on narrow winding roads, the glamorous old biddies extolling the splendor of old New England the whole time, we turned onto the dirt road we were looking for. Karen's Farm was a white house that needed paint, a gray weathered barn, tumbledown sheds, a sign said FRE SHEGGS. Behind the buildings, a cultivated south-sloping field, bordered on three sides by spring green woods, contained row upon row of herbs in dark raised beds. A dream, Val said. Karen was a square sturdy redhead in a green smock and dirty bare feet, she'd created her extensive garden from scratch, three small children still in pj's dogged her steps as she gave us a tour. Tiny Eleanor, in new white sneakers that looked enormous, took my arm with her clawlike hand as we shuffled slowly amongst the thriving plants. I'm sure I don't know a thing about herbs, she said, I just love being here. In full sun her crinkled skin looked tissue thin, as if it could easily tear. Val accompanied Marjorie, who knew the names of everything, chattering about plants with Karen as though sharing news about marvelous peculiar old friends. Now tell me if I'm right, Eleanor said, Val is married and you're going to be the doctor. I said of course that was right, she knew that was right. Now Marjorie you see has been telling me all morning that Val was to be the doctor and you were the married one, Eleanor said, I was beginning to doubt myself, she was so sure, I knew perfectly well it was Val, etc. Now I have one more question, dear, it's sisters-in-law, isn't it, not sisters, Marjorie wants to say sisters, you see, but actually you're sisters-in-law, aren't you? I told her she was right, we weren't sisters. We filled the car with sage, rosemary, lavender, oregano, thyme, dill, Charlie had dug up half the backyard, Val said, envisioning a new garden. On the way home both Eleanor and Marjorie nodded off, the day had grown warm, we rolled the windows partway down, I'm sorry about what happened, I've missed you, Val said, smiling forthrightly, okay? We walked the ladies safely to their back door, they could never thank us enough, they'd had a lovely time, they said good-bye as though, now that this day was done, they didn't expect to see either of us again. Val invited me home for supper, just Charlie's famous all-American hamburgers on the grill, she said, but my final exams began tomorrow, I had to hit the books. What was I doing for the summer? she asked, so I told her about my new plan. The plan now was to meet Pauline at her brother's in Denver the first week in June, I had my ticket, we would rent a car and travel through the West, camping along the way, New Mexico, Arizona, Utah, Wyoming, I was really excited about Wyoming, we would reach San Francisco by late July, we would stay with my mother until we set ourselves up across the bay, I would work until I was able to start school at Berkeley, we'd decided that it was crazy for us, me and my mother, to live apart, so far apart, she had discovered another suspicious lump a month ago, it was surgically removed and pronounced benign, but the incident had cost us long days of anxiety, which shouldn't have been so lonely. You're not coming back? she asked. You're going back to California? The alarm in her voice surprised me. I don't want you to go, she said, I want you to stay. She regained her composure, she was sure Berkeley would be wonderful, she was sure it was a good decision, my mother must be happy, etc. We had turned onto Val's broad street, the most direct route to my place. There's Charlie, she pointed. Just ahead on the green common, Charlie, purple T-shirt and red shorts, was hustling backward in a sideways scramble, reaching backward overhead to snag the high pop fly a boy had batted from his hand to the several other players on the field, their son and his friends, I'm sure. Val tooted the horn hurray, almost blushing, I thought. Dancing on the balls of his feet, both arms raised as in a cheer, Charlie caught sight of us as we passed, a wildman grin on his red face. I waved, gave the thumbs-up sign, then waved again. Still smiling, Val said, He hates baseball.